PRIMROSE

by

Kieran York

Scarlet Clover Publishers, L.L.C.

Littleton, Colorado

Covers Design Director – Karen D. Badger
Interior Design and Formatting – Karen D. Badger
Cover Artwork – Kelly Jo Stevens

Edited by – Martha Ryan, Kathie Solie, and Barbara Oatley
All Chapter Lyrics Written by – Kieran York

Published by Scarlet Clover Publishers L.L.C.
P.O. Box 621002
Littleton, Colorado 80162

Printed and bound in the United States of America, UK, and Europe

ISBN-13: 978-0692563878
ISBN-10: 0692563873

PRIMROSE

by

Kieran York

Books Also Written by Kieran York

Trevar's Team: 1 (A Beryl Trevar Mystery)
Within Our Celebration (Short Stories)
Touring Kelly's Poem
Loitering on the Frontier
Night Without Time
Earthen Trinkets
Careful Flowers
Appointment with a Smile
Shinney Forest Cloaks: Book 3 (A Royce Madison Mystery)
Crystal Mountain Veils: Book 2 (A Royce Madison Mystery)
Timber City Masks: Book 1 (A Royce Madison Mystery)
Sugar With Spice (Short Stories)
Blushing Aspen (Poetry)
Realm of Belonging (Poetry)

Astray (Forthcoming)
Ballad of Raindrops (Forthcoming)

Kieran York

Dedication with love to my friend – Sandra Moran

She is a great writer – I know because I have read her books- and hope to read many, many more.

She is a great educator – I know because I've had the privilege of sitting-in (via phone) on one of her lectures.

She is a great woman – I know because her friends and family adore her. They also know she is great.

She is a brave woman and is a woman with a sense of humor – she is the observer of pork rinds, the searcher of runaway socks, and a finder of mischief along crime-ridden jogging trails. She knows her DBAP public service announcements by heart. She is an expert at pie charts. Her favorite color is neon, and her photography is Abstract Expressionism, on the blurry side. She loves black cats, and they love her.

I asked her if she'd be interested in taking over as publisher of Scarlet Clover Publishers – after the new company is it built up a little. She responded with a tease that we need to keep the Kansas Legacy going.

But I think she is her own Kansas Legacy.

I'm proud of her and proud of her accomplishments. And certainly proud of what she's done for Kansas, and women's literature.

I'm also proud she calls me her Kansas Sister.

ACKNOWLEDGEMENTS

My thanks to Karen D. Badger, Kelly Jo Stevens, Martha Ryan, Kathie Solie, and Barbara Oatley for their artistry in making Primrose into a book.

Also my appreciation to all those who have worked as part of the Scarlet Clover Publishers Team.

As always, I acknowledge my appreciation for my family. I am blessed with the very best family - a sister, brother-in-law, two nephews, two niece-in-laws, and nine great nieces and nephews. I thank each of you for the love and happiness you've given my life. You are my life's blessings.

For my friends – you're always there. And for decades I've loved you all!

Kieran York

Cheyenne, Wyoming

Chapter 1

Please don't tell me anything that has to do with love.
When you're counting sweethearts, make sure I'm not part of
The trail of broken dreams that you used to leave behind.
'Cause I'll go on ahead and find someone I'll call mine.

- BlueJean's Blues

Change is drifting time.

It is most recognizable in fields of flowers or great shadowy skies.

Megan Holloway also knew it through the counting of heartbeats. For that is where her music began. She also knew all the ramifications of change. There was the kind that she was aware of and the kind that snuck up to kick her backside.

Megan's dreams had taken a multitude of spurs and spills along the way. She'd been bucked off and trampled by life. She now felt the reins of promise slipping from her grasp. She clutched the guitar case's familiar, worn handle. Within her enwrapping fist was the squeeze of security. Tugging the strap of her garment bag, she twisted it onto her shoulder. Her hand then dipped to fold around the double-web handle of her oversized rectangular duffle bag.

She was now carrying every belonging she owned.

Megan owned two pairs of Western boots. One pair she wore. They were battered mule-skin, and adhered to her feet as if she'd been born in them. Her newer pair, packed securely inside the duffle bag, was custom lizard-skin. Over the rumpled, faded denim shirt was a buckskin leather jacket with fringe hanging lifelessly. Her Levi button-fly, boot cut 501 denims clung to her frame. She had another three exactly like the ones she wore rolled up inside her bag, along with a patched denim jacket, half a dozen shirts, another half dozen T-shirts, and assorted underwear and socks. Stuffed in one side of her garment bag was a scored notebook with hastily entered songs. On the other side was a compartment jammed with a few sundries, a silver hat decoration, a bolo tie, and a small treasury of women poets. Two pair of dress slacks were tightly packed, and hung in the center of the bag. They were as decorous as the young entertainer got.

Megan traveled light, yet appeared burdened. She eased the tiny red hot candy between her lips. A cinnamon burst moistened her mouth with its warm bite. The candy was a comfort.

Her glance at the bus terminal's outer limits reminded her that every depot seemed nearly the same. The nuances of loneliness and tedium were always there. She brooded as she scanned the Wyoming skyline. Cheyenne was yet another stop. Under this sky of blue and blooming clouds with a mist of smog across the horizon - this place and the women of Primrose might improve her future.

Thoughts suddenly collided with truth. Although she would be afforded one more slim chance, it was to be a tradeoff. She would miss the solitude of being away from the city's bustle; being away from the road's travel. But at this stage in her career, she welcomed companionship. There was no other emotion as deep as the cohesion that was a band.

Primrose wasn't just any musical group. This band was a downtrodden as Megan. The country-western group was without momentum. Although there was undoubtedly raw talent, it had not been launched. Similar to Megan's story, the all-women group had never made it out of the chute.

It was in its third year on the circuit. Megan was in her thirteenth year as a drifting singer, songwriter, and musician.

She had started touring in her seventeenth year. Dreams had been given up, put on hold, and nearly forgotten numerous times. Both the group and Megan were either too early or too late for fame. Now perhaps, at thirty years of age, Megan's time for success was at hand. *But were the women band members a match*, she wondered to herself. There seemed no margin for error this trip.

Megan crossed the oil-stained street. Her slim, willowy frame plodded with the cumbersome burden of luggage and of doubt. Her boots gave added steepness to her five-eight height. A dented silver belt buckle blinked with its reflection of a dull day's glare. Her walk was proud yet her shoulders slightly slackened with weariness. Megan's walk was without hesitation. Her tanned face was sullen. She grimaced as she gazed across the street.

There, with a layer of time and of grime, was the coffee shop where she was scheduled to meet the manager of Primrose. More somber than usual, her dark bronze-hued eyes blinked at the sun suffused through the cloud cover. With a quick tip backward of the rim of her tannish ivory Stetson, her attractive face was more visible. That face was surrounded by long, ebony-brown hair that swayed in wavelets when she sang. The curtain of hair always appeared to keep time with her tapping boot. A brittle gloom was revealed by her firm jawline, pouting full lips and thickly-lashed eyes. But when she smiled, Megan's brightly shimmering teeth flashed a smile of sultry beauty. Charm was understood. Its message was there with a vulnerable softness beneath.

A discontented glare, mixed with sorrow seemed a necessary barricade to protect Megan's sensitivity. For the same reason she integrated an arsenal of protection into her songs. But no matter how pitiful the depiction might be, her lyrics never showed how truly sad her wail was. That, she conceded was the ultimate truth. She had only explored for a contrition deep enough to get her by.

She stacked her bags on the opposite booth seat. Megan glanced down at her guitar case. With reverential tenderness she placed the Ovation on the inside of the booth before she sank onto the cushioned seat. It had been a very long trip. She hoped she wouldn't appear too haggard. She was to meet with Fran Tobias, Primrose's founder and road manager. Fran would be looking for someone with energy and enthusiasm. Megan's emotions were running on empty. She calculated Fran would be arriving in ten or fifteen minutes. She nervously glanced back down at her turquoise-trimmed, silver wristwatch. The secondhand only increased the emptiness of waiting.

Waiting never spared her the sweet crazies.

* * *

"Cammy, you know there's nothing more important to me than Primrose. I wouldn't have recommended Megan if I thought there was a chance of her screwing up. BlueJean swore to Fran that Megan's clean," Selina Nesbitt defended. "Give it a chance. If Megan messes up, she's gone. Fran won't allow trouble. I promise." She reached to touch Camille's creamy, light face.

She so loved that face. From the moment she met Camille Ward, she loved her.

Camille's appearance was soft. Her expressions were properly restrained. Yet that aristocratic reserve that was a legacy of wealth and propriety, transformed into an unequaled sexiness when she entertained. Her sky-blue eyes sparkled when she sang. Her rosy pink lips were lush - her white smile dazzled audiences. Long, pale blonde hair fluffed in ringlets around her lovely features. With a sweep of perfectly manicured fingernails across her forehead, she would swing those curls that fell softly on her shoulders. Selina loved Camille's delicacy. Camille was barely five-three, petite, and her body was well-exercised.

Selina was first attracted to Camille's loveliness. Then she found there was so much more. "Cammy, the least we can do is to give her a chance."

"Selina, Megan has a shaky past."

"Trust me, sweetheart," Selina said as she crouched down beside her lover. "It's gonna work."

Light from a naked stage bulb diffused brightly. They would be performing on this empty elevated platform tonight, Camille considered. She would be dealing with an unknown quantity in the form of an erratically charged Megan Holloway. They had never even rehearsed together. Although Camille hated the vacuity of rehearsal, she dreaded the possibility of a poor performance. Scanning her lover's optimistic face she saw the gentleness that made her fall in love with Selina.

"I do trust you, Selina," Camille confirmed. "But I've heard Megan is trouble. And we've got enough trouble just keeping the band together."

"BlueJean swears that..."

"BlueJean is scarcely the best source on dependability. She's the cause of Megan's grief. I don't need to remind you that she is why Megan took her half-year hiatus from humanity. BlueJean also very nearly ruined your life." Camille wasn't certain why she felt the need to remind Selina of the heartbreak handed her by BlueJean. "And Megan hasn't even performed in over six months."

"And?"

"I'm uncertain how it will all play out with the band," she said with irritation. Selina and the other two female members of Primrose sang backup. Camille was the lead singer and played guitar and fiddle. She enjoyed having the center spotlight. That was a freedom to vocalize how she felt. A duo may or may not offer her that.

"We needed a lead guitarist. And Megan is terrific. And you heard her. She can sing."

"I'm feeling threatened," Camilla confessed looking away. "I haven't been with the band that long."

"When you sang along with Megan's demo tape it was wonderful." Selina had mentioned how their voices blended like silk and sultry magic. "Hell, babe, we all got goose bumps. Even Fran."

"And Megan was hired." Camille's words were edged with a discouraged acceptance. She had heard about Megan Holloway from Selina for the past year that they were together. She'd been told what a rare and wondrous woman Megan was.

Told by Selina; told by BlueJean. Selina and BlueJean had been lovers. A leading country and western radio personality-disc jockey, the glamorous BlueJean had broken Selina's heart over three years ago when BlueJean met Megan. The heartbreak was duplicated when she dropped Megan last year. Brokenhearted, Megan had left Nashville's country entertainment world for six months of being a recluse.

"You'll be great together." Selina leaned nearer and allowed her gangly legs to hang from the edge of the stage. She wrapped her arms around her lover.

"Selina, the woman walked off a stage. That's huge. She walked out on her audience."

"She was devastated. But she says she found peace in her little cabin back in the Colorado high country. She healed her wounds with solitude and a case of bourbon. She bragged that she'd emptied those bottles with great therapeutic accuracy." Megan had written songs and told Selina that she had done a tour of her mind. When composing songs, she traveled her past with BlueJean. Then, via music, she attempted to sort the pain. "Cammy, I remember how it was to get dumped by BlueJean. Megan went over one kinda ledge and I went over another."

"You checked into a sleazy motel and took a bottle of pills. And if it weren't for an allergic reaction it would have killed you."

"The allergy saved my body. You saved my heart and soul."

Camille smiled. "That was my pleasure. You know how much I love you." She studied her tall, lean lover. A year ago her friendship with Selina had strayed toward love. Camille had been won over by Selina's loving, kind disposition. She loved Selina's strong Texas accent and the way she walked, as well as the way she was.

Camille's warm touch against Sara's mid-length auburn hair was reassuring. Selina kissed Camille's hand. "I love you, too."

"Selina, I want Primrose to happen. We've been playing barrooms, fairs, and rodeos from Albuquerque to Albany. The big break just hasn't come."

"You heard Fran. We needed the right formula. Now the vocal combo is right. When Fran claims you two could be the leading duo vocalist act in country-western, she means it." Selina stood, extended her hand and helped Camille to her feet. She gazed into Camille's light blue eyes. Selina could always see the sky in those eyes. "You're the best kinda brightness my life has ever known, Camille Ward. I got sunshine all over me when you're near. Baby, it will all change when Megan is with the group. You'll see." Selina's gray-green eyes narrowed and her forehead wrinkled. "You aren't sorry you left that slick bunch of rockers to join up with a batch of shit-kickin' cowgirls, are you?"

"Naw," Camille's mock drawl ended with a laugh. "You've just about got this California surf-bunny tamed out."

"Was it my bluegrass?" Selina asked as she snuggled near to kiss the tip of Camille's nose. "Or was it my two-step?"

"It must have been your honky-tonk," Camille replied. Her arms lifted to surround Selina's shoulders. Her fingers locked around her lover's neck as though they were a chain. Or, she considered, perhaps more of a lifeline.

* * *

After a quick cup of coffee Megan and Fran left the coffee shop. Megan smiled when she saw the Primrose bus. Scripted on strategic areas of its side panels were huge, multicolored, brightly-painted primroses. The group's name was scrolled in chipped gold paint. The dilapidated lavender bus had obviously charted mileage. Fran always made certain it was cleaned and shined. Through stalls of buses and curling exhaust fumes, Megan realized she was entering a new phase in her life.

"Haul it in," Fran said as she pressed open the folding door. "We got the back seats taken out to use it for stashin' our luggage and instruments. Middle seats convert to mini-beds with cot-sized mattresses. Cozy as I can make it for you gals."

Megan saw that the three sets of seats behind the driver's seat were the only hint that the old bus had not simply been a long panel truck. She delivered her gear to the back, and then returned to slide into the front seat opposite the driver's area. Fran gave a hearty crank to the ignition key.

"All the comforts of home," Megan commented as the bus pulled out onto the street.

"Hell, yep. Care to imbibe? There's a sweet little bar on our way. Well, a couple blocks from the motel. And after your journey I just bet you have a case of parched throat."

"I've been cutting back, but why not? I can use a little buzz before meeting everyone."

"You okay with booze now?"

"I don't get falling down drunk now. Not since getting BlueJean out of my system."

Megan studied the front window's reflection of Fran's image. Her short, stocky build appeared too short to reach the pedals. But with great dexterity, Fran maneuvered the vehicle.

Fran's closely-cut, beige-gray curly hair famed a circle around her leathered, puffy face. From piercing dark-green eyes came an unexpected force of survival. Megan had heard rumors of Fran's past as a hard-driving, harder drinking manager. Both showed in her late-fifty's facial crevices. Wrinkles were so deep they looked as if they had been etched with a fork's tines. Her face had lived a very long time.

Fran cackled loudly. "Nothin' wrong with a drink or two. Hell, line up the empty glasses of mine and it would reach around the world. A couple of times, maybe." Fran glanced back into the rearview mirror. "We all got us some stories. I'm outta Kansas. Farm life wasn't for me. I found a guitar-strummin' lesbian drifter. She was a rhinestone cowgirl. I took a real shine to that little gal. Over thirty-five years ago. That's how I got into the business. I was her promoter and road manager. We were together for ten years when she was killed in a motorcycle accident. Broke my damn heart in half. I got busy and put a group together. They made it to the charts. Found themselves a flashier manager."

"That was lousy," Megan commented. Betrayal was one of Megan's strongest dislikes. Loyalty was deeply meshed with her soul. "Well, you have Primrose now."

"Yep. And were gonna make it big. I got that feelin' deep in my bones. I couldn't take another letdown. After I lost my lady and my band, I drank my way through the country and half-heartedly promoted various groups. Took all this time to rebuild my heart. Now I know we can hit the charts."

Fran ushered the bus into a large slot in a roadside tavern parking area. As they walked inside, Megan gathered herself together. She acknowledged that she belonged back at her cabin of loneliness. But she was now here, out of necessity. The women sat at the wooden bar on matching high-backed bar stools. Every western town seemed to have been decorated by the same designer, Megan thought. But it did add to her comfort level.

"Welcome to Cheyenne!" Fran toasted with her shot of whiskey.

Megan lifted her frothy mug of beer. "Good returning to civilization."

Fran's head reeled back with her rolling laughter. "Cheyenne is barely civilization."

"Not civilized as long as we're here, huh?"

"Yep. We're a wild bunch. Only gonna be here for a couple of weeks. After Frontier Days, we got a gig in Denver, Santa Fe, Albuquerque, and Amarillo - and so on," Fran recited the first leg of the tour. "I book some more gigs as we go. Don't turn away opportunity. We usually try to work alongside of rodeos and fairs. Might go on down to San Antonio on our way back to Nashville. Guess BlueJean told you Nashville's our home base?"

"She mentioned it."

"Hot damn, but you're gorgeous," Fran muttered with a grin. "You and Cammy are gonna look mighty luscious up there on stage. Your dark hair waggin' and Camille's blonde hair! Whew!" She gulped the final sip of booze, and quickly followed with a swallow of a beer chaser. She looked down to fidget with the buttons on her western shirt. Her penetrating eyes then zoomed in on Megan. "You got yourself really together now? I mean, we're hitting Denver next, and BlueJean is gonna be interviewing you all."

"I told you, I've recovered. Selina's probably told you that BlueJean leaves victims in her wake. It takes a little time."

"I don't wanna have problems. We have this agenda and we gotta win." Fran ordered another round of drinks with a side of pickled-eggs and chips.

Self-doubt stabbed Megan when thinking about seeing BlueJean again. She had been allowed to believe in love. They had exchanged mutual brands. BlueJean was seared against Megan's heart. During their three years in Nashville, BlueJean had appeared to settle down. She worked at local radio station. Megan stopped touring so that she could be with her lover. She did studio backup singing, a few stage gigs, and worked wherever a guitarist-singer might be hired. Selina's visits to Nashville were strained at first. Then she stayed with Megan and BlueJean, and their friendship grew.

"In my wilderness months, I traipsed all those pine-needle paths and cried into all those columbines," Megan said so softly it was nearly a whisper. She recalled trekking the mountain paths. Tears had dried and whimpers had faded. Quaking aspen soothed her with a pastoral message of tranquil sounds. Snow had cooled her soul. The heart sting had lessened with time. "I'm okay now. I swear I'll never walk off another stage."

"When we get to Denver, you stickin' by that?"

"Yes. You have my word." BlueJean had left Nashville with the rodeo champion. She ended up in Denver after Megan had retreated to her cabin. Then BlueJean also dumped the bucking bronco queen. That gave Megan some consolation. Megan grinned briefly, "BlueJean discarding the interloper was about the right combination to make me feel better."

"Enough better?"

She gazed into the time-toughened face of Fran. Fran was probing her resolve. "Sure. Absolutely." Megan considered her answer. "BlueJean has called many times trying to begin again. I told her I only wanted work. That's when she set things up with Primrose."

"She's got her a mighty sexy voice to be turning down,"

Fran said with a snicker.

"People fall in love with her voice." Seeing her only reinforced their infatuation. Megan closed her eyes briefly and envisioned BlueJean's shapely form, her dark-eyes and streaked-blonde hair, her flawless features, and the snap of her sexy wink. The voice of satin was only a bonus.

"She said she'll give us all the air time we want," Fran boasted.

"Fine." Megan felt a security in sharing her history with Fran. Fran extracted trust. "I can't make excuses for walking out on an audience. There are none. And I'm not saying I'm totally immune to BlueJean. But I promise I won't let you down." She bit into the rubbery pickled-egg. "I don't make many promises, because I mean them."

"I got your word, that's good enough for me."

Both women knew how much was hinging on Megan's vow.

"We'll get smoothed out on the circuit," Fran calculated. "By the time we get to Nashville, we'll be ready to cut a demo."

Megan's soft smile flickered. "I've got a case filled with sheets of music."

"Hot damn, girl, you sing with that same look in your eyes as when you say the word music?"

"Lyrics can blast the heart out of a singer," Megan replied. Megan was well aware that her eyes showed the miles of endless indigo highways that she'd drifted. They also reflected the omission of fame.

Hell yes, there was flavor to Megan's sultriness, Fran considered. "You got yourself a home, Megan."

"I am my home."

Chapter 2

It's a world filed with strangers and promises weaved
Into a land where I once believed.
So if my reach doesn't seem complete
Remember I once felt a lover's defeat.

- Strangers and Promises

Camille watched as Selina swung Megan inside her hug. Perhaps, she considered, it had been their similarly inflicted wounds that bonded the friends. While Camille wasn't concerned about it being a romantic threat, she did find uneasiness. Megan was as lovely as they had portrayed her. Camille extended her hand as she cordially smiled. Megan's handshake was warm. She was also every bit the charmer everyone raved about. Camille realized that when Megan kissed the cheeks of the two youngest members of the group, Elena Montoya and Jesse Applegate were mesmerized by the band's newest member. With dissatisfaction well-hidden, Camille watched as Megan's magnetism lured them. The younger women were coaxed into nervous laughter when Megan complimented them.

Megan began by questioning them about their joining the band. Camille was certain she'd already been told the information by Selina, BlueJean, or maybe Fran. Regardless, Megan extracted their version. Elena was recruited from a San Antonio bar. She played guitar, percussion, and an assortment of instruments. Her glib, youthful showbiz personality enhanced the group. Jesse Applegate played guitar, banjo and fiddle. She hailed from a remote area in Montana and had lived on her family's ranch until she signed up with Primrose. When Fran discovered the shy youth, Jesse had been selling musical instruments in a small local music shop. Fran always knew exactly what she was looking for, Selina believed.

Each of the five musicians was glad to begin playing immediately after they tuned up. Fran gave a rapid count and they began with a song that had been on Megan's demo tape. She had written the song after the BlueJean breakup. It was a slow number called, "Strangers and Promises."

Camille neared the microphone. It was the first time the duo would share their voices and Camille wanted it as good as possible. It annoyed her when Megan popped a tiny red hot candy into her mouth. As Camille inhaled the cinnamon scent she scowled.

While they played the intro Megan whispered, "Lighten up, it isn't that bad a song."

Awkwardly, at first, the women's voices blended into the soulful rendition. As they leaned nearer they fueled one another's lyrics. Camille was aware of Megan's sensuality, but was determined not to put up with Megan's prima donna act. Their eyes chained with musical commands. It frightened Camille that they were so vocally well-suited. Camille's frown continued through the song. When it ended she quickly moved away from the microphone she had shared with Megan. "I'm going to need my own mic," she muttered.

"Hot damn! Whatever you want," Fran yelled up at them. "I just thought the nearer you two were – it might be good for the music. Hot damn!" she then squealed again. "We got us angels up there. Magic. We got some magic turnin' loose." She gave each of them a bear hug. Then she turned back to the keyboard and commented, "Selina, it's as good as you said it was gonna be."

Selina's smile widened, beaming approval. "Sizzle," she exclaimed with a whistle between her teeth. "And you two look terrific up there together," she commented as she approached Camille's side.

Coolly Camille snapped, "We're not showgirls. We're singers. I'm more concerned about the sound."

"You sounded better than you looked," Selina playfully redeemed herself. "I bet Fran even got those chills she gets."

Fran chuckled, "I got 'em. I tell you, my chills even got their own chills."

"Amen, sisters!" Elena chanted. "Big time, here we come." Elena's round, cherub-like face was meant for jubilation. Her huge, lovely dark eyes were attributed to her to her Hispanic background. Shoulder-length hair fell thick and free, matching the deep brown of her lush eyelashes. Elena's mouth was animated. It decorated her plush face with sweetness. Short, with a rotund body, Elena's energetic vibrancy maintained constant motion. She was quick to laugh, and quick to cry. Fran attributed her skills as a musician to her quality of rapid-fire emotion.

Jesse's bass guitar twanged a background agreement. Jesse had always found it easier to communicate though music. Her stammer disappeared when she sang backup. She combed her thin fingers through white-blonde hair. Short, back at the sides and off to one side over the forehead, that hair took the brunt of her nervousness when her hands weren't busy creating music. "On our w-way," she faltered with the words.

With a quick side-glance Camille became aware from the look in Fran's eyes, that the manager had seen the spark of electricity that went off between the duo. *It was just for stage*, she wanted to relay. But her words were simple. "It felt fine."

"I've always aspired to sound fine," Megan sarcastically uttered.

"Sounded hell of a lot better than fine," Fran hooted. "We want to be on the charts. We want all of it! Album, awards!"

As they began another set, Megan offered Camille a red hot candy. "I can't sing without them."

"I can't sing with them," Camille declined.

"Soothes my throat." Then with a grin Megan's eyebrows lifted. "And cinnamon is great for disguising booze-breath and white, furry tongue after a night with the bottle."

Camille's jaw clamped tightly. With a trace of disapproval, she looked away. She recalled leaving her last lover. The woman had a drug problem. That was not only ruinous to their relationship but also to the all-woman rock band they were a part of. Perhaps, she had conceded, that was part of her immediate attraction to Selina's clean-cut, moderate behavior. Camille words were bricks building her belief, "I try to conduct myself without over-indulging in anything."

"I'll just bet you do," Megan chided. Her teeth bit down on the red hot candy with a loud crunch. "Red hots are an evil habit. I'd hate to see you addicted to them."

Camille glared. She planned on issuing a warning that she wouldn't stand for Megan's placating insults. She wasn't about to be toyed with by this down-and-out lush. Her smoky blue eyes narrowed. She wrapped the neck of her guitar tightly with shaking fingers. "Let's sing," she commanded.

In spite of tension, the women harmonized throughout the rest of the makeshift rehearsal.

Camille quietly packed her guitar while the others entertained themselves with stories of BlueJean's antics. Camille endured the group's chattering about previous band escapades. She predicted they would all probably get loaded. With the exception of Selina.

Camille stilled a shudder that was building as she worried about how she would handle performing with a drunk. Old resentments cropped up. She resented being on the road. She despised cheap motels and tawdry tour life. She had never really been at home with country-western music. But she was at home with Selina.

* * *

"Hope you don't mind bunkin' with me," Fran said while pitching back the bedspread on the twin bed opposite the one where Megan sat. She leaned back into the cove of pillows. "We squeeze a lot of silver dollars outta our nickels."

"Fine by me. All I care about is a place to hang my garment bag and a corner to lean my guitar."

"We been splittin' rooms like this 'cause Camille and Selina are a couple. So they take one room. The kids take another. Elena claims we bunk by age. Cammy is twenty-eight and Selina is three years older. Elena is barely twenty-two and Jesse just turned twenty-one."

"Are they together?"

"Naw. Basically they're buddies. They have women along the way. They might do a little messin' around to release tension. Nice kids. Elena is our comic. She's taught us some ranchero stuff. We play it in Texas and California. Audience eats it up like good candy. We'll teach you any you might not know. For tonight we'll go with standards and the songs of yours we rehearsed. Might kinda need to fake it for a couple weeks. Then we'll be caught up."

Megan stood to unzip her garment bag. After her outfits were carefully hung in the makeshift closet, she gave a shake to the buckskin leather jacket. Fringe waved and then settled. Next she ritualistically took her best boots, blew on the leather, and then ran the tops across her denims with a buffing motion.

"Glad I don't have a huge wardrobe to haul around."

"We'll get us a few matching shirts and neck scarves later."

"That would be nice. I've never worked with a band with any kind of uniform look to it," Megan said.

Megan turned back to Fran. She studied the weariness in the stocky woman's face. Fran's arms were folded behind her head. She suddenly was energized. Sitting up, she pulled a bottle from the nightstand drawer. "There are a couple of glasses in the bathroom. Want a mid-afternoon nip?" Fran asked.

"Sure." Megan retrieved the glasses. She watched Fran unwrap the glasses and pour the splashing liquid. "What time do we go on?"

"From nine to about one in the morning. Long night. By the time we pack up, have a little breakfast and unwind, it might be after three by the time we get back." She extended the glass to Megan. "This'll help you relax. Sometimes we take a little afternoon nap. A couple hours of shuteye helps."

Megan's arm bridged across. "I've been weaning myself off the hard stuff. Drink beer mostly." There was a sudden curve to her lips. She moistened them with a quick lick. "Everyone needs at least one bad habit. And I don't smoke."

"I keep up as danged many bad habits as I can," Fran remarked. "I like my smokes almost as much as I like my drinks." Fran gave a raspy cough demonstrating the point. "See, I got the hack to prove it. But the booze is medicinal. Cures my throat." Her laugh became a long sputter. "Aw, I've been round the block a time or two. Mind if I smoke in here? I sure don't wanna ruin your vocal chords."

"It doesn't bother me. I give my voice so much abuse when I'm singing, it won't make any difference."

Fran's hand fished the drawer. She pulled out a crumpled pack of cigarettes. "Yep, I noticed you reach for them notes like you was goin' for the world's greatest orgasm. Hell, you don't get accused of holding back. Wallop those lyrics. Even in rehearsal. Mighty soulful sound. BlueJean claims you have the best natural voice in the business. Hot damn, woman, you can twirl those lyrics."

"I've never had much training. Camille's voice is excellent. She's the real singer."

"She's had the best training." Fran lit her cigarette and inhaled deeply. She tipped ashes into the ashtray with an extension of her nicotine-stained index finger. There was something expressive about her stubby, adroit fingers. They became her statement when she talked.

Megan noticed hands. Her own fingers were long, tapered and agilely adept at forming difficult chords. Camille's hands were lovely, artistic. They had the confidence of having been musically trained. Selina had mentioned that Camille began with the violin. She reluctantly joined in when the group needed her to fiddle. Even Selina had sensed that Camille considered it to be a transgression.

"Camille seems to believe I'm a degenerate," Megan suddenly blurted. She took a quick gulp of her drink. "I pick up on those things."

"Naw. That's just Camille's way. A little too wholesome, girl-next-door type. But she had a real bad time with her ex. Some rock singer. Hooked. Cammy walked away from a load of hurt and bad days."

"I figured a woman like her would be the one inflicting the hurt."

"Nope. She loved this gal, but couldn't save her. Hell, Cammy's parents rejoiced when she left the gal. They said their dreams came true. But not for long. Cammy remained lesbian and not an operatic lesbian at that."

"Does she give a damn about what her parents say?"

"Not so you'd notice. Parents are loaded with dough. They wanted her to marry a banker or something. She cooled their cookies," Fran said with a laugh. "Teamed up with a wild rocker. Then us."

"At least her parents care. Selina's were alcoholics. She raised herself. That's probably why she doesn't make too many trips to the distillery."

"Yep. I never could see Selina and BlueJean together. BlueJean parties plenty."

"Our business churns out a great variety of drifters. BlueJean has her fun, but doesn't do much drinking. No drugging," Megan noted. "We all have our stories. Our rhymes and reasons. Maybe we don't want to allow anyone too much like ourselves to remind us who we are."

"You're getting too deep for me," Fran declared as she stubbed out her cigarette. "Maybe we all should issue disclaimers."

Megan nodded as she took the bottle from Fran's outstretched hand. She poured a couple of inches into her glass. "And what about you? You have a woman tucked away somewhere?"

"Naw. Bein' road manager and tour bus driver keeps me too busy to chase. Back in my day I chased plenty. Now I got my visions to live with. Memories. Keepin' herd over Primrose takes nearly all my energy." She sat up and began to cackle. "Almost forgot my other important duty. I'm a hell of a bouncer. Some of them horny cowboys think my women are nothing but a pair of boobs attached to a singing cowgirl. I gotta pitch their balls out. I tell the assholes not to waste their saliva on my women. We ain't, none of us, interested."

Megan chuckled. "I'll bet you hammer them."

"Damn betcha. One cowboy comes to me askin' if I can get him a date with Camille. 'Hell,' I screech, 'what you think I am a fuckin' procuress?' I pick up the nearest beer bottle and chase his ass out. Cammy insulates herself pretty good by shooting them down with one-liners. She's too damn regal to put up with shit."

Megan dryly agreed, "I can well imagine."

"Aw, hell, you'll like her. Took me time to get on with her. You'll like all the women. We're family."

"I like you," Megan stated. "Yes, I'll be fine with all of them."

"Are you gonna be fine when you meet up with BlueJean again?" Fran took a final swig of whiskey.

"I promised you. I'll keep my promise. I'll be there when I'm needed."

"I'll keep askin' until I'm sure I'm getting what's inside you."

Megan pulled off her boots with an annoyed tug. "Right now there is only weariness inside." When her head sank against the pillow, she experienced the exhaustion of travel added to the pressure of meeting her new family. She soon heard Fran's whistling snores begin. Megan considered that if she were alone she would grab her guitar and prompt a song from the lonesome ache of this moment. She would make use of those random, tainted blues in her soul to create lyrics. For there was a gloom about the dull afternoon light that spilled into the stained and squalid motel room. Shadows were wasps projecting quivers from trembling draperies. These were the sweet crazies she thought. The soul becomes devoid of life's lace and loveliness. Megan hated the foul mustiness of cheap motel rooms. She hated not being able to convert her despair into a song. She scribbled lyrics into her memory. That would get her by.

* * *

Camille turned into the comfortable embrace of Selina. Their mini-nap had converted into Camille's rest time. But it wasn't restful. She leaned nearer to kiss Selina's familiar, moist lips. She wanted Selina to awaken. She needed the fervent press of her lips. Thoughts of tonight's first duo performance unnerved her. There was a desire to be sexually invigorated. Although she hated the thought of sex by stopwatch, she knew time was creeping nearer to leaving for the country dance club. She cuddled Selina's long, thin torso. After another deeply passionate kiss, Selina was stirred awake. She whispered, "Selina, I want you." She rotated softly against Selina.

"Baby, what a way to be awakened. Sake's alive!" Selina drawled. Camille was directing her lover's lean body over her own. Her arms caressed Selina's back. Their bodies tangled gently, wrapping and rocking. Passion built as they wedged. Camille never failed to be enraptured by her lover's tender cadence. Selina seemed to know the blending by heart, just as she knew music by ear.

It was this artful, sweetness that so impressed Camille when first sharing love with Selina. It was the only love Camille had ever experience that was consuming, building, and complete. Their tempo built until Camille experience released with her first of a series of orgasms. As they weaved together, Selina's kiss against her neck excited her until their bodies rippled with a deep pulsating orgasm. Selina collapsed against Camille's shoulder.

"Whew!" Selina exhaled. "I'll never get tired of loving you. You're my sunshine."

"And you're mine. I do love you, cowgirl."

Selina sighed heavily as she kissed Camille's temple. "I don't believe our love is perishable. I feel like I'm breathing your air." Selina unbuttoned her soul to Camille as she had to no other lover. "I never want our love to go out of tune."

Camille failed to share the symbolism. The finer the instrument, the easier it was to slip its gear. She quickly quashed her musing. Fine instruments can be re-tuned. Strings could be replaced; frets could be fixed; even bowed bridges could be restored. But it had to be an extraordinary instrument, or it wouldn't be worth the bother.

Chapter 3

You tell me that time is sure to erase
Those memories of our goodbye embrace.
But love doesn't fade away with the years
Or blot away all of my spent-out tears.

- Goodbye Embrace

Looking into one another's eyes for cues to Megan's song, "Goodbye Embrace," the duo sang the melodic lyrics in perfect harmony. Megan cherished her own words, for beneath them churned the pain of losing BlueJean. Those lyrics were carved with great accuracy and matched the soulful agony in her brown eyes.

Megan's erect carriage reflected fierce pride, but the pain within her face was never far away. It gave way with measured vulnerability. Her makeup was scant, and often she didn't even bother with it. The lighting gave a soft glow to her complexion. As she sang, her emotions changed. Sensitivity was never in doubt with her audience. Even Camille understood that Megan had traveled to hell once too often.

Fran was amazed, and exalted, by the way the duo melded music. Their physical contrast was stark. Each woman was lovely in her own way. Megan's gleaming charismatic smile charmed. Camille's eye contact of intrigue held the audience. Their cohesive voices were perfectly matched. Jovial songs ignited clapping; brooding melodies burned. Megan's olive complexion and dark hair was the opposite intensity of Camille's ivory skin and blondeness.

Although their dress hadn't been planned, Megan had

selected an off-white, satin-sheen, fringed shirt, blue slacks, and dark boots. Camille wore a sapphire outfit with oyster-colored collar. Each member of the group wore lavender neck scarves that had been purchased at the last minute by a proud Fran.

Throughout the set Megan's absorptive eyes provided a power that Camille felt. Each time their glance would begin to bind them to a familiar force, Camille's eye snapped back toward the audience or another member of Primrose.

By the end of the final set the bar was still crowded. After an encore, and Megan's final words of so long, sweethearts, the group exited. Fran could tell it had finally registered with the younger women. There was an awe connected with the way Megan grasped an audience. And connecting with the audience was what had happened. Fran knew that to dissect the emotion would be to forfeit it. She called it magic. That combination exists so rarely, as she knew, it becomes a mesmerizing event. Her eyes shone as she whistled through her teeth. The glimmer in her eyes was understood by the band.

After loading their instruments in the back of the bus, the woman's triumph continued.

They had decided to stop on the way back to the motel to get a celebratory stash of booze. Camille went silent after her comment about being off to the distillery again didn't register with the others in the group. But after arriving at the motel, and unloading, it was evident that she had cooled to the idea of a gala.

"I'd rather just go to our room," she murmured to Selina.

Megan slipped her arm playfully around Camille's waist. "Camille, let's perform as a group and let's play as a group. Aw, come on, just one drink. We were better than great."

Camille twisted away from Megan's outstretched arm. "I'm not declining the invitation on the basis of our performance. I'm tired." With an uncomfortable glance away, her jaws tensed.

"Let's toast our first gig," Megan persisted. "Just a quick drink."

"I despise quick anything," Camille's words were curt.

"I didn't invite you to a quick anything," Megan teased.

Camille hated being toyed with. There was a snarl in her

voice as she said, "And don't." Her body tensed as her eyes glared into Megan's.

Although Selina heard the encounter, she elected not to comment. She gave a weak smile. It had not escaped Camille. Camille whirled around. "Selina, are you coming with me or going to celebrate with your pals?"

"Cammy, sweetheart, you know I'm with you," Selina acquiesced. She gave an exultant wave to the others. "See, ya'all in the morning."

Fran slapped Megan's back, "Come on, we'll have us a party without them two. Like I say, you gotta get to know Camille."

"What's a party without a society snob?" Megan joked. "Hell, the little snoot could have at least let Selina off leash for a drink or two with us."

"It isn't that bad," Elena defended. She leaned the case of beer up against the motel wall while Fran unlocked the door. As they entered, she added, "At least Selina is happy."

"I got my heart twisted out of my chest by a woman I venerated. Maybe I resent controls in relationships." Megan leaned her guitar in the corner. The moment's silence made her soul feel vacant. She referred to that emotion as poetic pathos. One must, she reminded herself, chant one's own passion. She bent her thoughts toward home. She wondered why this moment, surrounded by new friends, seemed as desolate as when she was in her cabin alone. "I don't want any relationship." A partial smile escaped. "I'm the romance warrior. My last battle was lost."

"Megan, you'll fall in love again," Jesse comforted. "We all do."

"I'm immune," Megan replied. "I'm immune to heartbreak. I've been vaccinated by the all-time princess of western romance." Megan's laugh exploded.

Fran added, "An' that leaves nothin' at all to lose."

Megan slipped a red hot candy between her lips. Tasting the bursting flavor made her think of sparkles being let go in her mouth. She liked the flavor zing produced.

"The night is young, but I'm not," Fran joked. "So let's knock the caps offa the beers so's we can chase a little whiskey. And Megan, you shouldn't be too paranoid about women. Shit, you can hurt yourself on some of 'em. But that's all over and done with now. My granny used to say that you should never start a party with a grumble on your lips. So let's drink to a little fun along the way."

"Yes," Megan replied with a chuckle. "Hell, tortured artists don't have it all."

As the women popped caps and poured, they laughed.

Megan's father always told her when she was a child that one must look into the eyes of a person to take measure of that person's soul. Megan scrutinized each of the pairs of eyes. She was convinced of each woman's dedication to the band; and the devotion to the friendship that was forging. Defining others was less tricky than mapping herself.

* * *

"What a debut," Selina bellowed as she lifted Camille off the floor in a tight embrace. "We are a hit! A hit!" Her words were not only exuberant, but also filled with astonishment.

Camille agreed, "It was a high. When the audience reacts like that there is an electrical charge. I've never experienced that strong of a charge before though."

"It was like some mystical mixer in the sky wired us together," Selina exclaimed. "All on the mark."

"It's the right musical combination now. We just need a break or two. And we need to keep the Red Hot out of trouble."

"Red Hot?" Selina's quizzical frown amused Camille.

"Megan."

Selina massaged Camille's shoulders. "Sweetheart, she's tryin' to make good. I know she's moody and sarcastic sometimes. But, babe, we can keep her level."

"No one can promise she won't bolt. It isn't even that threat. She's just so damned surly."

"We've got to try to understand her more. After a few weeks, she'll settle down. Just think, if we're this terrific now,

25

think how great we'll be in a couple weeks."

"I'm thinking about when we reach Denver. If Megan is this messed up about BlueJean now, how do we expect to keep her settled down then?" Camille asked.

"We need a demo tape for when we roll into Nashville. BlueJean can get us set up with a recording session. She knows industry people. They have some good studios in Denver. And she's tried to get Megan help with studio execs before. Megan never had the right backup or arrangements before. I offered to help her with the arrangements, but by that time BlueJean was chasing around, so Megan was going into the dumpster."

"It sounds as if BlueJean requires a dumping ground for her ex-lovers."

Selina grinned. "Yep. She flirts with fans right in front of her lovers. I just left sooner than Megan did. Megan kept believing." Selina removed the scarf from around her neck and tossed it on the dresser top. "BlueJean is notorious. And I 'spose you'd say she's irresistible."

"She messes with people's emotions. You call that irresistible?"

"I know she sounds unsavory, but there is something about her." Selina smiled down at Camille. She lifted her lover's chin. They leaned into a kiss. "Cammy, I love you. If BlueJean wouldn't have moved along, I wouldn't have you in my life."

Selina's kiss never seared, Camille thought as their lips again met. It offered secure warmth. Camille never shivered with excitement when they shared romance. But she attributed that to her stodgy, conservative upbringing. Burning affection was out of the question. It existed, but she had never experienced it. She had orgasms; provided them. But that was about it.

That great passionate epiphany eluded her. And undoubtedly would continue to do so. She knew only too well that good qualities disappear beneath great ones. And good was so much better than anything she had ever before known. Camille had not been bred to be a comparison shopper.

* * *

The celebrating foursome stacked a castle of empty beer cans. Hours had worn away with stories of lost loves, tales of gigs gone wrong, and dreams unfinished.

After Elena and Jesse left, Megan snapped open another couple of beers. As she passed one to Fran she commented, "Nice kids."

"They're the best. That Elena is a pistol. She was trying for a date with you. In case you never noticed," Fran chuckled.

Megan smiled. "I noticed. But I told her that I'm a love vagabond." Elena had pressed her fleshy body near Megan's several times that night. "Tempting as loneliness makes it, I don't have any intentions of quick sexual gratification. It would only mean trouble. I'm trying to make trouble my adversary." She took a swig of beer.

"Elena's a funny kid. She probably thinks I'm a funny old broad," Fran snorted. "Nothin' in the world like being a young troubadour out there cruising your denims off."

Megan wiped suds from her upper lip. "Guess I just never took advantage of the opportunities. I was fairly well-behaved compared to now. A decade ago was a world away. The kids now would consider me a sweet, old-fashioned thing."

"I been out there three plus decades, and I gotta say, we were plenty fuckin' wild back then, too. Hell, now I got me more wrinkles than a desert has arroyos. Doesn't keep me from wishin' backwards sometimes. Kids aren't so bad these days. I get on good with Elena and Jesse."

"Jesse is mighty quiet."

"She had a bad time as a kid." Fran pulled another beer from the ice-filled wastebasket. "A horrible bad time."

"Would it breach a confidence to tell me?"

"Hell, you're Primrose now. When she was ten it happened. Like I said, she was raised on a ranch up in Montana. It belongs to her family. Harvest time they had these field laborers. One of 'em takes her. Rapes her. Binds her wrists and ankles with barbwire. Left her for dead in a ravine. Anyways, her daddy gets a search party together. They never found her until early the next morning. She was just barely hanging on. Her daddy goes nuts. Chases down the laborer. Shoots him dead. Well, the law never bothered with arresting her daddy."

"They shouldn't have charged her dad."

"Back in the old days they left the victim's justice alone. But her daddy was never the same. It messed him up so bad he never cared much about anything. They nearly lost the family ranch, but her momma and brothers kept things goin'. A few years ago her daddy kills himself. Thought he was responsible for protecting his family. And figured he should have been responsible for protecting his only daughter. Anyway, Jesse has scars on her wrists, arms, and ankles. And her heart. She loved her daddy. Then she felt some crazy responsibility. A ten-year old kid ain't responsible for shit. No woman is." Fran's eyes filled. "Jesse sometimes wakes in the night screamin' and bawlin'."

"Shit!" Megan uttered, turning her head away from Fran's weeping face. She felt a hollowed-out ache. "Shit," she repeated. She then took a couple of gulps of beer.

"I hear tell that it probably messed her up in the sex department, too. Real inhibited. Sort of a sex rookie if you know what I mean."

"That would do it." Megan tipped as she stood. "I'm going to bed," she declared. She heard Fran retreat to her bed. Megan stumbled toward the mirror that was directly opposite her gloom-filled face. She silently cursed into the image.

She had passed out on her bed for about an hour when her eyes burst open. BlueJean.

The dream was about BlueJean. About their lips brushing and the urgency of their love. The first time they made love. Megan remembered the sound of the snaps as she pulled open BlueJean's sequined blouse. The flush of her face when they snuggled together was recalled. Clothing was scattered as their impatience intensified with passion. No words were spoken as the women twisted together in a sudsy shower. Megan heard the crackle of the downy suds. The women enticed one another with playful nibbles and kisses that covered the length of their torsos. It was the greatest throb of passion she had ever experienced. BlueJean loved lifting veils. She had extracted Megan's total trust.

Megan wanted every woman to have that emotion. She wanted Jesse to be touched and to touch with unencumbered love.

She tried to shake herself from sleep to reality. Glancing across the room she saw Fran's frame synchronizing with her snores. Megan picked up her warm can of beer to sip. Then she stood. Rubbing her eyes with her fingers, she quickly pulled the left hand away from her eyelid.

Each fingertip was capped by a hardened callous. These were the musical badges of a guitarist. She recalled BlueJean kissing her fingertips. And BlueJean insisted that they felt sensual on her skin. Megan though about Jesse's scars. She'd only caught glimpses of them when the young woman's sleeve cuff slipped upward.

Megan ambled outside onto the sidewalk in her stocking feet. The moon reflected only veiled lighting. The first cast of sunlight was seeping across the horizon. Its gauzy dimness meant another day of clouds cluttering the sky. Her thoughts raced. The Creator had a lot to answer for. She cursed under her breath, "Damn it to hell! We are such lonely strangers. We have all come here to live. And here hurts."

Chapter 4

Whiskey morning coming on.
Starless daybreak tricking dawn.
Guitar gals are singing out,
Telling us what love's about.

- Whiskey Morning

"Mighty sad looking pair of damsels," Fran spoke as she pivoted her backside against the seat of the diner's knotty-pine booth.

Camille tossed the menu on the table. "I'll have the same as yesterday, please," she ordered.

Fran nodded. "I'd like the scrambled eggs, bacon, and a little sausage. Couple of your hotcakes, too. Coffee. Hot and a lot," she added with a chuckle.

Selina finally glanced up. "Same for me." She handed the menu back to the waitress. "Thanks," she said as she slumped back. "Cammy, lighten up, sweetheart."

"You two battling so early?" Fran quizzed. "Both of you are actin' like you got rode hard and put away wet."

Selina explained, "She's worried about Megan. She thinks Megan is going to start up with one of the kids."

Camille steamed, "It's obvious. They're both taken with her. Jesse just turned twenty-one. I don't care about Megan's conquests, but indiscretion within the group is bound to create a problem."

"Jesse and Elena went back to their room alone," Fran quickly defended. "Camille, baby doll, we can't have squabbles amongst our lead singers. I don't wanna see this thing unravel.

Megan doesn't want that."

Camille's eyelids clamped shut. Her hand became an awning to shade her face. She'd seen a group go sour before. And it was caused by drugs and dueling romance. She also knew the pain of attempting to resurrect a band after the complications of affairs. She wondered why it seemed mandatory for a group to be fragile to be excellent. She also couldn't understand why Selina insisted on fortress duty for Megan. They had primarily been long distance friends.

Selina's gaze shifted. "Cammy, Megan was with Fran. She's not going after Jesse or Elena."

Camille opened her eyes. After a moment's hesitation, she announced, "Fine. I'm not a chaperone. I'm only noting that they are both smitten with Megan. And Megan is certainly not doing anything to discourage their attentiveness. In case of a maelstrom, I did issue a warning."

"Megan just had a few brews with 'em." Fran's propeller sentences continued to excuse Megan. "It ain't like she's flirting with 'em. Hell, Elena said that her patron saint was on overtime when she saw Megan's publicity photo. Before they ever met. The youngsters got 'em a little crush." Fran broke with a raucous chuckle. "I swear Jesse never even stuttered when she danced with Megan."

"They were dancing?" Camille probed.

"Radio was on. A song came on that Megan liked so she danced with the youngsters. What the hell, she didn't lay 'em. And like I say, Jesse never even stuttered once."

With playful sarcasm, Camille's mood finally broke when she spoke. "Megan probably kept her too busy to talk."

"Busy?" Selina questioned with a frown.

"Teaching Jesse her official lesbian handbook's reference material," Camille answered with a tease in her voice. Camille wondered if her own acrimony was concealed, or was beginning to dissipate. She sipped warm tea. Either way, she was going to attempt to keep things tranquil, for both Selina and Primrose.

* * *

The group had been silent as the bus swayed to a halt in front of the club. After unloading, the women set up for their rehearsal. Megan wondered why everyone seemed so restrained. She guessed that the younger women had hangovers. Selina and Camille had not wanted to rehearse early, so they decided on a quick rehearsal right before performing. They had slept in, and after awaking, they had a late breakfast with Fran.

When Primrose was ready to perform, things were still tense.

Elena's springy gallop skidded to a stop as she approached Megan. She leaned near to whisper into Megan's ear, "Camille is nervous about you getting too familiar with Jesse and me. And keeping us up drinking until the wee hours."

"Are you sure?" Megan questioned. Her eyes flickered with a comedic gleam, "Why?"

"This morning at breakfast she mentioned her concern to Fran."

"If I'm not loving her lady, what difference does it make to her?"

"She doesn't want anyone messing up the group. Camille seems to think we'll have problems," Elena explained. "We've celebrated after work more times than I can count. She's never objected before so I don't really think that is the reason."

"Partying didn't bother her, so it must mean she doesn't like you partying with me."

"That's my read," Elena agreed.

"I know she isn't my welcoming committee, but why does she want to be on the censorship committee?" Megan issued an accompanying grin with her statement. "Let me guess, she thinks I might bring you and Jesse out?"

"Late for that one," Elena said with a chuckle.

Megan caught Camille's glance across the room. With relish, a sexy grin covered Megan's face. It went without response. Camille's lithe figure rapidly turned. She tapped the microphone.

Elena cackled, "She may be worried about your sleeping around with Jesse, Selina, and me, but nobody needs to worry about her sleeping with you."

"Appears not," Megan replied. "Well, the blonde den-mommy can object to anything she wants. She isn't guardian of my chastity belt."

Megan wished she understood the intricacies of relationships. She hadn't gone out of her way to insult Camille. Words and music were what meant the most to Megan. Words were her catalysts to express the emotions that spurted through her nerves. Music was her personal dialogue conveying her soul's contents. Yet, she was struck by her own inability to communicate with Camille. Megan didn't wish to risk wild speculation. After all, while performing on stage, Camille was warm. Off stage she became a glacier.

Megan gave Elena's thick, dark hair a tug. "Don't let it bother you. She'll settle down when she figures out that you and Jesse are way too old for me. Eighteen is about right," Megan joked.

"Last time she was like this was when we went to a lesbian bar. A real dive. Camille was pissed. She didn't want any part of it. Wouldn't even order a drink."

"I don't suppose that drove the bar out of business."

"Nope. The bar was filled with women. We passed out flyers announcing our show. Fran said she'd arrived in bull-dyke heaven."

Megan laughed. Then with a swagger to her voice she whispered, "We don't need her approval to be friends. We'll party whenever we want. Party until the floorboards give way. For now, let's play music."

Tuning up was without words. Camille nodded when she'd matched her D-string. "Ready?" she asked.

"Always ready for a lovely lady," Megan chided.

"Keep your suggestive innuendoes to yourself. I'm not interested in hearing any of it."

"Funny, I've been hearing that you're interested in my love life. Or should I say my vulgarities." Megan flashed a consoling smile. "Let's go for a truce. I'll curtail my vulgar habits if you stop being concerned. Or if you stop being concerned, I won't need to harness my trashy ways."

Camille departed from her anger long enough for an automatic smile to appear. Her head lowered. "Okay, I suppose I am being a badass."

"From where I stand yours is definitely not bad."

Megan's fingers squeezed the frets as she leaned into their opening song. She was well aware that, indeed, Camille's posterior was better than fine. That consideration only provided another helping of isolation when Camille looked thoroughly disgusted by her comment.

* * *

Camille's upbringing had prepared her for life among the privileged. Her family's time boundary was simple - birth begins with millions and should end with billions. There is a need to keep ahead of inflation. Her father had taken wealth - then created mega wealth. He lectured his three daughters that they must continue as his family champions. He never wanted his monetary legacy to dissipate through the generations. Another lesson plan was that they must learn to read people and understand their signals. To this end each daughter received a Vassar education. They were denied nothing.

Her two older sisters had accepted their roles. They had listened; properly assessed signals; made their family proud. They married well and beyond. They were raising families of their own. Handing down their family philosophy, they were doing what expectations insisted upon.

Camille's parents could not understand her dismissal of Ward tradition. She had never been a rebellious child. Now all they could say about her wild streak was that she had at least concealed her failure by not becoming famous. Although they disapproved when she worked with the rock group, they held out hope she would again find significance. When the band split apart, Camille's father was optimistic. Then she relocated to Nashville for country-western music. The only optimistic thing about that, her mother declared, was at least she was no longer in their backyard. Tennessee was fairly well-hidden from

California's elite.

Their precious youngest daughter had missed all the signals. Their disapproval was not born of reprehension, but primarily of anger from her disloyalty. They began with tolerance, hoping she would outgrow her lifestyle. Their hope of a concert violinist in the family was rapidly disappearing.

When she announced she was living the lesbian life with a rocker, they were stunned. Even on the verge of clamping shut the estate door. Camille understood their dissatisfaction. But she didn't understand why they rejected Selina. Selina was personable, fresh-scrubbed, drug and alcohol free, and didn't even smoke. Camille argued her lover's case to no avail. All her parents could find to complain about was Selina's lack of money and formal education.

These were the very elements Camille most admired. Selina Nesbitt had been on her own from childhood. It had been a dismal, deprived existence. Selina's only salvation was music. She was gifted. From the moment she picked up an instrument, there seemed an automatic command of it. Her mind could quickly arrange music. She played each instrument with spirituality. With such an enormous rapture, Camille understood that Selina converted musical notation into what Thomas Carlyle called 'the speech of angels.' Camille had studied musicology; her lover produced magic. Camille performed classical; Selina presented a treasury of her soul.

Beyond that, Camille considered, Selina was honest, dedicated, and kind. That should have impressed the ultra-conservative Ward elders. It did not. Camille felt the security of Selina's devotion and love. That should have impressed her family. It did not.

Wistfully, Camille gazed out of the bus window. The call from her family that morning had produced an amalgam of emotional remembrances.

Elena perched next to Camille. "You seem quiet."

"I was thinking about my family."

"I thought maybe you were pissed because of Megan. You know, during lunch break when she offered you potato chips and you said no, so she says about being fresh out of truffles."

Camille sighed deeply. "She gets on my nerves." Camille wasn't exposing the fact that she hated being ambushed by Megan in regard to her background. It would only give over additional ammunition accusing her of being stuffy. But each encounter put Camille more on edge. She hated being the joke. Her older sisters had teased the beautiful child unmercifully. Now Megan was doing the same. It violated Camille. "No," she disputed, "I'm not upset. Just tired."

"You and Megan are terrific together. You're both so spontaneous."

With a resigned smile, Camille remarked, "Maybe I should make the effort to be more spontaneous off stage as well." Glancing over her shoulder Camille observed Selina. Her lover was bent down on one knee fanning scores of sheet music. She and Megan had been together for half an hour working on arrangements. Megan and Selina savored music. Camille felt she was different. Although she loved music, it remained only a part of her life - not life itself. She had never seen Selina so involved, so enthusiastic about the band. "It's important to Selina. The band. Before Megan arrived Selina was so nonchalant about it. Now she's glistens when she's involved with music."

"We all do now," Elena confirmed.

"Yes."

"And it seems to be coming together," Elena gushed, grinning widely. "Fran said after filling the place last night, management wants us to do a Sunday afternoon gig, too. They made an offer Fran couldn't refuse."

Camille bristled. She had wanted Sunday afternoon to belong to Selina and her. Perhaps escape on an outing. They could attend the rodeo. As Jesse passed by, Camille asked, "Is it definite about working Sunday?"

"Fran says we should," Jesse answered.

Elena defended, "Only a couple of sets. Management said there wasn't a deserter in the crowd last night. They want us to pull in a different audience this week. And the crowd isn't as rowdy on Sundays. Not like that drunken cowhand last night, huh, Jesse?"

"You hear t-the guy hollerin' about your boobs?" Jesse asked Camille.

"No."

"Crazy buckaroo yelled out that you have sweet boobs," Elena disclosed.

"I rarely hear anything but the music when I'm up there. I was busy keeping up the harmony with Megan. Sweet boobs," Camille repeated with a brief smile.

"T-that's why Elena and me were l-laughing. I turn to Elena and she was jiggling her boobs for him. Then she gives him the finger."

Elena's oval face burst into a smile. "I saw Megan glare at him, so I figured I'd defuse it. I was just glad Jesse was doing her banjo number so I was on the bass guitar. If I'd had my drumsticks flying I might have done myself some damage when I flipped him off."

Camille laughed. She shook her head and confessed, "I don't know how I could have missed all that." She gave an obvious glance in the direction of Elena's full breasts.

"He was just a liquored-up cowpoke," Elena said. "My brothers are probably at least as stupid when they go out. But it really pissed Megan."

"She hates when men make passes," Jesse uttered. "I can t-tell the way she looks at 'em. I know how she feels. I d-don't like it either."

"As long as they keep their hands off of me," Camille stated, "I don't mind one way or the other. I just ignore them." She realized that the audience probably figured Jesse was lesbian. Fran was completely obvious. Elena and Selina might be sorted out by other lesbians, but fairly invisible to straights. Megan and Camille would have fooled anyone. Both came equipped with naturally feminine mannerisms.

"You two sure got the guys in the audience flipping out over you," Elena teased.

"At least that expensive finishing school wasn't a total failure," Camille made an attempt at self-deprecating humor. "All I know is that the audience is really backing us now.

Having support is much nicer with western music. In a rock group it becomes frightening when the fans get riled. I never knew if they were going to destroy the instruments or the women."

"I'd hate that," Elena commented.

"I did hate it. Sometimes it was as if we were little more than background music. They often appeared to have their own agenda. By the time our rock band was coming together musically, the rest was deteriorating to bedlam. Everything was lost," Camille recalled with pain. She had skirmished with such determination to help her lover overcome her drug problem. She cringed with recollections. "I hope Primrose never slides like that."

"We're more t-together than ever," Jesse confirmed.

Camille suppressed her response.

Fran's husky voice ordered the women back from break with her familiar line, "Let's hear it. Let's make 'em think we care."

With a clap of her hands, the band began singing to an empty hall. But their voices were not empty. Camille read that signal without apprehension.

* * *

In rehearsal, they had barely started the new set of songs when Megan stopped playing. "You might try singing the lyrics the way I wrote them," she criticized loudly. Looking back toward the keyboard, Megan expected Selina to reinforce her complaint. Selina knew the implication of one singer in a duet altering the lyrics. When there was no comment, Megan's squint swayed back to Camille's furious face. The rehearsal was silenced.

Selina swung around on the piano stool where she had been awaiting a countdown for a repeat of Megan's ragtime number. The neck of Jesse's banjo was lowered. Elena leaned back from the keyboard. Squaring off, still tightly griping their guitar bridges, Megan and Camille glared at one another.

With a rapid clamping down of her teeth, Megan bit through a red hot candy. "Would you like to take it from the top? Try it the way it was written?"

"Had it been written the way I sang it, it would have been infinitely easier to sing," Camille protested.

Megan seethed with sarcasm, "It wasn't written to be easy. I wrote the goddamn song, but by all means, you tinker away with my lyrics whenever you want. Feel free to go through all my sheet music with your red pen."

"If you would try it the way I sang it, you'd see I'm correct about it being less complicated."

"By all means, let's make it less complicated whenever possible. Why change your lifestyle now. Easy living. Less complicated songs. Hell, yes." She watched Camille flinch. "You are some kind of camp director, lady."

"With someone like you around, the group needs a camp director," Camille dueled.

"That's right. I get bagged, I cruise, and I even curse. Not much redeeming value in a lowlife like me. My plus column is simple. Easy! Uncomplicated! I write songs. And I don't need a tight-assed, blue-blooded censor. And I don't need a fucking lyric editor." Megan's face heated with rage.

"I didn't figure it would take you long to erupt." Camille thumped the face of her guitar, and then strummed. "I'll make every attempt to sing the correct lyrics, the way they were written."

With a sultry sigh, Megan muttered, "Fine. That means you can concentrate on what those words express. Maybe your inhibition won't blunt my meaning."

Camille lifted her guitar strap over her head. "I need a break," she said as she wheeled around rushing from the stage.

"We all could do with a little break," Fran agreed. She pulled a bottle from her back pocket. After a long swig of whiskey she walked to a backstage table. With a lumbering plop, she sat. Megan followed her, sat across from her, and then looked away. Fran's husky voice queried, "Megan, you got your head up your ass?"

"Maybe so."

"Still got that bottle of swamp juice in your bag?" Fran asked. She then emptied her pint in one gulp.

Megan tugged out a bottle. Handing it to Fran, she contritely spoke, "Sorry I snarled at her. I'll apologize." Megan was well-aware that Fran had been warned about her mercurial moods. Fran deserved better. "I apologize to you, too."

"At all costs, we gotta keep this together. Don't you know how special this sound is? It's more than a couple of transposed words. Hell, blends like this don't come around for donkey's years. I may just be an old coot, but I know when special comes along. Life is packed with booby-traps. You get yourself clobbered by too many, and it's over. You're sleeping on a sewer grate. So think of this group as a winning lottery ticket. The ticket is torn in six pieces. We each hold our own little ole stub. You take a look at that woman over there. She's part of your winnin' ticket. Our ticket. You go the distance with her, and we end up big time. Money can't buy happiness, but it sure as hell can rent a little fun. You two keep this up, we kiss the jackpot goodbye. Back to nowhere-ville. You get what I'm sayin'?"

Megan gazed over at Camille and Selina. Selina was standing over Camille with hands on hips, and leaning into their commiseration. Camille's face was less than radiant. Selina's shoulders straightened when she linked frowns with Megan.

Elena and Jesse had taken advantage of the break to walk outside. Megan needed fresh air, wishing she could be with them, and sad that she wasn't. She inhaled the stench of stale tobacco and booze. With a surge of gallantry, Megan stood. "I'll take care of it, Fran."

"You do that. You're nothing but a couple a little huff cakes."

Megan nodded and then smiled down at Fran. "Thanks for putting up with me."

She ambled toward Camille. "I apologize," she mumbled down. "I'll try not to get crazy about my lyrics in the future. We can try it your way," she acquiesced. "See how it plays."

"That isn't necessary." Camille stood, extended her hand,

and then smiled. "I'll sing it exactly as you wrote it. And I'll never mess up your lyrics again."

Megan took Camille's hand. Selina wrapped her own hand around their handshake. "Now we got the battle line erased," Selina drawled, "we can get back to business."

"I'm really sorry," Megan said looking directly at Camille. "I'll make an effort not to lose my temper again."

"I just don't get you two," Selina disclosed. "On stage you trade looks like a couple of lovers. Step off stage and it is assault and battery time."

Megan shrugged. "Fran just called us a couple of little huff cakes."

The trio shared a laugh, and then Selina suggested that just the two of them find a corner to work out the ragged passages of the song. Megan retrieved her guitar. When she sat opposite Camille she released a smile. She admitted that they, indeed, did trade off passionate glances. She chastised herself for making it so difficult for Camille.

Megan began, "After we know one another better, maybe it will smooth out."

"Megan, it's okay. You know much more about me than I know about you."

"Not much to know."

"You're from Colorado, right?"

"Born and raised in a small community in the mountains, not far from Denver. My folks are divorced. I'm the daughter my mother doesn't talk about." Megan knew the conversation was cumbersome. She hoped it was not upsetting to Camille that she found it difficult to discuss her past.

"They are aware you're lesbian?"

"I try not to clutter my life with pretense. Admittedly, I could have done them a favor by being more discrete. My mother has very little to do with me."

Camille disclosed, "I wanted to please my parents. I even lived with a football star while I was in college. Only for a couple of months. He was everything my family wanted for me." Camille's glance lowered. "He was perfect. He made my family's wealth look pathetic."

Megan grinned. "You're telling me he made your bucks look like chump change? Whew!"

Camille chuckled. "Difficult to believe, but yes. However, I cared for him because he was in the same sad scenario I was in - parent pleasing. The breakup wasn't his fault. It was mine. I'd read about orgasms, but thought it must be made up. Then I was at a college party. In strutted this wild woman rocker. Her group performed. She winked at me. God, I must have blushed pure crimson. Then after her performance she tapped my shoulder. It took my breath away when she whispered all the things she'd like to do to me."

"She must have had a great line and a great delivery."

"Oh, yes. When she found out I was a music major, on the verge of graduation, she invited me to join the group. Via her bed. After college, I looked her up, joined the group, and suddenly my world came crashing around my head."

"Why a rock band?"

"Believe it or not, I found it exciting. But the pace is wearing. There was such an incredible intensity. The voice can't last long in that environment. Drugs didn't make sense. I wasn't cut out for that scene. Maybe that was a part of the trouble. I didn't fit. And I didn't want to tear up my throat attempting."

"Your voice is terrific. I mean it. I've noticed how you work it to the max. I never really learned vocal command. I just open up my mouth and let the words spill out. Words pour from my heart to my throat."

"Yours is a natural sound. Never apologize for that," Camille offered. "And you're one of the best guitarists I've ever heard."

"I think you're a terrific guitarist, too. I'm a one instrument woman. I truly admire Selina and the others being able to make music on numerous instruments. You also play a great fiddle."

"Thanks. I trained to work the symphony circuit. My parents consider anything out of a concert hall to be musical flotsam and jetsam. Naturally they feel I'm wasting my education."

"My parents didn't pay for mine, so they have nothing to

say. I was an English Literature major. I loved writing. I fell in love with words - their power. Lit offers elusive romance." Megan gave a toss of her head. Her dark sienna eyes sparkled under the lighting. "Tough to wail a sonnet, but I do draw some of my vulgarities from the Elizabethans."

Camille's lips curved. "You finished college?"

"Amazing, but true. Put myself through college by working gigs. Songs for soup."

"Well, with your songs, I'd hate to think you might be teaching poetry classes for the remainder of your life."

"The Lake Poets will have to go it without my contributions," Megan remarked. "I'm glad I'm with Primrose. I think we can do some good."

Spontaneously, Camille probed, "Have you always known you're Sapphic?"

"Always. Sapphistry 101! I started celebrating Lesbian Appreciation Day early. At fifteen I was rolling around a hillside with my best girlfriend. During college there were a couple of affairs. Then, when I began drifting, I tried not to spend too many nights alone. After a few years of one-night stands, I met BlueJean. That brings us up to date." Their stare disconnected. Megan's eyes clamped shut. "I don't suppose I'm a representative lesbie," she admitted.

"There's loneliness in your songs."

"That's because there's often loneliness in my heart." Megan lifted her guitar. For a brief moment she wondered if hurling insults wouldn't be more comfortable. Camille's eyes told her it would no longer be possible. There was no satisfaction to be derived from sharpened barbs.

Chapter 5

You can only blow kisses for just so long,
And then you gotta make contact.
You can only stage a handshake scene just once,
And then you gotta change your act.

- Blowin' Kisses

Selina had left earlier with Fran to pick up a new microphone. Camille was glad for the time alone. She stretched out on the motel bed, yawning contentedly. Sun filtered through the blinds. The sunrise glow of morning afforded her time to consider how her feelings had changed.

Perhaps, Camille decided, her first impression of Megan was badly flawed. She hadn't made an attempt to know Megan. This, she ruminated, was evidenced by the relative calm of the past few day. Hostilities had ended as quickly as their bumpy start had begun. Their exchange, that unbuttoning of secrets, was the key. She had speculated that Megan was secretive, but then she had never delved. She certainly hadn't expected the somber singer to announce intimate details of her life. No more than she had expected herself to confide in Megan.

Their sharing hadn't been as a confidence. Both told one another of her history as if delivering a dry newscast. Megan's eyes held only a hint of regret. Camille had shared the fact that she'd attempted heterosexuality. She had been reluctant to share this fact in the past. She knew when musical groups allow their secrets to surface, those previously classified tidbits congeal as a bonding agent. The band's spirit forms as trust is extracted.

When Camille heard a rap on the door she quickly pulled

her robe around her nude body. She heard Jesse's voice and invited her inside.

"I'm goin' across the street to get something t-to eat." Jesse entered the room with a bashful plod. "Thought you might wanna get a sandwich or something?"

"Sure. Where did Elena go?"

"Sleepin' in."

"I'll throw on some clothes. I'm ravenous." Camille wanted to shed the stuffiness of the motel room. She hated its confinement. Even a trip to the small diner across the street offered a rescue. She watched Jesse nod, and then timidly turn her face toward the wall. Camille smiled as she slipped on a pair of lace panties. With a quick tug over her shapely hips, she towed up her denims. Then, without worrying about a bra, she slipped a coral, cotton top over her head. She didn't mind wearing baggy tops with no bra, even though Selina teased her. The tall Texan would playfully accuse that she was going to give those cowboys a stiff zipper.

"I like your bright colors," Jesse complimented.

"Thanks." She gave Jesse's thin waist a sisterly squeeze. "Let's go graze, as Fran says. I can't wait to get out of here."

They made their way across the street. Their strides were completely different. Camille's promenade had springiness. Her well-trained glide was very nearly runway perfect. Jesse, in faded denims, plodded. She opened the door for Camille, and then followed the singer to a back booth.

"I'm glad you came," Jesse remarked.

"Glad you invited me." Camille's smile widened. "Hon, you are the cutest baby butch in town." She tapped Jesse's hand. "How are you feeling about Megan?" she pried.

"We're friends. 'Spose I got a crush on her. M-mostly just a crush. Elena, too."

"Crush?"

"I trust her." Jesse's lower lip trembled slightly as her lips parted. "I hope you t-two are okay now."

"We are. We had a talk." Camille was not totally secure with Megan's volatility. She hoped that their dialogue was a step toward friendship.

Jesse lifted the salt and pepper shakers as the waitress swabbed the tabletop. "Hamburger, fries, and root beer."

"Chef's salad, blue cheese dressing on the side, please. And iced tea," Camille requested. She took a sip of water, then inquired, "It's very important to you that we're all friends, isn't it?"

"Yeah." Jesse's eyes lowered into emotion. "I care for you 'cause you're a w-wonderful musician and singer. I care for Megan 'cause she writes my feelings in her songs."

"Honey, it isn't any of my business, but I don't recommend you get hung up on her. A crush is one thing, but deeper feelings could potentially hurt you," Camille cautioned. "I think too much of you to see her or anyone harm you."

"We're friends. I know she d-doesn't love me." Jesse's lips attempted to form the next word. They were then still.

Camille saw the look of being caged within Jesse's young eyes. "As long as you know that she's still in love with BlueJean."

"How do you know?"

"I just do."

Jesse's mouth wobbled, "She m-matters to me. But I sort of could tell about BlueJean. Megan is sad when anyone says her name."

Camille wished she hadn't told Jesse she was famished. She took her time spreading the salad dressing and stirring the iced tea. She had lost her appetite.

* * *

Megan's mouth tasted like felt fabric. She blinked the cascading light away from her eyes as she began to stir her limbs. She'd had a few too many brews, she admitted, but what the hell. At least it had shut down dreams of holding BlueJean; of bodies enfolding tightly; of BlueJean's cushiony breasts against her own. When living with BlueJean, she always tried to awake before her so she might watch her lover reel in breath. Love entitled Megan to voyeurism. She loved every breath

BlueJean took.

Megan twitched her body awake. She shivered. She reached to get a sip of beer to clear her morning throat. The empty can on the bed stand drizzled only a few drops of warm suds into her mouth. She pitched it onto the pile of spent cans in the middle of the room that mounded from the wastebasket. Tipping as she stood, she attempted to clear her throat. Once balanced, Megan reached in the cooler to pull out a lukewarm beer. She snapped the tab and sipped. Bubbles melted in her mouth. She thought about Patsy Cline's song, "Sweet Dreams," and she mumbled the lyrics to herself.

BlueJean had been on her mind. But that was not news. Now, however, they were only days from Denver, and that concern startled her. Days away from the heartache of seeing BlueJean again, Megan thought. She still had unshed tears. Leftover snippets of memory, she confessed. Her honeyed voice lifted as she toasted her image in the mirror, "The foibles of loving. The taste of summer. Who the hell gets over loving?" She unbridled her thoughts to silence. Her soulful eyes lowered. Each decade sets down a new format of rules. She reached thirty this year, and she wondered what the real cache of life might be. Survival? Quirky, those meditative glances at one's one image.

Megan remembered her conversation with Elena while they were drinking last night. They had discussed fiesta and the heart of fiesta. Jesse had been somber. When Megan inquired, Jesse said that her meaning of fiesta was simply being safe.

With that recollection, Megan wondered how the younger women were this morning. She quickly threw on her clothing. She went in search of company. Elena sprung open the door.

Megan glanced around. "Did Jesse go with Fran and Selina?" she inquired.

"Nope," Elena answered. She sat on the side of her bed, rubbing her eyes. "She must have gone over for some chow. Maybe she's with Camille." She stretched, exposing her cantaloupe breasts.

Megan teased, "Better cover up, I haven't showered yet. I might suggest we take one together. Save water. But that wouldn't be such a hot idea."

Elena stood, walked to the bathroom, and turned the shower's faucet on. She challenged, "Well, let's conserve water."

Megan kicked off her boots. She then stripped. "Pretend we're in a girl's gym class. I need to behave," she warned.

"I went to a Catholic school," Elena said with a protesting face. "I was always getting crushes on my older brother's girlfriends. I knew their bodies better than my brother knew them." She giggled. "Those gym shower scenes are burned in my memory."

"Catholic, huh?"

Testing the water temperature, Elena answered, "Yep. But the first time I kissed a lady I put my rosary into retirement. I figured my patron saint was gonna appear and kick the crap out of me."

"And now?"

Elena entered the shower stall. "Now all I know was that Mary never screwed men either."

Megan chuckled while soaping suds over her body. She made certain to keep it innocent, even when exchanging back scrubs.

"I wasn't religious. I did know that being lesbian was considered socially unacceptable."

"Society isn't always right."

"No. Not always," Megan repeated. Within the order of the universe, the laws of the planet, she surmised, some opinions just aren't significant. And within her boundary of time, it was only the inspiration of artistry that mattered. The harmony of thought, emotion and song, Megan believed. Loneliness is a cavernous moment that empties out the heart, she considered. Shower drops drizzled down as she rapidly lathered her body a second time.

* * *

Elena had quickly wrapped her body in a towel when she

heard the door slam. Her mouth hung as she witnessed both Jesse and Camille enter. Then she noticed Camille's expression of shock when Megan appeared in the doorway nude.

With jovial composure Megan quizzed, "Is this a scavenger hunt?"

Elena and Jesse gave embarrassed giggles at Megan's antics. Megan made no attempt to hide her exquisite form. Elena scurried to toss on a long blouse. Megan's dark hair was the only thing encircling her shoulders. There were strands of hair clutching her neck. Camille looked away from Megan's glistening body as the singer began to dry herself.

Camille suddenly felt the need to mask her desire. She went to the bathroom, slamming the door shut behind her. After relieving herself, she splashed water on her face. She scanned her image in the mirror. She was had heated and a rosy red covered her face. She resented Megan's roughish response. She hoped that her own smoldering lust had been hidden. "Damn," she whispered to her reflection. She flushed the toilet with a vengeance. Hoping that Megan had the good graces to dress, she exited the porcelain sanctuary.

Megan had slipped into a long denim shirt. She hadn't, however, taken time to button the top buttons that exposed her cleavage, nor to cover her long, luscious legs. Camille veiled her sudden craving. She felt confusion. She wondered why seeing Megan was turning her on. For there was no denying that her own breasts swelled, and there was moistness between her legs. She swallowed in an attempt to regain her presence of mind.

Reaching for answers, she assumed it was because Megan was an attractive woman. Camille's own anxiety added to the fact that Megan's nudity was sensual. That must account for the arousal, she attempted to convince herself. She was so stunned by her reaction that she continued to play touch tag with Megan's somber eyes. In the dim light those eyes had the soft sheen of pewter. Camille didn't want to search out mutual arousal. However, she did want to appear nonchalant, and emotionally unencumbered. She reluctantly took a seat on the edge of the bed opposite the bed upon which Elena had slumped down. Megan reclined next to Elena as Jesse quickly took a seat on the desk chair.

Megan propped pillows behind her back, as she flashed a rapid fire smile in Camille's direction. Camille read the smile as one of politeness, rather than sensuality. Camille wondered if Megan sensed her attraction. She hoped Megan had only seen embarrassment. Camille's mind rushed. Her glance tracked Megan's leg. When she realized Megan had seen her line of vision, Camille hastily riveted her gaze to the wall. She would rather they all believe that she was appalled by the promiscuity than that she felt passion for Megan.

Megan reached into her shirt pocket, plucked out a bag of red hot candies, and offered them around. Camille leaned across with her palm opened. Megan noticed her hand was damp. Wanting to spare Camille red stain, she lifted a red hot and gently guided it into Camille's mouth. As it squeezed by her lips, Camille felt her throat constrict. She swallowed the cinnamon juice.

Elena began jabbering excuses about water conservation. Jesse laughed adding, "You know what Fran always says about excuses are l-like assholes. Everybody's got one."

Camille hoped no one noticed the prickles of perspiration on her forehead and the tremors in her hand. She wanted to speak, but her mouth was frozen. Awkwardly, she stood and finally said, "Elena, it isn't any of my business what you two were doing. I should get back to my room. Selina will be returning and I need to press our outfits for tonight."

Megan continued dressing. She hopped as she rushed to put on her denims and boots. "Wait up, I'm going, too."

When they reached the parking lot, Camille turned. "Megan, I don't know what happened between you and Elena, but Jesse has an enormous crush on you."

"Jesse knows Elena and I didn't do a damn thing but get clean. We showered together. Case closed. I know better than to become intimate with either of them. And they both understand that."

"Why do you assume that Jesse knows?"

"She can read people." Megan's hands dipped inside the pockets of her button-fly Levi's "I know because I can also read people. And Jesse was fine with it all. Hell, we're like a family. This is like a locker room deal where the team showers in the open. And besides, I would have owned up to my emotions."

Camille felt the hidden confrontation, but wasn't going to acknowledge it. "It isn't any of my business," she clamored before Megan turned away from her.

Walking back to her room seemed to take Camille forever. An inward probe was stirring holes through her confused heart. The cinnamon flavor was a reminder. Once safely in her room, Camille brushed her teeth. She hungered for the toothpaste's mint flavor. She scrubbed her teeth with ferocious strokes. Even her breathing was discordant. She watched as telluric light slivers crowded through the blinds.

Everything would be fine when Selina returned. She thumbed through a magazine, oblivious to anything on the pages. Her mind was stampeding. Derailed for a final time, she covered her eye with delicate, trembling fingers. With the other hand, she tossed the magazine across the room.

Consoling herself, she speculated that it meant nothing. Her ponderings snagged. She reminded herself that she would never risk hurting Selina for anyone or anything in the world. Maybe Selina's pulse had rushed for other women. Maybe her palms had sweat. Maybe Selina had been aroused by someone other than Camille.

But probably not.

Chapter 6

I remember when loneliness dressed up in empty skies.
And days of tryin' to get tearstains from my eyes.
Where were you when candlelight was all I had to give?
You told me that you had to break away and had to live.

- The Clouds Have Broken

After rehearsal Fran had taken Camille, Elena, and Jesse back to the motel. Selina and Megan had stayed behind to work on new arrangements. Selina wanted to use the piano to score in the instrumentation on Megan's latest song. They were also anxious to see the new photos of the band.

Fran would be picking up the new promotional photographs of Primrose. These were the first photos of what Fran called her new and improved Primrose. Their promo placards featured the photo surrounded by an artist's rendering of the delicate primrose. The promotional copy was flush left and included the band's name along with credits and review excerpts. After picking up the new artwork, she planned to swing back by the rehearsal hall for the two women.

Megan and Selina discussed their excitement to see the new photos.

"I like the primrose border," Selina commented.

"I'd go for just a handful of flowers sprinkled in the corners, but Fran wanted a bushel of primrose." Megan smiled. The bus demonstrated Fran's love of primrose - why would their promo placards and press releases be any different. "But Fran knows what she's doing."

"Back to business," Selina instructed as she played several

intro notes.

Megan strummed a variety of chords before she was satisfied. She released a heavy sigh. "Okay, I'm transposing to D - that should get us there."

"Banjo with our intro," Selina declared. "Jesse'll like that."

"Nice touch," Megan praised. "Perfect. It sure felt great last night."

"Yep. That honky-tonk set had 'em on their feet clapping. You and Cammy swayed those hips. No wonder Camille always calls you Red Hot. You two looked like a couple of Red Hot women."

Amused, Megan placed her guitar down. "Red Hot? For my songs, my temper, or my candy?"

"My best guess is all three. Seems to be working better now for the two of you." Selina crossed her arms. Her hair shone a sorrel cast under the dim lighting.

"We're trying to be civil now."

"You even look like you're a couple."

"It's nothing like that, just show biz," Megan quickly defended.

"I didn't mean it that way. I trust Cammy. I've never wanted to electronically tag my woman. Just trust. You two got off to such a miserable start. I always meant to say that you shouldn't take it personal. Cammy has a ton of venom in storage for BlueJean, too."

"Why BlueJean?"

"Once she told me she isn't sure my romance with BlueJean was extinguished. Extinguished. That was her word. But Cammy knows she doesn't ever need to worry about me. Hell, I'm the luckiest woman alive. Past bullshit in my life doesn't matter anymore. My life is without hurt since Cammy."

Megan realized that Selina's background had better prepared her for prison than for Primrose. She had been battered, abused, and kicked around as a kid. Her childhood had placed hurdles before her. Somehow she had cleared them. She had been understandably left with a difficulty in trusting. After falling in love with BlueJean, she discovered the potential for trust. That gift had been shattered. Then Camille entered her life, and Selina's trust was harder won. But finally, and completely, it was issued.

"I'm glad you have Camille," Megan remarked with a simultaneous pat on her friend's arm. Her touch entreated a smile.

"She's turned my life around. It evens the score for those early miserable times."

"She loves you."

Selina playfully divulged with an impish grin, "After last night, I should say. Cammy was never so damned turned on."

Megan reeled her hand back. She had noticed Camille being overly attentive to Selina. But Megan also noticed electrical sparks scattering when Camille examined her nude body. Megan was certain that there was lust when her body had been perused, rather than with the disapproval Camille had been trying to reflect. There was downright hunger portrayed in the eyes of the lovely blonde.

"Here's Fran now," Selina exclaimed.

Fran's face was puffed and rose-colored from the past evening of drinking. Her eyes were rimmed with waxy lashes. She often joked that the doctor's diagnosed her to be within hours of dying if she didn't stop drinking and smoking. Fran told the story, then slapped her leg and laughed. She said she'd outlasted the doc's call on her life by at least twenty years.

She pulled the group photos from an envelope. Waving them overhead, she shouted approval. "Hot damn, women, we got us some damn nice pictures." She spread them on the table. "What you think?"

"Lovely," Megan remarked. Her eyes chained to the smiling image of Camille. She felt a strange burning anger inside. It torched her soul. Seemingly, it was a mixture of rejection with hopelessness. She had felt that way when BlueJean left their apartment for the final time. She often experienced it on frosty mornings at her cabin. She would split firewood. As the ax hammered, splinters of pine flew through the air simulating her heart. She questioned why she felt that way now. She surveyed the photos again.

Fran read her discomfort. "What's got you down in the mouth?"

"Nothing. Just weary."

"We'll be getting off early Sunday night. Told 'em that we'd only do an early show 'cause my women need them a little R&R. That'll give us time to go out to rope some of them rodeo queens." Fran chuckled. "Gonna be lots a happenin' Big dance and all. Hot damn, what I wouldn't give to be your age and look like you. Bar the door. Ready to party?"

"You bet," Megan ratified. With a wink, she asked Selina, "Guess you and Camille will be enjoying a night in?"

"Snuggle city," Selina reported. "After last night, yes indeed. Never been so great," she disclosed.

"If Cammy was my little filly," Fran sputtered, "I sure as hell wouldn't let her off my rangeland."

"As a couple it seems better to just be around people you trust." Selina picked up the sheets of music she'd been working on. She waved them in the air. "And we have Megan's new song worked out. Sizzlin' sounds."

Fran's glance connected with Megan. "How about we drop Selina back with her woman so's you and me can get us an engine full of steam?" Fran suggested. "I got the devil at my elbow."

"Count me in," Megan answered. "A drink or two will relax me for tonight's performance."

Selina kidded, "After all that booze last night? You two aren't retiring from elbow-bending."

"Naw," Fran gave a huff. "Well, Red Hot, what you say?"

"Ready, willing, and able," Megan retorted. She smiled, asking, "So you know my new nickname, too?"

"It fits doesn't it?" Fran questioned.

Selina chuckled. "Wait 'til Cammy hears she's got everyone calling Megan 'Red Hot' now."

Megan swallowed. "Glad I don't eat horehound candy."

* * *

"I'm absolutely livid," Camille blustered. She glared across the cramped dressing room. Selina, Jesse, and Elena were scurrying to tune their instruments. They had picked up Megan's outfit from her room. They then had hastily written a note telling Fran and Megan that one of the motel's employees had delivered them to the club. Fran and Megan were to drive to the club directly. "They," she fumed, "are out socking down sauce, and we are here worrying."

"They'll be here in time," Selina offered.

"I'm angrier at Megan than at Fran," Camille seethed. "We all know Fran is a boozer, but she's never been back late from cocktail hour to pick us up. And she's usually with someone who will do the driving."

"Here they come now," Elena chimed. "Hey, partners, she greeted the wobbly women. "We're glad you got here."

Camille glared at Megan. "Look at her. She's been drinking all afternoon. And I'm supposed to sing with her like that."

"She'll be okay," Selina interceded with a dubious tone. Selina's concerned glance back at Megan made her spirit topple. Megan was clearly smashed. "Cammy," she whispered, "we'll pick up the pieces if need be."

Loudly enough for Megan to hear, Camille's voice snapped, "This isn't preschool. It isn't rehearsal. We're on in a few minutes." She was angry at Megan, and angry at herself for allowing Megan to entreat her trust. Again, Megan became her nemesis. "You know as well as I do that liquor and drugs burn through any layer of self-control. And she has very little self-control to start with."

"Come on, babe," Selina murmured. "Let's get through the night. We'll talk with them tomorrow."

Camille passed by Megan in the narrow hallway. "If you're not doing one of your famous stage vanishing acts, you're falling down drunk."

Megan contritely staggered behind the other members as they went on stage. She fumbled with her guitar strap. Camille reached to assist. "I've got it," Megan insisted.

"I hope you've stuck a red hot candy in your mouth. You smell terrible." Her stern scowl prompted a comedic shrug from

Megan. "I'm serious."

"You sure as hell are. You're one of the most serious people I ever met." Megan's lopsided grin challenged. "And I've met a shit load of very serious folks." Megan reached in her pocket, pulled out a couple of tiny red hots. She popped them in her mouth. "There. Now you won't need to put up with beer fumes, Princess."

Camille issued a remote glare. She began to respond. Fran had moved to the microphone. She covered it. Whispering, she spoke to the lead singers. "There's a guy out there who just requested we include "Over the Rainbow," during this set. She motioned toward a barrel-chested Texan at the bar. His decorated Stetson was tipped toward the women. Large, ornate rings decorated his fingers.

"Bet he can't rope a steer with all that jeweled hardware on his fingers," Megan said with a giggle.

"Hold on a minute," Fran scolded. "He offered us a C-note to play it. We're doin' it second song. Hell, I'm a workhorse, not a racehorse, and that's taught me how money is mighty important. It is chicken one day, feathers the next in this business. And look 'em in the eyes when you sing it."

Panic pricked Camille's nerves. She hated requests. It meant that they were for sale. "I'm not sure of the lyrics," Camille answered. "And she'll be lucky to make it through what we did rehearse," she said with a nod in Megan's direction.

Fran spoke gruffly, "We can use that money."

"I'll sing the song myself," Megan declared. To Camille, she uttered, "You just stand back. Quit acting like such a flipping grump. On the refrain you can maybe give me a little backup. I'll pull the sonofabitch down."

Fran gave the mic a tap to make certain it was live. "Ladies and gents, here's Primrose." To the band she muttered, "Women, let's make 'em think we care."

Camille whispered to Megan. "Don't you dare leave me standing without lyrics. You want to look like a fool, do it on your own time."

"Ever read the love letters of Thomas Carlyle and Jane Welsh?"

"What?" Camille asked incredulously.

"They just don't train snobs like they used to." Megan's grin took Camille off guard. Megan cited, "Even in my most lugubrious humor." She then laughed as the intro began.

Camille's heart was pounding with anger and with fear. She thought about the rock group when they were so drugged up. "Just don't screw this up," Camille commanded.

She was amazed that they got through the opener without problems. Megan's guitar strumming began the introduction with intricate fretwork. Camille realized that Megan was actually doing a superb job with guitar. Then her melancholy voice began. A suspended note was formed from the very heart of Megan's soul. She magnified her pain, and her promise, through a universal teardrop within the song. Megan opened the tap on her voice as well as her heart. The group's music began to braid behind her. They were experiencing an emotional interchange as they never had before.

When Megan concluded the lyrics, there were several moments of complete silence. Then the patrons were on their feet applauding. Camille turned to see the band members also clapping. Her glance magnetically drew back to Megan. She joined in the rousing applause.

"Excellent. Just plain excellent," she murmured to Megan.

* * *

Megan's apology was strained. The band had graciously accepted. Megan was completely sober for the Sunday afternoon performance. She remained contrite and quiet. After the last set Megan asked if Fran minded dropping her off at a small country and western, lesbian bar. She hadn't wanted to go with Fran, Elena, and Jesse to a big gay rodeo dance. After Fran dropped Camille and Selina back at the motel, the others continued on. Megan wished the trio a fun time, and apologized for not wanting to accompany them. They seemed to understand when she begged out by telling them that she needed to treat her loner personality to a night away.

Megan hadn't been at the dingy bar long when she felt arms wrapping around her. "Howdy, Megan Holloway!" Kasey Colby clamored as she planted a kiss on Megan's mouth.

"Colby!" Megan bellowed. "You're an entry in the rodeo?"

"Damn betcha. And I hear you're playin' with Primrose now."

"Right. I didn't know if you'd be here or not. Last I heard you'd re-injured."

"Got more goddamn staples in my ass. I pass a magnetic force and I'm goin' butt first," Colby cackled. "But I'm not about to miss Frontier Days."

Megan pointed to the barstool next to hers. "Sit that cute little metal ass right down."

Kasey Colby's eyes sparkled. She was an adorable rodeo star with long, bright mahogany curls, freckles, and kiwi-pulp-colored, iridescent eyes. She was also a favorite of the rodeo circuit. Known for her trim, 5'5" sexy spunk, she could ride, rope, and wrestle with the best of them. Still only in her mid-twenties, she never turned down a challenge. Media called her fearless. When BlueJean and Megan were a couple, BlueJean had interviewed Kasey Colby. The deejay called the rodeo darling too good to pass up. So she hadn't. That was when Megan and BlueJean split.

Megan ordered Colby a beer, then complemented, "You don't look any the worse for wear."

"Hell, heroes don't need a shove," she joked. "I keep after it."

"The purse treating you okay?"

"Bull-doggn' was fine. Did some great qualifying. A couple of dirt dives, but no real scalp scratchers. One fuckin' bronc gave me a britches burner. I knew he was trouble when he tried to iron me against the chute. Hell, it was profitable enough for the bruises."

"Glad you survived it."

"Yep. Reckon when I get to rodeo heaven I'm gonna get the shit spurred outta me by a bunch of ornery four-legs," she said with a laugh. She took a quick gulp of beer then wiped her face. "Sorry about things with BlueJean. I figured you'd get back together."

Megan forced a smile. "Forever is a long time to spend with a hot-blooded woman. BlueJean goes in for the Whitman's Sampler of dating." She turned her cool bottle of beer around several times. She had hoped that time would tame their love, but it hadn't. Now she wanted for the hurting to end. But her heart had been ripped out by the roots. "BlueJean needs to do her own thing. She recommended me for this gig with Primrose. She had been with one of the members. Selina Nesbitt."

"Nice woman. Selina."

"She's been a good friend."

"I'm alone; you're alone. How about a couple drinks and dances? Then maybe head over to a steakhouse I discovered. Biggest damned platter of beef in town. I got my truck outside."

Megan nodded her approval. "What are you doing alone? I figured those buckle bunnies would be hot after you."

"Fresh outta buckle bunnies tonight. And why are you alone? Where's your band?"

"It all just got to be too much closeness. I'm sort of in Coventry anyway. The quick remorse edition is that I got tanked before a performance the other night. I opened my heart and allowed the contents to spill out, but it wasn't enough. Detention hasn't helped much."

"Band pissed?"

"Just Selina's woman."

"She looks tender enough to thaw a rock."

Megan chuckled. "Actually, looks are deceiving. She can be hell's ambassador. Way too regal and elegant for a country band. She acts like we should throw bananas to country-western audiences."

Colby roared. "You do need to get away. Come on, let's dance."

Megan found Colby's body warm as it grazed hers. The dance floor was filled, and that crowed them together. Megan didn't mind, she was glad for the company, the conversation, and the laughs they shared.

By midnight they decided on dinner. The meal, Megan

agreed, was excellent. The platter was filled with a huge steak, and seasoned steak fries. Although she had been reluctant to talk about Primrose, Megan had loosened up after a few drinks. She had expressed optimism about the band's sound. As they crawled into the truck's cab, Megan flashed a smile in Colby's direction. She wasn't surprised when Colby requested Megan share a motel room with her.

"Got kicked outta my room last night," the rodeo star explained. "Rip-snortin' loud. I really got a skin full. Figured I'd spend up some of that prize money by celebrating. Anyway, we might be able to find a room somewhere."

"Probably not with Frontier Days. Come on back where I'm staying," Megan suggested. "If nothing else, we can bunk in the bus."

"They aren't gonna have a problem with you bringing me?"

"Naw. Most of them won't anyway. They should be used to my Bacchus worshipping by now. Speaking of which, there's a little liquor store on the corner there. Might as well stock up."

After the stop, they headed to the motel. Megan heard muffled laughter behind Fran's door. She knocked. Jesse and Elena had joined the road manager for a party. The radio was playing country. Fran had already passed out. Megan was glad when Elena suggested that she could take Colby to their room and the younger women would stay behind in Fran and Megan's room. Megan was pleased that Camille and Selina had made an early night of it. She hated the thought of Camille's disapproving side-glances.

Megan had never had a relationship with anyone in BlueJean's past. Although she didn't fault Colby, the affair had caused the severing of her relationship with BlueJean. Mostly she put the blame for that on BlueJean. She knew that Kacey Colby had only been the toy. They had all been BlueJean's toys. But while in BlueJean's arms it had felt wondrous and glorious, and one sensed a feeling of importance to the illustrious radio personality. It had felt brand new each time BlueJean touched Megan. Megan's heart sprinted for a moment. The pounding flooded her being and her face flushed.

Megan considered the past while sliding the key out of the

lock. The door sprung open. "There's some icy beer in the cooler." Megan pointed toward the Coleman. When Colby handed her a brew, Megan asked, "You've probably seen BlueJean since I have. She's okay?"

"She's still everyone's mystery." Colby's eyes flickered in the low light. "Saw her when I was down at the fair. Still got her string of fans lined around the world. You still have feelings for her?"

Heavy-lidded, Megan looked away. She wondered if her soul would forever be sewn to BlueJean's vagabond heart. For many moments her hypnotic trance flipped through memories. She studied the marionette show of shadows. There was the night BlueJean called to make her excuses. Kacey Colby was in the hospital. She'd broken her leg while barrel racing. The lower portion of Colby's leg was in a cast. The fact that Colby was in traction had not stopped BlueJean from hungering after the rodeo star. A friend divulged the performance to Megan. It had been cuddling, and fondling, kissy-facing, etc., the friend relayed to a broken-hearted Megan. Now, Megan considered, she was sitting in a motel room with the rodeo star.

"BlueJean was my past," Megan retorted. "Now it is only phantasmal love. That's all."

"Hell, folks think bull-riding is dangerous. Trying to work a relationship with BlueJean is true danger. I'd rather take a face-plant off a charging bull any day," Colby quipped. She unknotted the silk tie from her neck. "She still loves you. She told me she didn't want to hold you back. When you were with her you'd never go on the road. She said you turned down opening for some pretty powerful acts. She said that you had stopped intimacy before she bedded me."

"Bird in the cage theory. How goddamned considerate of her. She opened the cage to fling me out into the world. What crap!" Megan unsnapped her shirt. "She did it for me. That doesn't sell. She wanted to make love to every woman in the world. That's what she flipping wanted."

"There's rodeo lingo called the hole. It's the inside of a spinning bull. When we enter the hole it usually means you're going on a britches burn. Sorta like being inside a tornado. Well, BlueJean is that kinda danger. When she winks it's like entering a buckin' chute. Another expression is seein' daylight. That's when you come loose from a bucking animal. You're up so high the spectators can see daylight between rider and animal. There's this technique called floating where you look like you're being bucked off with every jump. You see, I think that's how BlueJean works the drama of romance. Like she's on display even with the person she loves."

"I didn't have time to psychoanalyze her," Megan said with bitterness. "Three years wasn't near enough time to understand her."

"She still carries your photo in her wallet. The only photo she saves."

"That thought certainly chases away the loneliness she left me with." Megan hated being transparent but knew her cynical words were properly interpreted as caring.

"Still wanna have a good time? I mean, you don't wanna lie fallow too long or you'll forget how."

"Even a broken clock is correct twice a day. Let's take a long, warm shower. After that, let's be a couple of degenerate women in a night of unbridled lust," Megan invited with a sexy smile.

"BlueJean always said you were the best."

"Can we forget BlueJean for the night?"

"I can."

Megan covered Colby's lips with her kiss. "One of the infinite tasks of the human heart is redemptive love."

Colby laughed. "Shit! You better talk my language 'cause I got no idea what the hell you're spouting. I was just hoping I can satisfy you. That's all."

"Ride 'em, cowgirl," Megan lulled.

* * *

Flashes of sunlight penetrated Camille's shaded eyes as she walked toward Elena and Jesse's motel room.

Just when Camille had believed Megan to be civilized, the

woman went on stage totally loaded. Megan's raw talent had rescued her. Camille admitted that the performance had been extraordinary. Although disapproving, she'd agreed to put it aside. Megan had promised never to go on after drinking.

Camille knocked on the door. She guessed Elena was showering, and perhaps Jesse had gone on for an early breakfast.

"Oh lord," she exclaimed as she entered the room. Her head rotated to another direction. She heard the moans of pleasure halt as Kasey Colby's burrowing head bolted upward from between Megan's thighs. Colby's arms were looped around Megan's hips. "I'm sorry. Jesse and Elena told me to wake them. I did knock."

"It's okay," Megan called to her. She slid up against the pillows. Lifting a crumpled sheet that had fallen to the floor, she tossed it around Colby. Then she bolted to the chair to gather a robe. Once she had secured the robe's belt, she glanced into Camille's shocked face. "Elena and Jesse are in Fran's room. They had a little party over there last night. They suggested we trade rooms."

"Obviously the party continued here as well. Look, I apologize, but they did ask me to stop by for them. We'd planned on breakfast."

Colby giggle. "Yeah, well I was just having breakfast."

"Camille Ward," Megan introduced, "I'd like you to meet Kasey Colby. Of rodeo fame."

"I've heard the name," Camille acknowledged as she attempted to produce a smile.

"Howdy," Colby greeted her. "Care to join us?"

Megan's head sagged into her hands. "Colby, Camille is with Selina."

Camille's face went as crimson as her blouse. Her embarrassment was obvious to the other women. She had wanted to run the moment the door flapped open. "I'd better get back and see if Selina has awakened yet." She had given Megan a searing glower before slamming the door behind her. She rushed across the graveled lot toward Selina.

She wanted to bury herself in her lover's arms. She wanted to hide away forever. She had never walked in on two women making love before. Even when with the rock band was at its wildest. It didn't seem to upset Megan until Kacey Colby recommended a threesome. Perhaps that had upset Megan because of her friendship with Selina.

"Sweetheart, what's wrong?" Selina asked as she opened the door.

"I just walked in on Megan and Kacey Colby making love."

Selina wrapped Camille in her embrace. She kissed her temple. "Colby? The rodeo darling?"

"The same. I've never been so damned embarrassed in my life."

"You sure they even noticed you?" Selina asked with a bemused smile.

"Of course they noticed," she snapped.

"Then they must not have been too involved."

"Damn it, they were involved. Then that Kasey person asked me if I wanted to join them. How insulting."

"Take it easy, sweetheart. Megan's real open-minded about these things." Selina whistled through her teeth. "BlueJean ran off with Colby. I'm amazed Megan would touch her. You know, seein' as how BlueJean messed around with the woman. She musta been drunked up."

"Who *hasn't* made love with BlueJean!" she chaffed.

Sara grinned. "You and Fran. Oh, and the youngsters. Don't think she's made it with Jesse and Elena. Yet." Selina registered the concern in Camille's eyes. "It isn't the end of the world. We're family. We should be glad that Megan is finding some comfort."

"Comfort scarcely describes it. I want to close the world out."

Selina caressed her temple. "I love you, babe." Selina took Camille in her arms. "I'm gonna show you how much I love you."

An hour of passion, spent on pleasing one another, went by all too quickly. Camille cherished Selina's tender calm. After love-sharing, they snuggled. Camille felt protected in Selina's embrace. She wanted their love to obliterate all of the morning's events. She wanted more than that. She wanted her feelings from Selina authenticated through her touch. Megan's image invaded her thoughts. She wanted to end that invasion.

For the next drowsy half hour, Camille attempted to extrapolate reasons for her anger. She felt anger with Megan. She delved. Was it because Megan was making love? Camille's eyes misted. She felt the captive tears along her eyelids. She continued questioning her anger. Her stomach tumbled and pitched. Had she been mortified by seeing the two nude women? Or was she concerned that her true emotions showed? Just as they had the first time she saw Megan's nudeness.

Camille gave a lengthy sigh. No, she had made her adoration of Selina visible. She showered her love on Selina. Whatever Megan was doing was Megan's concern. After all, the brooding singer had been celibate for half a year. She was now enjoying and being enjoyed by a beautiful rodeo queen. And why not? Megan didn't require Camille's imprimatur.

Camille's introspection gathered strength. She wanted to confront her own truth. She continued questioning her motives. Suddenly she caught her breath. Had she wanted to be the one making love with Megan? Had she wanted to gather Megan's supple body near her lips? Had she wanted Megan's mouth, her breasts, and her orgasm? Her love?

Snuggling her face against Selina's shoulder, Camille's eyes squeezed shut. She could not grapple for a truth she would forever deny. She would never harm Selina. "Please," she implored as she embraced Selina, "never let me go."

Chapter 7

Here I am, all alone again.
Feeling my mind go lonely.
Finding life has closed on in,
I'm reaching, and all alone again.
I was always gonna remember where I been.
I wasn't 'spose to fall in love again.

- All Alone Again

"What's a flesh adventure without a guest dropping by?" Megan said with a chuckle. Leaning into the conversation with Colby, Elena, and Jesse, Megan proudly added, "Voyeurism at its very best!" She lowered her voice so none of the coffee shop's patrons would hear. "We were in a wonderful tangle at the time."

"W-what did you do?" Jesse queried.

"I asked her if she wanted to join us," Colby beamed as she reported, "Hell, she looks plenty good to me."

"Live porn," Elena said as she slid down against the back of the booth laughing in giggling gulps.

"It's funny now, but I'm not sure the princess thought it was proper," Megan said with a sputter. "If she'd dropped by to inspect the troops, she got an amazing inspection opportunity."

Colby teased, "Hell, anytime I get a good response, I figure I must be doin' something amazing."

"I'm guessing rave reviews, but then Camille's reviews aren't in yet," Megan said.

"Yeah," Colby agreed, "and from that sour look on her face, I might be getting trashed. She's a looker, but I bet she can get mighty uppity." She stabbed the fork into steaming hash browns. "I'd a liked to have had the chance to see if she's that uppity in bed. Bet she's got steamin' loins."

Megan's head dipped. Her perusal of the menu camouflaged anger over the thought of Colby with Camille. Camille's virtue needed no champion. She was well-armored with a sense of loyalty to Selina. Megan was lumbered with the consideration that she might be experiencing some strange jealousy. She wondered if being protective of her friend's relationship was a cover. Megan hated veils. Was it, she thought, that she didn't want Colby near Camille? "Don't even think about Camille. She's with Selina. They're tight. That's the way they both like it." Her scowl then softened. "I need some strong coffee."

Colby's arm orbed Megan's shoulder. As the clasp tightened, Megan glance toward the booth directly opposite the aisle. Fran, Selina, and Camille were being seated. After a swarm of greetings, Camille's glanced latched with Megan's. The crystalline shimmer of Camille's blue eyes fascinated Megan. She sealed any emotion those eyes might have produced while they were on stage.

The waitress threaded through a cluster of tables to get the women a fresh pot of coffee.

Selina lifted her cup high to toast, "Here's to Primrose!"

Each cup was lifted. Megan hated the way Colby was leering at Camille's plunging neckline. The brightly colored tank top displayed Camille's cleavage. Colby made a point of nudging Megan when they entered. Megan's slow burning anger seemed to intensify, then dissipate as she reigned in her emotion. Her back stiffened, her teeth clamped, and then she allowed her body to release the tension. The aroma of bacon reminded Megan she hadn't finished her breakfast. It was a welcome interruption.

Banter continued with small talk until Colby leaned across the aisle in Camille's direction. "You comin' back for a second feature this afternoon?"

Ruffled, Camille's smile faded. She glanced away. That only fueled Colby's flirting.

But before she could continue, Megan gave her arm a tug. "Drop it," she insisted.

"Just letting her know that my offer stands."

Selina had been munching toast. She took it with her normal good-natured charm. She reached for the creamer, poured cream into her coffee, and then passed the cream and sugar to Fran. It was Megan's steely glare that became noticed by everyone.

Colby continued, "You're welcome anytime."

"Don't you have a cow to ride?" Camille jabbed. She stood, threw her napkin down. Rapidly, she headed for the door.

Selina corrected, "Bull. She rides bulls, sweetheart." But Camille had not heard her.

Megan gave Colby a shove. She scooted out of the booth. "You wait here for me while I apologize for your ignorance."

Megan dashed behind Camille. When she caught up, Camille whirled around. She seemed astonished that it was Megan instead of Selina. "Keep your little tramp to yourself," she spat. She wheeled back around. "She's perfect for you. A true matched set."

Megan followed. "Camille, I'm sorry about what she said. But why are you attacking me?" She reached for Camille's arm. "Please believe me, I didn't know she was going to say those things. I'll dump her. Will that do?"

"Don't drop her on my account." Camille's eyes flared. She blazed, "You just make certain that she shows some respect for my relationship with Selina. You got that?"

Megan sighed deeply. "I'll make certain it doesn't happen again."

"Your little bronco dolly is waiting for you."

Megan felt Camille's arm pull from her hand. Her shoulders lowered. "I don't want you or Selina hurt."

When her eyes drifted back to Camille's face Megan saw a portrait of someone as confused as she was. Camille's words wrenched slowly from her heart, "I would never want Selina hurt. And I would never hurt her."

Megan rummaged through her emotions. Her glance tethered to Camille's. Megan saw a flash within Camille's eyes that told of her wound. Then there was a glimmer of love, or perhaps forgiveness, Megan couldn't differentiate. Camille twirled her petite frame. She sprinted toward the motel.

Stranded, Megan's outstretched hand sagged to her side. She felt that Camille's warmth had shined on her for one brief moment. And then it was forever gone.

* * *

Fran was reclined on the double bed. Her boots were crossed at her ankles, her Stetson dipped over her face, and snores heaved her body. Camille entered. She started to leave, then saw Fran stir. "'Mon in," Fran mumbled. She tapped her hat back, then grilled, "Cammy, baby doll, you finished rehearsing?"

"I am. Selina and Megan are in our room working on a new arrangement, as usual. They're leaning over sheaves of notated scores. I had nothing to contribute, so I thought I'd see if you might want to grab a cup of coffee across the street."

"I just got comfortable. My breathing's been playin' up. I heard that primrose oil was once used by Native Americans as a medicinal remedy. Wonder if it would cure my gaspin' and chokin'?" She coughed. "But you can grab a soft drink in the cooler, and pull me out a beer. Did the kids go to the rodeo with Colby?"

"Yes," Camille answered with an edge to her voice. Digging around in the cooler, she pulled bottled water for herself and a beer for Fran. "Maybe you wouldn't need primrose oil if you'd quit smoking," she suggested as she handed the beer to Fran.

"Thanks, baby doll." Fran pulled the tab and then took a long swig. "I'm too danged old to be giving up bad habits." With a huge grin, she added, "Anyway, they'd never give me up."

"Last night I had a little trouble with my voice on the encore number," Camille complained.

"We been pushin' it with so many rehearsals. Even the

calluses on Megan's fingers are showing wear. Well, when we get to Denver, we can cut back on our rehearsal time." Fran sat up as she took a long swig of beer. She then opened the bedside table drawer to extract a quart of whiskey. "My favorite drink has always been the next one," she quipped with a laugh that converted into a sputter. After the rattling cough dipped, Fran eased the rim of the bottle to her lips.

"Maybe the drinking irritates you."

"Hell, they call me a hard drinker, but there ain't anything hard about puttin' a little booze down your throat."

Camille broached the subject slowly. "It might be better for your health if you could ease up on the drinking."

Fran gave a harsh cackle before slumping back down against her pillow. "I began drinking about loneliness. Fortify with a drink or two. Before that it was a bunch of damned gallivanting with nothing to show for it. But maybe now bright days are gonna break for all of us. I have a feeling it is about to finally pay. Primrose can make all those dusty trails and black nights worth it. All along, I just wanted me one winner. Sure, there have been plenty of near hits. But someone always came into the picture as soon as the group got going. Nothing in my life has been a win." She wheezed. "But Primrose is different."

"Selina thinks we'll be ready to cut a demo in Denver."

"BlueJean has the connections. We got our repertoire." Fran stretched. "Mixin' a good demo is tricky as hell. We need a good recording studio."

"BlueJean knows her way around the recording business. I'm sure she will select the best available."

"Havin' a great track before we hit Nashville won't hurt. We can lay down enough songs for an album."

"I hope we can include the new song Megan's writing. It's titled 'Red Hot Blues' after her nickname."

"If she finishes it in time, we'll include it for sure."

"Selina said it ought to be finished on the trip to Denver."

Fran's glance zeroed in on Camille. "We got the sound and now we need to get the look. With extra work, we got us a few extra bucks in the kitty. We'll get some new, matchin' duds."

Camille nodded. "That will be nice. A little accent color."

"Are things with you and Megan better?"

"I'm even tolerating Colby," Camille divulged with a hasty grin. "That hasn't been easy. I guess she's on her way down to Tulsa tomorrow. And we're headed for Denver, so maybe Megan's little fling has flung."

Fran glanced down at her scuffed boots. "Cammy, you know what we got is real special. You and Megan are magic. I been waiting all my life for this combination. We can win. I may never have this again." Fran lapsed into a trance. "You know that, don't you?"

"I can tell it is special."

"It's magic. You two are like no other duo I've seen. The way you two sing. Even the way that your moves are synchronized is great. Megan isn't a bad woman. You two had me worried a little while back when you were bickering."

"We don't always understand one another." Camille inhaled deeply. Fran's gaze was nailing her to the wall. "It has just taken some time. We're both trying to get along."

With slow, pensive words, Fran offered, "Cammy, you know that even if Selina wasn't around, Megan isn't your sort. She's moody. Drinks too much for your tastes. She may be a beauty, but she's got trouble in her heart." Fran's stare was encroaching.

Camille asked, "Why are you telling me all of this?"

"Just telling it," Fran disclosed. The remainder of the statement was silence. They both knew that not much could get by Fran's hillbilly scrutiny.

* * *

After their performance, the group disbanded. Megan and Colby had started their final night together with a drinking bout before a love-making session. Megan had been impatient, and her usual tenderness became indifference. She crawled from their bed. She leaned against the wall. Lifting the blinds enough to peek out into the darkness of night, she sighed. This night was murkily smudged. The flash from lit up beer signage depressed Megan.

"Out there on stage tonight Primrose was connecting," Megan slurred.

Colby sat up. "You were terrific. I love the sound of your voice, Megan. It is country, but damned if you couldn't cross over to pop."

"I'm not interested in pop."

Unsteadily the nude rodeo star walked to Megan's side. "Good, 'cause I like country best." Her hand grazed Megan's face with a caress. She eased Megan's nakedness against her own, into her clasp. Her lips were against Megan's ear. "I want you." Her body pressed Megan against the wall as her mouth hungrily kissed her lips. "Let's continue."

Megan reached for Colby's hand. She led her back to the disheveled bed. Megan pulled Colby against the length of her flesh. After many minutes of frustration, Megan felt a chill. Her heart raced, but she realized it was useless. Passion had dissolved. Megan drew back, unable to satiate her desire.

Colby scoffed, "You too drunk or am I the wrong woman?"

"I don't need BlueJean to have a climax," Megan growled her response. She pulled away from Colby's clutch.

"I wasn't talkin' about BlueJean. I mean your little blonde singing buddy. I see how the two of you look at each other. Maybe you need to pretend I'm Camille."

Before Colby got another word out, Megan threw her from the bed. Enraged, she pitched Colby's clothing at her. "Get the fuck out of here." When Colby sat immobile, Megan lunged at her, pulling the rodeo star to her feet. Colby began to struggle with Megan as she was being pulled toward the door. Megan fought off Colby's scratching. She opened the door. Then she tossed Colby out onto the sidewalk. She wildly pitched Colby's clothing and boots at her. With a fury Megan stepped into her own denims, rolled a t-shirt over her head, and began throwing Colby's luggage out onto the sidewalk.

Colby haphazardly dressed. As her duffle bag flew past her, she turned. She flung herself, scratching, at Megan. Blood curdling screams were unintelligible. Rebuffing Colby's pounding fists, Megan attempted to get back into the room. She felt her hair being pulled as she swung around. She tried to throw Colby back against the ground. Colby tripped the drunken Megan. As they fell, Colby attacked her with a blizzard of slaps. From the corner of her eye, Megan saw Jesse running from one side and a partially clad Selina from the other. Selina's shirt was flying from her body as she reached Megan. She pulled Megan back away from Colby's sprawled frame.

"Cut it the hell out, you two. You're gonna wake everyone," Selina chastised. She quickly admonished, "Now stop it before someone calls the law."

Jesse had pinned Colby to the gravel. Colby spat, "Just let me at her. Nobody does that to Kasey Colby."

"Nobody smart would get near enough to you," Megan charged. She then again lunged for Colby.

Selina restrained her. "What's going on?" she demanded.

Megan's jet eyes swayed to Camille. Clad in her robe, she was rushing across the parking lot toward them. Megan muttered, "Not a damn thing. Just a lover's spat."

Camille approached. She seethed, "You two are going to get us all thrown out of here. If Fran finds out about this…"

"It's over, sweetheart," Selina replied. She moved back, releasing Megan. "Listen, Red Hot, Fran is hell on this kinda thing. She always jokes that guzzlers are acceptable as long as there's not any brawling. You break up your hands, it shuts the band down. Band rule - no fighting, ever."

Colby stood, brushing dust from her denims. "She went berserk. Wigged out."

"What started it?" Selina questioned. The air was electric with tension.

"Hot stuff there couldn't get going," Colby charged. "You know the old saying, don't go huntin' if you can't kill. She couldn't do it. I tell her she must need her blonde partner to get it off…"

Again Megan lurched in her direction with the quickness of whiplash. It took both Selina and Jesse to restrain her. "Get her the hell out of my sight," Megan shouted.

After garbled expletives, Colby said, "I need to get the rest of my stuff."

She followed Jesse back to the room so she could retrieve her makeup case and sundries.

Selina tried to settle Megan. "You've both been drinking too much."

Megan's eyes linked with Camille's anguished glance. It wasn't until Colby was safely in the cab of her truck that Selina released Megan's arm. Colby's truck roared off, but not before she shouted from her window, "Send that fuckin' bitch back to the pound." Dust rose, and the tires spit gravel in the distance.

Megan glared. "She's the flipping nut."

"Come on, she was just mouthing off." Selina gazed back at Camille. "It's absurd. She was the one hitting on Cammy. She wanted to cause a scuffle. She likes having a hissy fit. Hey, Red Hot, you know I trust you both. You're my friend."

Megan stepped back, stumbling. She looked down at her hands as her fingers splayed. Assessing the damage, her limpid eyes burned. She turned, staggering back to her room. After slamming the door behind her, she sat on the bed's soft ledge. She took out a half spent pint, pressed it to her lips, and drained it with one series of gulps. She pitched the empty at the wall. Shattering as it broke - the snapping crunch of glass reminded her of how fragile it all really is. Remaining was the splintered glass, another mess she would need to deal with in the morning.

She slipped into bed. After grappling with the blankets, she attempted to sleep. Her eyes snapped open. She gazed around the lethargic charcoal color of early morning. She couldn't halt the vision of Camille. In her mind was a hermetically sealed portrait of the singer and of her soul. Camille's wheat-hued hair draped over her shoulders. Metallic blue eyes were as tangled and lost as Megan's. There were the contours of Camille's body. There was the motion as their voices and spirits sang to one another. Megan's body thrashed against her dreams for remainder of the morning.

Selina trusted them both.

A rainstorm of tears accompanied Megan through the hours. Only once did she totally awaken to her own nightmare. Once awake she searched shelter.

Chapter 8

Put the past away, it belongs to yesterday.
And long ago is no longer so.
It isn't yours and no one assures
The past or tomorrow, no way to borrow
From what has been, and no way to lend
Our future way. All we own is today.

- Today

Morning was an intruder.

Camille had begun packing before they were to meet Fran at the bus. It had seemed a short night. Selina's loyalty to Megan patted down Camille's grievance against Megan. After all, Selina argued, Colby was trouble. She'd even been kicked out of the last motel she was in for being rowdy.

It was agreed that Fran wouldn't be alerted about the skirmish. Jesse and Elena quickly offered to take care of settling the bill so that Fran could grab a few more winks. The interceding young women listened to the motel manager's complaint against them. Apologies were made, the bill was paid, and Fran was none the wiser. Selina had even joked that the cowgirl rodeo star had been indeed dismounted by a Primrose wild bronco. With the problem averted the band members readied themselves for their journey.

"Passerby hearts. Passerby hearts," Selina remarked to Camille, "is the name BlueJean uses for band members and rodeo stars."

"I'm not a passerby anything," Camille disputed.

"No. Sweetheart, you're not. I'm sure one glad Texan that you're not. You give me a bushel full of rainbows each time I see your smile. I love you so much, Cammy."

Camille turned away from Selina. At times she felt a nightstick of honesty pounding her. For the first time she didn't want to hear Selina say those words. And she didn't want to repeat them back.

When the bus was being loaded Camille and Megan took the same path. With her Stetson dipped down across her forehead, Megan nodded. Megan's eyes were hidden behind sunglasses, and she wore her usual denims and faded western shirt. She stacked her garment bag with the other luggage. She placed her guitar case securely beside her.

After everything was packed and they were aboard, Megan leaned over to Selina. "I'm sorry about last night. Colby. I didn't have any idea she was going to cause a problem."

Fran turned the ignition key. The engine gave a grinding clatter before starting. "We're on our way," she bellowed. "Next stop, Denver."

Camille had originally thought Fran a crude, drunken, overtly masculine dyke. Time had changed her mind. The rough edges had been softened by the knowing of her heart. Camille now saw a woman who had dedicated her life to music and her own truth. If that was her agenda, Camille considered, she couldn't be all bad.

"Comfortable, babe?" Selina questioned as Camille leaned into the soft sanctuary of Selina's arm.

Over the rasp of the radio's music, Camille answered, "I'm fine." There was the rattle of voices, and miles ahead, so she snuggled tightly against Selina. "I was just thinking about how I've come to respect Fran."

"We all do eventually."

After the first hour Elena and Jess had stretched out on the back seats to rest. Camille was reading a magazine, and Megan had just asked that radio be turned down. In a whisper, Selina explained to Camille, "We're in range of BlueJean's station. I'm not sure Red Hot wants to hear her yet."

Megan took out her guitar and began working on chords as she scribbled lyrics into a battered notebook. Selina listened intently.

"Sounds great, Red Hot," she complimented when the song

was completed. "You are the sage of song." She moved to the bus seat across from Megan. Megan picked at the strings and then sang the latest version of "Red Hot Blues" for Selina.

When Selina offered a suggestion, Megan was impressed and quickly changed several notes. "Yes. Yes, that works better. You're brilliant, Selina," she offered. "Much better."

Camille watched the two women. She cased her mind in an attempt to unsnarl her emotions. The same type of close relationship she shared with Megan onstage was shared with Selina and Megan offstage. They could huddle together for hours working on lyrics and notation. Selina had the ability to take simplicity and form it into complex elegance. Camille admired that quality, for she considered herself a musical technician. But Selina's music was exultant annotation. She once told her lover it was as though each note was jumping out of a window to its freedom. As she watched Selina attentively becoming absorbed by the creative process, she felt a longing.

Megan had not taken off her sunglasses, nor had she glanced in Camille's direction. Camille wondered if it was because she had been unjustly accused of caring for Camille by the rodeo star.

She listened intently to the rhythm of Megan's latest song. She extracted the blues, blended with Megan's unique style of writing. The song offered a relaxing accompaniment to the highway. Pelted by repetition, Camille realized that the hilly view outside was a stimulant producing calm. There was time to feed her soul with increments of mellow wisdom. That encouraged her to be as remote from everything as possible.

Everything with the exception of Megan's lyrics.

* * *

Megan cherished the rocking gyration of the bus. What she wrote while traveling, she jokingly called her ode to the road. The interior of the bus had become a rumpled womb. It moved her across the landscape. After replacing her guitar in its case, she watched the frames of grassland. When she removed her sunglasses, she glanced across the aisle to see Camille staring out the window. Then Megan realized that Camille was surveying her reflection in the window's pane. She had been studying Megan.

Megan quickly slipped her shades back over her eyes.

Along with the gritty feeling of the road, Megan was experiencing the strain of a hangover. No one, thankfully, had mentioned the fight. And without doubt, would not. What Megan found distressing was that Colby had picked up on her feelings for Camille. If a stranger had guessed so quickly, how much of a secret could it stay from a group that was living and working together.

Megan hated debauchery. She despised doubt. Her friendship with Selina excluded any thought of ever being near Camille. She could never know Camille's softness. It would be futile to even entertain those dreams.

Watching hummocks flash by made Megan contemplate life's ridges. As the bars of gold sunshine splashed against the ranchland, she mused about her own life. She often felt as though she was continually against one ridge or another. There never seemed a way to reach the pinnacle. It was always the ridge; the cliff; and the loss. There never seemed to be a way to reshuffle the deck. Her feelings ravaged her. She hated her own anger.

Admittedly, the only times she felt true happiness was when performing, writing music and lyrics, and when she had been in BlueJean's arms. But looking into Camille's eyes and singing with her had also provided happiness. Each voice lifted the other to encourage perfect texture within their sounds. Megan chastised herself for the arousal when she traded smiles with Camille between songs. Although congeniality had started with the women smiling for the audience's benefit, Megan now meant each smile. When their searing wails would blend, it stunned them both. When their emotions snarled, both women ran for cover.

Kasey Colby had called it with great accuracy. Megan forced herself to concur. For each night Megan browsed Camille's face as they sang. Each night Megan's soul was being laced more tightly to impossibility. Camille made it abundantly clear she loved Selina.

"How's it goin'?" Jesse quizzed as she sat beside Megan.

"Great. How you doing?"

"Fine. I d-didn't mean to break in on your thinking and all."

"I welcome your company."

"I w-wanted to tell you that if you ever wanna talk, I'm here. I mean, about that woman BlueJean. They say you never got over her." Jesse reached giving Megan's arm a bracelet squeeze. "You keep lots of stuff inside. Like me. But you can trust me. If you wanna. You told me to come to you if I ever need to talk. W-well, you can talk to me about BlueJean."

Megan's hand reached. She caressed Jesse's thin fingers. "I'm not sure getting over BlueJean is possible. But for now, I'm fine. And thanks. I appreciate your offer. Colorado isn't an easy place for me to be. And maybe it might be even a harder place to be away from. I'm originally from Colorado."

"You get to see your family then?"

"I suppose so. Maybe tomorrow I'll venture up to my small hometown."

"Fran, Selina, and me, we gotta set up t-tomorrow morning. Maybe Elena and Camille can go with you. Or your friend BlueJean."

"BlueJean works in the morning. I'll just hop a bus. See my folks. Turn right around and head back to Denver."

Before they hit the outer-city's choked arteries of traffic, Jesse had returned to sit by Elena. Within minutes, Elena had scooted beside Megan. "Want me to go with you to see your family?" she offered

Megan was reluctant. "You don't need to."

"I'd be happy to."

Megan gave a half nod

Elena nudged Camille. "Megan and me are going up to see her family in the morning. You wanna come while the others set up?"

Quickly Megan muttered, "I'll just be stopping by my

mother's café. Then go over and see my father."

"It'll be fun," Elena added.

"No thanks. I'd better stick around and help," Camille replied.

"Sweetheart, go on," Selina insisted. "Those little tucked away mountain towns are wonderful. You can get out and enjoy the scenery. That great mountain air will do your lungs a world of good. There's nothing for you to do while we set up."

"I'd really rather not."

"Aw, go on, babe. We'll be fine without you," Selina encouraged. "When you get back, you can give me a report about Megan's sister. And if she's as pretty as Megan, I'll have a backup in case you run off."

"I'm not going to run off," Camille retorted coolly.

"Just kiddin', babe. Look, go on up there and get fresh air. Clean out your lungs. You been complaining how you hate being in stuffy motel rooms and in the bars. Here's your chance to see a Colorado mountain town."

"My family skied in Vail and Aspen."

"Come on," Elena prodded. "It'll be fun."

Camille finally conceded. "Are you certain we'll be back in time?"

"Be back by six so's we can go through last minute prep," Fran barked. "We don't go on 'til eight."

Megan slipped down against the bus seat. She crossed her arms as her hat plunged down nearly covering her face. She didn't want to view Denver coming into sight. She didn't want to hear BlueJean on the radio every morning. She didn't want to visit her family. And she certainly didn't want Camille there when she did. Her speck-on-the-mountain hometown would never be mistaken for Vail or for Aspen.

* * *

Their bus was filled with tourists. It climbed, lifting up the curves of ribbed mountains. Camille watched silently as they passed the unfolding meadows that were pocketed between evergreens. Calibrating vertical walls were layered. Camille remarked about the beauty of the tundra, brush, and wildflowers beside the swollen stream that edged the highway. Megan had shrugged with indifference.

She was even more edgy, Camille noticed, when Elena decided to stay back with the others after having downed an excess of boilermakers last night. Camille then tried to decline the trip again, but Selina seemed insistent that Megan not journey alone. Camille was well aware that

Megan wanted to be alone. And Camille would prefer not being the interloper.

When they debarked Camille noticed the flavor of the small town. The air was heavy with the scent of pine sap. It reminded her of the Christmas season.

They walked across the street. Megan's arms spread out. "This is my hometown," Megan said with a pensive sigh.

"Excited to see your family again?"

"Not really," Megan murmured with a brooding voice. "It's an obligation. I'm a displaced person as far as my family goes." She pointed to the corner café. "That's the only benefit of living in a town this size. It doesn't take long to get anywhere. Flip-side of the coin. There isn't really anywhere you want to get to."

Megan opened the café door for Camille, and then followed her inside. Scattered throughout were tables topped with red and white checked table clothes. Several men garbed in western attire were seated at the counter.

A woman in her late fifties was behind the counter. She glanced up. Her eyes were coal black. Thick dark hair was pulled back into a bun. Her face was haggard. Camille was not expecting Megan's mother to be this woman. This dowdy, unpleasant woman with a lackluster voice shocked Camille.

"Look what the cat drug in. You broke?"

"No." Megan's voice was sullen; nervous. "I have a job. With a group. This is Camille. She's a singer with the band."

With restraint, Megan's mother nodded. "How do ya do?"

"Nice to meet you, Mrs. Holloway." Camille realized that Megan's mother was scrutinizing her.

There was no exchange of hugs, endearments, Camille noted with disbelief. Her family always displayed their affection. Megan's mother was barely even showing civility. She gave a shrug toward a table. "Sit down over there. I'll get you some coffee and breakfast."

"We've eaten," Megan quickly declined.

"What'd you come for?"

"Just to see you. After we finish the gig in Denver we'll be out on the road for several months. I thought I should stop by." Megan's explanation trailed to a halt.

"Grab the pot of coffee and a couple mugs and go over and sit down. I'll be with you in a minute," her mother directed.

Megan's eyes filled. A sigh was smothered between her lips. The bitter burn of humiliation flushed her face. Camille studied her in silence. Megan's uneasiness was obvious. When her mother finally returned, she had brought another pot of coffee.

"Fresh. Top 'er up?" her mother asked. Megan lifted her cup. "Your sister's gonna be upset she didn't get to see you. She's over in Grand Junction visiting your aunt."

"We aren't staying long. We need to be back later this afternoon. We have a performance tonight."

"Big star, huh?" her mother grumbled. Resentment simmered, and then it erupted. "Mitch had big dreams, too."

Camille glanced at Megan. Megan explained, "Mitch is my older brother."

"Another dreamer, drifter," Megan's mother spat. "We don't talk about him 'cause he's over in Canyon City."

"Incarcerated," Megan's jaw clamped as she said the word.

"That's right. No good came to his escapades." Megan's mother twisted her hands as she spoke. "Your sister is useless. And you, you bust your backside goin' off to school. We could have used you around here helping. But no. No, you go off and get all that learning. Then what do you do? You go off to spend the rest of your days being a no-account barroom singer. Playin' and singin' to a bunch of drunk cowboys. Riffraff. You're your father's daughter."

Megan's shoulders drooped as she eased back. Blinking,

she looked away. "I make music. That isn't a crime. And I'm doing something."

"Maybe it isn't a crime. But how you live, girl. You know what I mean." Her eyes narrowed as she scowled at her daughter. "You know full well what I'm talking about. This way of life you got yourself into."

"Not now, please," Megan implored.

"Not now," her mother mimicked. "When? Next time you drop in here givin' me the time of day? When? When hell freezes over? Maybe then you'll get yourself sorted."

Megan stood. "We're leaving."

"Come up here among decent folks. Bringing your dolly…"

"She isn't my dolly. She isn't a dolly. She's a respectable woman. A refined woman with class," Megan affirmed though her teeth. "Come on, Camille. This was a mistake."

As they reached the door they could hear her mother's rantings. "You're the mistake, Megan Holloway. You're the mistake."

Camille was grateful to be out in the open air again. She felt a sharp ache when she scanned Megan's face. "Maybe it would have gone better if I wouldn't have been with you."

Megan answered, "No. That wouldn't have mattered. She's always like this. Let's go see my father."

They trudged back across the street. Camille thought of how different Megan was than her mother. Warmth was exuded by Megan. Her mother was cold. Her eyes were icy. Megan's eyes blazed with passion.

Megan declared, "I told you this was not going to be fun."

"I'm so sorry."

"I don't imagine she's anything like your mother."

"No." Even the fact that her mother was disappointed in her daughter's lifestyle didn't dim her love for her daughter. Although Camille was made to feel inadequate by not meeting their expectations, she was always warmly greeted. And loved.

"My parents are separated. My mother lives over the café and my father has an apartment. I'm not sure that they were ever really together," Megan explained. They entered a grimy stairway that led to an apartment over a vacant storefront. Megan leaped the stairs two at a time. She rapped on the door.

When the door opened, a bent, stooping man in his mid-sixties peered out at them. "Meggy," he hooted. "You come back for good?" He clasped his daughter to him. His eyes overflowed with tears. Tears toppled down his gaunt face. Short whiskers were stubble on the lower portion of his face.

"Just visiting," Megan answered with tenderness.

He motioned the women in, directing them to a kitchenette table. When they sat, Megan introduced her father. His tall thinness was exaggerated by a rumpled western shirt and faded denims. His cowboy boots were worn and turned up at the toes. He removed a six-pack from the small portable refrigerator. After passing the women a beer, he sat. With great gusto he flipped the tab and then toasted. "Glad to see you, little girl."

Camille sipped slowly. She observed Megan's father in an attempt to understand Megan. Tired, puffy eyes told the story of his history of drinking heavily. Although drained, those eyes showed warmth. His thinning hair had once been the same color as Megan's. It was apparent from the structure of his face and his smile that he had once been a very handsome man. The smile was also Megan's smile, Camille calculated.

He tapped his foot to the Johnny Cash music that was playing from a radio up the hall in his bedroom. Although the rooms were small and cluttered, Camille noted that things were systematically placed in order, and in their proper places. His coat was neatly hung on a hanger.

Rows of books were carefully arranged on pine shelving. From Homer to Thoreau, his tastes were classic. It was obvious from the multitude of poetry books that he had a penchant for verse. In the corner a tower of newspapers leaned. Violets, under their plant lights, were on a shelf.

"You still singing and writing songs?" he asked.

"Yes. Still trying to write songs."

"My troubadour daughter," he said with a mixture of apprehension and pride. "You aren't in any trouble, are you?"

"No. I'm with a group called Primrose. We're playing in

Denver beginning tonight. I just wanted to visit you. We were over at the café earlier."

Grimacing, her father then smiled. "She gave you a bad way to go, Meggy?"

"Same as always," Megan sighed. "She put food in my mouth, clothes on my body, and shoes on my feet, and this is how I repay her. Swinging hash has never been a thrill, and now she only has disappointment in place of children." More burdened by her words than embitterment, Megan inspected her beer can for many moments. "Maybe she has a right to be angry. First Mitch, then me, and now it looks like Martha isn't even living up to her expectations."

"She runs the socks off poor Martha. She's a good kid, like you. But sooner or later your ma will chase her away too."

"Ever hear from Mitch?" Megan asked.

"Not since I quit sending him money for smokes."

"I call him a couple times a year. Other than that," Megan confessed, "it's almost as if he isn't even alive. I guess you could say he hasn't got a life anymore."

"Your mother wanted all of you to have the best." He reached over to touch his daughter's hand. Hers curled around and into his. "Meggy, I couldn't ever give her enough. Other than trouble. Maybe that's why she expected so much of you three. No matter. Just give it your best. Nothing else is important. Live with everything you got. Bite life whole and swallow it down. Love, laugh…all the rest…everything. Give it all you can. You always loved music. There are worse vocations." He smiled. "One thing I ask of you."

"Yes?"

"Meggy, believe that you can be whatever you want. Don't let anything your ma or anyone else says tear you down."

Megan spoke with deliberation, "Dad, I only want to write songs and be loved. That's all I want."

"Then you keep on singing and searching."

"It's not easy," Megan expressed with a deep, resonant sigh.

Her father pondered. "Well, Whitman said that to have

great poets there needs to be great audiences. Maybe folks are ready for your songs now. And Emerson said that no man ever followed his genius 'til it misled him." Nonplussed, with a baffled grin, he quickly added, "Guess he meant that for women as well."

Megan laughed. "Good to see your consciousness-raising courses paid off."

"There's no law says that mountain folks can't be accepting." He paused. "I'm trying hard to understand how it is with you women. You know, how it is with your kind."

"It isn't always necessary to understand as long as there is acceptance," Megan related. "And I appreciate even that much."

Her father canvassed her expression. He then checked over Camille. "You take care of my daughter."

"I'm a friend," Camille attempted to clarify. "We're a duet."

Megan's father shook his head, laughing. It was a contagious, rich laugh, so like Megan's. "A duet, huh?" he repeated. "That's a new name for it."

Although Megan was amused, she also displayed an obvious discomfort. She had never talked about women with her father. They had gone around the issue, often pretending it didn't exist. "Dad, our bus back to Denver is due. We've got to leave. I'm not sure when I'll be back. We're headed south to Dallas, then on to Nashville."

They moved to the door. He gave his daughter another hug. "Don't you forget to put your heart in every single lyric of those songs. I love you, Meggy. Take that with you on your journey."

"I love you, Dad. Thanks for accepting. And encouraging. Take care," Megan requested.

Megan darted to the street. She moved rapidly toward the bus stop. Camille rushed to keep up with her. "I didn't know you have a brother."

"I never talk about Mitch. Guess that doesn't make me very accepting."

"I understand."

"He was always in trouble with the law."

"What is he in for?"

"Murder. He got life without the possibility of release. He was cornered while in the commission of a robbery. He took out a bank guard."

When they reached the bus stop marker, Megan leaned back against the post. Her body slid down until she was crouching on the ground. Anguish squeezed her.

Camille knelt beside her. Her arms enfolded Megan. Their cheeks touched for the first time. Megan slowly drifted back away from Camille. Her words gnawed their way out. They stung them both. "Guess you'll think twice next time you're cordially invited to visit the Red Hot Shrine."

Chapter 9

We both know that someday you'll need to choose.
I'll be left lonesome with my Red Hot blues.
Reason relates this love isn't very smart,
But I've already lost this Red Hot's heart.

- Red Hot Blues

Fran had blustered that they would need to get into those songs for opening night. Sell them, she insisted. Fetch every bit of sparkle, she stressed. Megan was fresh out of heart. Her soul felt sluggish. However, when the lights went on, the announcement made, and Primrose burst into music - she seemed to ignite. Megan issued a faint smile when she glanced into Camille's eyes. Things seemed very different.

She was aware that spiritual intimacy always changes relationships much more so than physical intimacy. This was an experience she'd never felt. Something had changed her. Profoundly, she acknowledged. Selina then announced that band would be introducing "Red Hot Blues" for the first time before a live audience. Megan heard the piano introduction. Then there was a rumbling bass guitar along with the slide of steel. Elena began blowing her harmonica. Megan and Camille locked eyes as the song built. Gently their voices ambled through a corridor of lyrics. They sang "Red Hot Blues" with fervor. Lyrics palpitated, throbbed, fluttered, and they became a tremor that rocked the band and their audience.

After concluding the song neither Megan nor Camille had noticed the cheering crowd. When the applause continued, Megan glanced to her side. Fran was hooting. The audience was stamping their feet, whistling, and clapping more loudly than

Megan could ever recall. It was a moment of bringing down the house. The Primrose circle closed. Each women was laughing with elation. Jesse gave the thumbs up sign. It was as if the women were experiencing some mystical high that nothing else had ever provided. They grinned, shook their heads, and felt emotionally solved. Megan recalled an old-timer once told her that the magic moment in show biz is just that. It is brief; it is elusive. And while it is there, no other feeling can compare.

After the performance was complete, the group found that offstage was even wilder. Fran gave them each a bear hug. Selina lifted Camille off the ground. She swung her around in her arms and the kiss they shared was passionate.

"We got us a hit!" Elena wailed.

"Hot damn!" Fran exclaimed. "It's got number one written on it."

"I suppose so," Megan ratified. She listened as the applause continued. "No more encores. My voice is shot," she complained.

"You get the last stanza of that song finished, girl," Fran clamored. "We're puttin' 'Red Hot Blues' on the demo tape for certain."

Megan walked alone through the musty hallway toward their dressing room. Before getting there she saw the door to a storeroom. She entered the small confined space. Hoisting herself onto a storage counter, she covered her eyes. She'd written those lyrics to replicate her heart's situation. They were the contents of her soul. Additional lyrics were unavailable. They were secret. They were unresolved. She wasn't ready to expose more of her heart. She wouldn't allow more self-excavation into that hidden corner of her soul, even if she were able. She inhaled the disinfectant scents that mingled with booze and stale cigarette smoke.

She feared that forbidden, perhaps inevitable direction of her life. In her heart she was convinced that they, indeed, had the making of a hit. And, she meditated, burying her head against the crook of her arm, unless she reined her desire, her song would be prophetic. But she would finish the lyrics, basing them exclusively on hope.

"Hot damn, what you hiddin' away from?" Fran asked. "We been looking for you." She waved a bottle in the air.

Megan took the bottle allowing its contents to pour rapidly into her mouth. There was the warmth flowing down her throat. When she felt the fire within her, she handed the bottle back to Fran. The pain hadn't been extinguished. Not even nearly. A rush of despair nearly crushed her when she glanced into Camille's eyes.

"The group is waiting for you, Red Hot," Camille declared with a smile. There was no condemnation in her lantern gaze. She was only looking in at the darkness with concern.

* * *

For Camille there had been a missing ingredient. She realized that; accepted that. She nuzzled Selina's neck as they cuddled in the cradle of warmth. She loved sleeping near Selina. Their bodies always seemed to respond to one another's motion. But her soul seemed to have been washed up on some distant shore. She felt alone - even in their bed.

Loving Selina had never been an empty experience. There was always satisfaction. Selina was no stranger in her arms. She had belonged there from the beginning. But recently, Camille felt to be a stranger in her own heart.

"Tired, sweetheart?" Selina asked as they snuggled.

"Long day." She swayed one of her legs over Selina's outstretched thigh. Slowly, she fit against her lover as her head rested on Selina's shoulder. They had wrapped their naked limbs in love and now the passion faded into weariness. Camille was thankful that Selina had only asked if she felt tired. Their bond was so tight that either of the women knew if the other was pulling away emotionally. "The trip to the mountains was exhausting."

"How was Megan's home?"

"I'm not certain one could refer to it as a home. We saw her mother at the family café. She's nothing at all like Megan. Then we went to visit her father."

"Mountain folks are sometimes a little different."

"Her mother was cold."

"BlueJean once told me that Megan's mother has always been rough on her. Since the day she was born. Megan's resemblance to her father reminded her mom of her wayward husband. Guess Megan's dad was a good looking devil in his time. But he's been drinking hard for years now, so he's probably not looking great."

"I surmised that. And years have definitely worn him. Just as they will Megan if she doesn't put the bottle away. But her father was very kind to both of us."

"Guess she loves him, but her mother's something else." Selina recalled, "Megan's brother was the light of her mother's life. He gave them nothing but a hard time. Megan was the middle kid. Her mom sort of overlooked her. Then Megan's sister was born, and being the baby got what love her mother had left. Which from everything BlueJean says wasn't much. She told me a story about when Megan's dad bought her a guitar. In a rage her mother sold it off. It broke the kid's heart."

"Now Megan is writing about that heartbreak. All of her heartbreaks."

"Megan's heartbreaks aren't over. BlueJean called tonight. She couldn't make it to our opening, but she'll drop by tomorrow night. I say she's playing it coy. I could tell she really wanted to see Megan. She wants to do a remote from the club." Selina cuddled nearer her lover. "I know you think Megan drinks too much. And she is moody. But she's had some bad times."

"You've had far worse times," Camille refuted. "You don't booze your way through life."

"Megan is different. And besides, I believe that fortune is seasonal. I've found my good times now. Cammy, you're my treasure. When I'm with you, I feel like I've got life's first prize. It's like I got the grand prize wrapped in my embrace. I can't even remember any hurt when I'm with you."

Camille traced Selina's lips with her index finger. "Selina, I do love you." She nudged nearer into the cradling arms of her lover. "I'm lucky to have you. You're the finest person I've ever known."

Camille had only gotten those words out when she experienced a flutter in her throat. Selina was far too fine to be a consolation prize, she considered. Camille allowed the obvious to surface. She was becoming more entrenched in thoughts of Megan. She admonished herself. Fran must have been aware of that fact, because she had warned Camille that Megan was not for her.

Silence crowded Camille with questions. She had no idea why there was loneliness within her. She questioned the reason Megan's gaze performed some act of love with hers each night. Or so it felt. She wondered why her emotions seemed to be turning inside out. How difficult it was to render them invisible. And it was becoming impossible to suppress them.

That afternoon, the look in Megan's eyes as Camille bent to hold her had been one of deeply burning passion. When they sang Megan's songs their link seared. She longed to touch Megan and to be touched by her. Just once, she thought. She wanted to sob when Megan backed away from her. As if Megan was in a trance, Megan withdrew to the far side of her memories. Camille wanted to be there for her just once.

Camille scanned Selina's sleeping face. It was blissfully gentle. She suddenly regretted making love. She had been thinking of Megan. That somehow made her love for Selina shabby. And she wanted that least of anything. Anxiety pulverized her throughout the night. She would be listless in the morning. BlueJean would be dropping by and that was cause for concern.

Camille studied the shadow flecked ceiling. She realized that she couldn't hurt Selina. Nor could she ever leave Selina. The mere thought was blasphemy.

* * *

Fran was ready to topple. She lit another cigarette. Bobbing, she plunked down on the bed opposite Megan's. She chuckled briefly. "By Jez, you women are turnin' 'em on like lights. I love it when an audience goes wild."

"Like being caught up in a great poem," Megan confided. "You know, one that makes the tears drizzle at the same time your spirit is soaring."

"Or being caught up in a great woman," Fran declared with an accompanying whoop. Her face then flushed. Her eyes pressed a squint that also produced a spray of crosshatched wrinkles. "My woman was a knockout. She'd be singin' away. Cowboys loved her. But when they'd begin with her, I'd get pissed. I'm small in stature, but I'm a bouncer at heart. Shit, I loved that woman." Her eyes searched for immunity from memories. "But now I got Primrose. I don't need women in my life. Still, I think about her. She was Shangri-La and all the accompanying rigmarole!" Fran allowed a constricted smile to escape. "I only loved one woman. Bedded others, but that was just to keep the lonelies from pouncing on me. Only one was everything."

"BlueJean was my everything," Megan admitted.

"Was?"

"Love is somewhere out there waiting on us to arrive."

"You believe that?"

"I couldn't write a song if I didn't," Megan divulged. She wanted to pull up any long ago abandoned philosophy she could to ease the moment. It might, she deliberated, fortify her spirits. When they turned on the radio in the morning, it would be BlueJean's voice they would hear. Megan needed to confront the sexy twang and recollections of the promise of love. Promises, Megan considered, that were whispered into her ear repeatedly. Into her heart, as well.

BlueJean would be at their next performance. She would be accompanied by her harem of fans. They would be there with a treasure trove of goddess worship for their favorite country and western radio personality.

Fran staggered to her feet. She rummaged through a sack, finally pulling out a fresh bottle of bourbon. "Hell, love's well behind me." She returned to bed, steadying herself as she anchored her arms on the mattress. "Those wild days are long gone. You had yourself a time with that little bronco buster."

Megan watched Fran's weaving head. "Fran, she was a warm body. And that's about all. She was a no-assembly-required kind of sex."

Fran poured, filling her glass halfway to the rim, then passed the bottle to Megan. "Looks like for some reason or 'nother you need this more 'n I do."

Megan's fingers wrapped around the base of the bottle. She then poured her glass liberally, draining it immediately. As she twisted the cap back on, Megan gave a sigh. As if her heart had become cast iron, she wanted to seal herself away from humanity. There was a sudden requirement for isolation. "I left some music out on the bus. I want to give it the onceover." She bolted for the door. "I'll be back in a few."

Megan's eyes closed briefly when she shut the motel door behind her. When they opened, her view took in the cool Denver evening. Stars were dotted sparklers. She began to stroll the length of the U-shaped motel. Her glance stopped at one room. Selina and Camille would be sleeping now. Or not. Maybe they were sharing the spicy redolence of sex. Perhaps they were reaching for the apex of an orgasm.

Life's intermission, Megan pondered, must be when one's alone. She hoped she wouldn't see the merging configuration of two women behind the drapes. She didn't want to hear their amplified pleasure.

She blinked rapidly as her head tipped upward. She gazed at the coruscating star map above. The day's events had depleted her. Her hometown was, and would forever be, a difficult journey. Her mother could always chip away at her with stinging words. Words from her early childhood rumbled through her memory. In a droning monotone, her mother scolded with vicious reprimands. Degradation and humiliation were pounded into Megan's psyche. She bitterly wondered how it would impact her mother if she did become famous.

Megan glanced at the cone of light beaming down from a light post. Memories coasted until Megan thought about how Camille had sensed her pain and knelt to hold her. The touch of Camille's softness frightened Megan.

Megan leaned against the fender of the bus. She yawned. She suddenly saw a figure exiting the room. With closer inspection she realized it was Camille. Megan stepped away from the fender.

"Camille, isn't it a little late for you to be out here?"

Clutching her robe, Camille passed Megan. "I needed to get my makeup case." Swinging the door open, she explained, "I just got my period. Didn't have any plugs with me." Turning, as Megan followed her up the bus steps, she delved, "What are you doing up so late?"

"I needed to get off by myself."

"I feel that way sometimes. Usually it's on the bus. I want to run," Camille admitted. "Touring is the part of this business I hate most."

"Most? Meaning you hate more of it?"

"Maybe if I'm honest, most of it. But traveling makes me homesick."

"For your family in California?"

"Yes. And for a home of my own – a stable place of tranquility. Selina and I plan to one day marry. When there's time." Camille quickly inserted, "But this is probably always going to be Selina's life. Our life."

"Maybe someday we'll be able to fly to our concerts."

"I wouldn't mind doing a few concerts. But not all the time. I'm basically a nesting kind of woman. I'd like to plant roses, light a fireplace in the evening, be comforted by knowing I'd be waking up in the same place every morning."

"You are in the wrong profession for that."

"I've hoped that we might get to a place where we could limit tours. That would satisfy Selina. I do enjoy some parts of entertaining. Audiences at times - like tonight. And I do love working in a recording studio. The road is the worst part for me."

"It's maybe what I love most. There's freedom. Writing songs is about a freedom of the soul. To tell what's inside."

"Megan, is that the only time you tell how you genuinely feel?" Camille quickly retreated, "I'm sorry. I didn't mean to say that in a negative way."

"It's the truth. The truth I can handle."

Camille slipped the case from under the seat. Megan bent to lift it for her. "I can get it."

"No bother, I'm headed back now anyway." Megan's fingers grazed Camille's. "I'll walk you right to your door, my lady."

"Selina's lady," Camille curtly corrected.

"Yes." Megan locked the bus. She turned to peer into Camille's face. "It's just a figure of speech. You shouldn't be out here alone." Moonlight was spilling against Camille's face. Her hair shone. Megan swallowed.

They walked slowly. Camille twisted toward Megan. "Thinking about BlueJean?"

After a few steps Megan answered, "No. I was thinking about you."

"Me?" She coiled, deflecting Megan's inspection.

"You were kind today. When my mother saw fit to annihilate my confidence, you were kind."

"With your swagger," Camille teased. "How could your confidence be annihilated?"

"Just because I act confident doesn't mean I am."

"I was referring to the fact that your song brought down the house tonight. That should have provided a multitude of confidence." At the door their line of sight made a direct hit. "Megan, your songs are special. You are special."

She handed the case to Camille. "Thank you."

"Thank you for seeing me back. Carrying my case. Megan," she spoke with hesitation. "I hope things are okay between you and BlueJean tomorrow."

Megan scrutinized Camille's lovely face. Her eyes shut a moment. As they did Camille leaned toward her to kiss Megan's cheek. Megan's eyes flashed open. "Things will be fine. I'll make them fine."

With the hint of a smile Camille exonerated Megan. "You aren't such a wild Red Hot after all."

Megan heard the safety chain's rattle as Camille locked the door from the inside. Megan's soul sputtered, Yes, I am. I am a wild Red Hot. She then returned to her room.

Chapter 10

Begin to feel the mountain air
As each day makes us aware
That we can chase a pinecone dream
Listen to a symphonic stream.
Begin to touch the rocky slope
As our hours have us hope
To follow a columbine request
And love each of our moment's best.

- Beginning Song

The doorway of Megan's memories was ajar. Camille could sense a withdrawal. Megan was becoming increasingly aloof after the first set had concluded. While Jesse and Fran worked on a microphone problem, Camille and Megan sat backstage. Camille finally spoke. "Megan, are you doing okay?"

"Fine. I thought you were being more quiet than usual."

Issuing a half-smile, Camille explained, "I just have the cramps. I always become a little pensive."

"I had to have a hysterectomy when I was twenty-two. Right after college, actually. I remember my mother told me she wished I'd had an early family. Guess she blamed me for getting an education instead of getting pregnant."

Camille grinned. "Now that is a different wrinkle."

"As you can confirm, my mother is definitely a different wrinkle."

"At least you're smiling, Red Hot."

"You are, too." Megan paused. "I thought you might be upset because BlueJean is dropping by for our last set."

"Why should it bother me?"

"Selina."

"No. Selina and I belong to one another. Exclusively. I was concerned about how you'll handle seeing her again."

"I'm no longer in her custody," Megan joked. "I remember once my brother held me down because I wouldn't apologize for some stupid thing. I must have been about seven or eight at the time. He's a couple of years older, and was always a bully. Anyway, he held my head down against an ant hill to break my spirit. No matter how I struggled, I couldn't break his hold. I was terrified of these goddamn ants. But I didn't break. Finally he lessened his hold enough and I kicked him in the balls." Megan chuckled. "Hard. Anyway, the story is analogous to my fighting to break BlueJean's hold. My spirit will somehow win the battle - one way or another."

"BlueJean doesn't have balls," Camille said with a laugh.

"Don't you believe it," Megan answered snickering.

"Seriously, I believe you're still vulnerable."

"BlueJean can inspire the sweet crazies. That's for sure."

Camille looked away from the gloom reflected in Megan's eyes. Camille knew she should be happy if Megan still had feelings for BlueJean. "From what I hear BlueJean doesn't take prisoners," Camille alleged with an edge to her voice.

"No treachery involved," Megan defended. "It's just that BlueJean is a beguiling woman. But when she's ready to move on, she moves on. There's a refreshing honesty to that."

"You make her fickleness sound idyllic. How about loyalty?"

"Maybe I didn't understand the complexities of her way of loving. And she damn well didn't understand mine."

There was resistant to unformed words. Camille disputed them by looking away. With a deep sigh she stood. "Well, she's definitely in a position to assist with our careers. I hope she'll like your new songs. And Primrose."

"Do you believe someone can love more than one person at a time?" Megan grilled as she followed Camille to the wing of the stage.

Camille watched as her lover gave the thumbs up sign. The microphone was back in commission. Camille glanced back into Megan's face. Their stare rooted them for many moments before she answered, "No, I don't think that's possible. Why?"

"Maybe I was hoping you might."

"Please don't say things like that." There was a pleading in her voice. Camille made her way to center stage.

Although the beginning was strained, they finished the set with complete aplomb. Just before their final set, BlueJean and her entourage entered. Camille felt her heart rush. She watched as Megan played and sang to the beautiful BlueJean. She watched Megan's eyes mist as her song went out to the radio personality. Camille felt left behind. She asked herself why that might be. She had no answer.

When the set ended Camille watched Megan's smile reach across the backstage area toward BlueJean's. The two women slowly paced across the empty hallway. They then stepped into the cove of one another's arms.

Camille was suddenly wounded. She wondered how Megan could look so serene in the arms of a woman who had hurt her. She felt an involuntary shiver course through her body.

* * *

Megan was perplexed by Camille. They had gathered together, and Megan was aware of the mutual attraction. But Camille's words had crushed any thought of allowing an attraction to be elevated to romance. She told Megan she didn't want to hear heart talk. When singing their eyes were aglow. All of life's best moments were reflected. Their voices synchronized; their bodies swayed in harmony; their boots tapped in unison. There were times when Megan felt her heart was being extracted by Camille.

But it was BlueJean's arms that protectively wrapped around her ex-lover. The Texan was responsive and then some. Megan knew BlueJean still had feelings for her. There was a bonding when they had stepped into one another's embrace.

Megan recalled what it was like to have been loved by the

tall, voluptuous, former beauty queen. It felt like being wrapped into all the love that existed. Now, Megan considered, it was the same. Her transient heart was always at home near BlueJean. The radio personality provided Megan her truest heart cottage.

BlueJean hadn't changed. She hadn't brought her followers, but there were always willing women on the outskirts. They eyed her with dreams. Her admirers chased her. Until they were caught. They knew that she reeled them in by night, and threw them back in the morning. Most of them knew BlueJean's philosophy was simple and basic. Life is a festival. Women she met were her feast.

BlueJean's kisses were temporary; her smile was fleeting; her eyes were faithless. Megan had so often sketched her ex-lover in song. Those lyrics explained how BlueJean could take a heart for ransom. She could imprison a lover's soul. It wasn't merely her enchanting beauty that was worshipped. It was BlueJean's spirit.

With a blazing exchange of warmth, Megan's smile lit the room. BlueJean had not changed. The frisky thirty-seven year old packed her fitted Levi's to perfection. Her sequined sapphire shirt was well-filled. The yolk fringe bobbed above magnificent breasts. A silk neck scarf brought a patterned splash of silver and blue. It was tied to the side. Her polished silver belt buckle flashed. A cocked dark Stetson was decorated with a spray of feathers that bloomed across its front panel. Under which streaked honey-blonde curls fell in tiers past her shoulders. Her boots were tri-shaded, and their sheen glowed. They were meant for that gliding walk - that sailing strut, across the dance floor. Her walk was sensuous, yet serious. She knew where she had been, and where she was going. She was a woman with authority. She knew her power. She used her power.

BlueJean's sexy dark bedroom eyes were playful. But they were also sure and confident. They were dynamic lanterns beneath thickly lashed eyelids. Her eyebrows lifted and dipped with precision. Her lips, with a slight pout, were full, expressive, and commanding. Her teeth were brilliantly white.

And the smile, as Megan once stated, was designed by angels.

Still being held by BlueJean, Megan inhaled the fresh, sweet fragrance that was BlueJean. And with a torrid, naughty laugh, that reminded Megan of a wind chime, she teased, "Megan, I want you right this very moment, darlin'."

Megan squeezed her waist. "There's a line," she challenged. Other members of Primrose surrounded the radio personality.

"You are all terrific!" BlueJean's Texas accent caressed as she nearly lifted Megan off the floor. "And you're still beautiful. I always knew you could do that to an audience. You took those folks higher than a Georgia pine."

Fran grinned, winking at Megan. "Well, BlueJean you're still even better than beautiful. An' damn if you ain't greater than gorgeous!" Fran gave her a warm hug. "Glad you like my band. You're in a position to give us a hand."

"Fran, I'll be doing everything in my power to help. This is one terrific group. You can bet I'll be telling my listening audience about you every chance I get. Monday through Friday. And I'll also taut Primrose on my new national weekend syndicated program." She glanced toward Selina, "And Selina may have mentioned that I know studio folks I'm going to want to introduce you to."

Selina nudged her way nearer, giving BlueJean a congenial, safe embrace. The handclasp and quick brush against Camille's cheek had been more reserved. BlueJean's arm then curved around Fran's shoulder. "You told me on the phone that you had the right combination this time, so I figured if they passed your inspection, they must be great. I just wasn't prepared for them being this great this quickly. You made a miracle, lady."

"Hell," Fran roared, "I do believe you liked the performance."

"What I just heard needs to top the charts," BlueJean affirmed. "And you have my word that I'll do everything within my power to see that it happens."

"Primrose has come of age," Selina whooped, then hugged Camille. "We just passed the critical test."

"I count five mighty sexy women to put on a CD cover.

How about we talk tomorrow afternoon? One of my people took a few minutes of video, and I'll send it off. I'll get with my recording studio pals and a couple of backers," BlueJean promised. "Now, I have a request. I want to sneak off with Megan for a private conversation." Her focus strayed over the length of Megan's figure, and she joked, "Issue a little invitation for a private performance tonight."

Megan returned her smile. "Great. Look, why don't you go on back to the dressing room with the others. Make arrangements. Chat. I'll be back in a few minutes. I need to get a little air. Unwind."

"Sure, darlin'." She understood Megan's space requirements. She eased around between Fran and Selina. Her arms gathered them in. "Let's get caught up, ladies."

Megan plunged through the backdoor, exiting out to the alley. She gasped for air. She needed to withdraw from the tumbling images and sounds. The thicket of an audience often encroached. She needed her comfort zone. She required an arm of silence to open wide and whisk away the jumble. Silence emptied the doubt and confusion. It was her only way of unchaining from the stage.

* * *

Elena covered her drums as Jesse assisted Fran with the scramble of wires and plugs.

Selina had disconnected her keyboard. She sorted sheet music with her usual reverence for each piece of paper. Camille had taken her guitar and case to a quiet corner. There she sat on a folding chair and removed her capo. She rested her guitar in its velvet case.

She had closed her eyes for only a moment. BlueJean had been signing autographs, but when Camille looked up she saw her. The shapely radio personality swung her leg over a chair opposite Camille's. The chair was positioned with its back to Camille, but BlueJean jauntily mounted it and rested her chin on its back.

With a breeziness to her voice, BlueJean lulled, "You and Megan make a terrific team."

"Vocally Megan's easy to work with."

"And not vocally?"

"Most of the time."

"She likes blondes," BlueJean remarked, giving her own hair a flip.

Without comment, Camille closely examined BlueJean. She was the beauty everyone spoke about. And, Camille considered, even more lovely in person. Although blonde, BlueJean's hair was darker in shade, but light flowed to the tips of her curls. Her dark eyes did sparkle just the way Selina had described. And her light bronze complexion made BlueJean's coloring exotic. Camille wondered if BlueJean might be referring to Camille's light coloring. She didn't like where the insinuation was going. She snapped shut her guitar case. Glancing back into BlueJean's teasing eyes, she spoke. "Megan is a member of the band. We pretty much limit our conversations to music. I really don't know, nor do I particularly care, what hair shade on women she prefers."

"Blonde."

"There is a wonderful selection of fans out there. I'm certain she'll find someone. She found you."

"I found her," BlueJean corrected. "I walked into a little dive and saw her working for tips and drinks. Fell like a ton of bricks. I knew then she was filled with potential. She plays a mean ax, and lord how she can sing. Her songs put a stake in my heart. I cried the first time I heard her sing 'Sweet Dreams.' I swear I never could stand anyone other than Cline singing that song. But Megan, yes. Well, I kept smiling at her. Then she did a bluegrass number and one of her finger picks flew off. I retrieved it for her. I walked up and handed it to her. She reached to take hold of it, but I held onto the tip. After the most glorious smile I'd ever witnessed, I allowed her to pull it from my grasp. After her show was over, I picked up the knapsack that was sitting at her side. I took her home with me."

Camille stood. She glared into BlueJean's eyes. "I don't know if you noticed, but Megan picked up her sweet dreams and a pint of whiskey that was in her back pocket and went out for a little post-performance nip. Why don't you go outside and reminisce with her?"

"Colby called to tell me Megan's been hitting the sauce again. Reported that Megan went bad tempered. The dismount must have created a bit of an altercation. She said she did a britches burner on the way out." BlueJean hesitated. "Megan didn't drink much we were together. She knows I don't like tipsy women."

"I didn't think she would put her bottle up for any woman."

"Megan drinks to keep from being sad. I drink rarely, and only when I'm happy. But, no, she didn't cork the bottle for me entirely. She just wasn't messed up."

"I have it on authority," Camille retorted with a trace of bitterness, "that she really climbed into the bottle because you stopped making her happy."

"She's a drifter. She needs her freedom to create. She needs the road to crank out songs. Needs misery to wring those lyrics from her soul. I can't nurture her. When she left the road, the songs stopped." BlueJean's sigh was one of frustration. "It was poison to her creativity. I was her hemlock."

"Selina's, too?" The question stung. It was meant to sting.

"Selina wanted my love, but she didn't want me. Not as is. I was wrong for her. We both knew that."

"So out of the goodness of your heart, you dumped her. Then with more heart goodness you dumped Megan."

"Selina's past made her susceptible to rejection. Mine just happened to be the one that put her over the top. I don't stalk my prey." BlueJean's shadowy eyes displayed sorrow. "I loved Selina. I didn't want her hurt. I was never dishonest with her."

"Her love for you nearly took her life."

"We're all born counting down life. I can only be responsible for my own life. Selina's fragility was what pushed her to the suicide attempt. Not me. There were no lies. Why should people stay together in order to achieve a high-number anniversary. Numbers that drift through years of unhappiness. I'm sorry that Selina was hurt. Sorry I couldn't be what she wanted me to be. But that isn't the part of me that I give up in loving. I don't relinquish myself. I don't require that of others. Megan understood that. It pained us both when we parted."

"And now? Are you going to be around to pick up the pieces if Megan needs another six months to get over you? This time you'll be taking the band down along with her."

"Is the band all you're concerned about?"

"I'm concerned about my singing partner. Her friendship."

"Don't be concerned about Megan. You have my word...No, she has my word. If she gives me another chance, I'll never hurt her again."

"Your word," Camille balked.

With exasperation, BlueJean sighed, "Look, darlin'..."

"I'm not your darling."

"Damn right, you're not," BlueJean fired back. "And you're not Megan's darling either. Maybe that's what is bothering you. But we know, if it is, you'll tease her, without pleasing her. Your panties probably strangle you when they shut."

Ruffled, Camille jabbed, "At least mine aren't accessible to any woman who looks good and in my direction."

BlueJean's eyes glimmered as the edges of her lips lifted. "I hit a sore spot. I'll bet you'd love a romp in the hay with Megan. See what her passion is all about. There's nothing like a regal tart in heat."

"I'm not the tart." Camille scowled. "Just do us all a favor and rustle up a little of that down-home integrity. Don't mess Megan over." With her jaw firmly set, her eyes narrowed. "Or maybe you would enjoy hearing it said a different way. The way a tart might say it. Don't fuck Megan over again."

"Whew!" BlueJean gave a mock pivot backward. "Bet we both enjoyed that little outburst. That word isn't even in my vocabulary. But then you're an elegant ex-rocker, and I'm a family radio deejay."

"Megan doesn't deserve to be hurt again."

"I'll let you in on a little secret." BlueJean's voice softened. "I still love her. I'll always love her. I love her too much to take away her gift. She wasn't writing those kinds of songs when we were together. Our love repressed her." BlueJean stood. She kicked the chair away from beneath her. "Someday when she's ready – not only when I'm ready - I'll take her back home with me for good."

* * *

Megan waded through the trash of an asphalt alley. She reached back for the bottle in her hip pocket. Tipping her head, she felt the streamer of heat as she gulped. She gazed at the building's exterior brick walls. They were filthy and worn, she contemplated. She felt worn. Her eyes trailed the spittle markings. After another long swig from the bottle, she wiped her mouth.

Glancing about fifteen yards down the alley she spied an elderly Native American. He was propped against the wall. She watched his torso sliding down into a crouch, and then he toppled to the side. Approaching him, Megan went down to one knee. She pulled him back up into a seated position. His matted eyes blinked. She handed him her bottle. He thirstily took several swallows. Reluctantly, he extended his hand to relinquish it.

Megan stood. "Keep it," she uttered. She returned to the backdoor. Turning, she watched as he finished the bottle He mumbled his gratitude.

Fran met her at the door. "Where you been?"

"Just needed to be by myself."

"Need to talk?" Fran's arms went around Megan's shoulder.

"His eyes were naked."

"What?"

"The guy out there. His eyes were vacant. Totally naked." Megan's own eyes filled with dampness. "It's nothing. Just that I'm going through the sweet crazies. A couple of deep breaths and I'll be fine."

"You still hooked on BlueJean?"

With a slice of doubt, Megan frowned. "I don't think my

heart will ever owe allegiance to anyone again."

"Ain't that what you want? To be a free agent?"

"That's the only thing that keeps me safe."

Fran shook her head. "Baby doll, love is the only security that exists."

Megan's eyes filled. "I'm frightened."

"Of her? Or of you?"

"There isn't any difference." Megan issued a forced smile. "I'll be okay."

"That's right, kid, you'll be okay." Fran laughed. "I know how some women are. Hell, I'd rather douche with battery acid than be hooked on a woman like BlueJean."

Megan nodded and she grinned.

They shared a laugh. Fran's deep stomach laugh rolled. She slapped Megan's back. "Hot damn, kid, you're okay. Tonight you goin' out with BlueJean? For old time's sake? Do a little grazin'?"

"Grazing?" Megan was amused.

"Home on the range!" Fran snickered loudly as they walked.

"I'll go home with her. Sure. But maybe now time has fenced off certain feelings. I'm not sure. Once we climbed into one another's hearts. A part of that exchange remains. Time impacts emotion."

"Is there anyone else," Fran asked, treading lightly, "impacting your emotions?"

"BlueJean says she's very single."

"I was talking about your side of the range."

Tentatively, Megan bristled. "No one in my life."

"You know you can always trust me. I'm Ma Confessor of this outfit. We're so close to being where we need to be. We're pullin' a demo. We're on our way. I don't want that busted all apart."

"It won't be. Fran, I'm damned tired of failure."

Chortling, Fran said, "We ain't even gonna consider failing." She reached in her shirt pocked to pull out a pack of cigarettes. Lighting up, she sucked in, and then exhaled a cloud. "We gotta be race horses. Ready when the gate opens. Then run our hearts out."

"Fran, why did you ask me about someone else?"

Fran ruffled her curly hair. Her eyes narrowed. "It's easy to get a hankering for someone when you sing love songs into their eyes. 'Specially when those eyes are as gawl darn pretty as Camille's."

"I was wondering if that was what you were asking." Megan gave Fran's back a reassuring pat. "That wouldn't be very smart of me. She's in love with Selina."

"That wasn't any answer."

"I got a date with one of the wonders of the world tonight. That should be answer enough."

"Tell this old lady, is BlueJean anywhere's near as good as she looks?"

"BlueJean is all the women I ever wanted. All in one."

"Have yourself a nice night," Fran said as she watched BlueJean walking toward them.

"Oh, yes." Megan issued a slight laugh. Then her laugh ceased. Her eyes locked with BlueJean's.

* * *

BlueJean's midnight blue, perfectly restored, AC Cobra 42 SC had just squealed out of the parking lot. With the sport's car top down, the two women's hair sprayed as they exited.

Camille had taken the bus seat next to Jesse. Jesse had been dreamily watching BlueJean. She drooped back when the roadster roared out of sight. "BlueJean. She's gorgeous. I w-wonder if she can sing. She's sure got a beautiful voice."

Camille gave Jesse's shoulder a playful shove. "A good voice is nothing more than an instrument. Like a good guitar. It doesn't always make good music. Needs tuning and training." Camille smiled as she glanced back at Elena. "So do you both have a crush on BlueJean?"

"I wouldn't mind being Megan," Elena answered through her sputter. "She's been away from BlueJean for nearly seven months. Think they'll remember how to make love?"

"They were hot and heavy lovers for three years. I doubt they'll forget," Selina remarked.

"I just hope Megan can handle it," Camille curtly added.

"She's aware BlueJean's love is perishable." Selina glanced up from the sheet music she was shuffling. "I just hope Megan watches the bottle. It's easier to get inside than to get out." She shifted, leaning across to Camille. "Sweetheart, did you get any reading when you talked with BlueJean?"

"I got a pathetic excuse for amputating love. In Megan's case it was emancipation. She didn't want to smother Megan's creativity." Camille wasn't going to tell Selina that BlueJean claimed Selina didn't love her for herself. "Did you get everything fixed?"

"The amp sounds like a concrete mixer getting its feeding. Might be the wiring needs some work. I'll get busy on it in the morning. We need to go more digital, but until we get money, this system has to do." Selina stretched. "The important thing is that we have this opportunity. Our big break is directly ahead of us. BlueJean never puts her reputation on the line for a loser. Not even ex-lovers."

"Primrose needs this break," Fran called over her shoulder. She guided the bus into the motel's parking lot. "There's plenty of agony to failure. Tomorrow we're gonna make it count," she stressed.

Selina's face became gaunt. She peered out the window. "Fran's right. Good fortune doesn't come back for you. One time shot."

Elena chatted, "BlueJean said she wants to have a picnic for us on her day off."

"Bet she's havin' herself a picnic tonight," Fran cackled.

Selina grinned. When she evaluated Camille's stern face, her smile dissolved. Camille noticed her lover's reaction. She reached to give Selina's hand a squeeze. "I love you," she mouthed.

"Sweetheart, you okay?" Selina grilled.

"Just weary. Not every day we see so much action."

"Hot damn!" Fran exclaimed with an accompanying whistle. "That BlueJean is all kinds of action. Hell, she even mentioned doing a remote from the club. She's got her some mighty good ideas. Told me about working on a video right off the bat. She's a mover."

"Bet she's moving right now," Elena bellowed. "Whew-ee!"

Camille's expression was stony. Sealed. She didn't want the contents of her heart examined by Selina. At most times she wanted to fully open her heart to her lover. This was not one of the times she could allow inspection. There was too much confusion.

The same mixed emotion as when she saw Megan and Colby together, she felt when seeing BlueJean's convertible speed away. Megan was going to another woman's bed. There would be a love session - an orgasmic parable. Camille withdrew from the clatter of conversation surrounding her on the bus. Megan's lyrics whirled through her thoughts. There was the way Megan pulled away from her when she was trying to comfort her in the mountains. There was the kiss on Megan's cheek last night. Camille shuddered with the thought of Megan's question about loving two people at one time. Had she lied to both of them when she asked Megan not to say those things? The deeper the inquiry, the deeper her pain became.

"Cammy, sweetheart, are you awake?" Selina asked as the bus snaked into its parking space.

"I'm awake," she replied. She slid her arms around her quixotic lover's neck. "Selina, just hold me a moment."

Elena chuckled. "Looks like you're gonna get lucky tonight, Selina."

"Anytime Cammy is in my arms, I'm lucky," Selina reported.

Camille buried her face against the retreat of Selina's shoulder. "I'm the lucky one."

* * *

Roaring down the Valley Highway, BlueJean piloted her Cobra with a bold assurance. "You anywhere near as happy to see me as I am to see you?" she yelled through the rush of wind.

Megan's arms unfolded. She slipped her fingers into BlueJean's outstretched hand. "It's good to see you."

"Darlin', it's wonderful to see you." She drove rapidly, proficiently. She took the exit with skill. "Wonderful," she repeated.

Megan felt the silken touch of BlueJean's fingertips. They excited Megan. Steamy glances had been exchanged when BlueJean pulled into her assigned parking space. She turned off the ignition. "Megan, I'm glad you decided to come home with me. I was frightened you might not. It means more to me than you'll ever know."

Megan would not allow her emotions to stray. Not this time. "I'm needing some great hot sex."

"I'm needing you." BlueJean's eyes were no longer flashing sensual signals. Hushed, the moment served to ground them both. "Megan, the last months I've never been with anyone and not needed to pretend she was you. I just want you to know that. To know how I feel."

"Is that the way you feel?" Megan coolly inquired. "You had the real thing. You kicked me out so you could do some cheap imitation number on other people? That's not only illogical, it pales as an excuse. Why don't you stick with the line about needing space and lots of variety? I'd buy into that. But let's not stretch credence to its limit."

"The one thing you can't accuse me of is lying," she disputed. "And it's important to me that you believe what I say. I've never felt the way I feel about you with anyone else."

"Let's assume you'll keep up the good search. Maybe you'll find someone much better."

"There is no one better." BlueJean's bronze eyes lowered. With resignation, she spoke, "I want you to be happy." She eased back in the leather seat. Her head dug against the headrest. She gazed up at the stars. Then she surveyed Megan's face. "We both knew you had other things to do."

"It was more that you had other people to do," Megan jousted.

"I'll never convince you that there's much more to it.

Megan, you were being stifled."

BlueJean's hand lifted. Her fingers drifted across Megan's glum face. The caress was petal soft. "I love you," BlueJean continued. "I'm still in love with you. I've never said those words to anyone else before. You never got around to saying them to me. I'm glad I could at least feel a portion of your love through our lovemaking." She allowed a smile to emerge. "We can have that again, can't we?"

"What we can do," Megan stiffly offered, "is go to bed together."

"I want to share love with you."

With a laugh Megan murmured, "I just want a meaningful lay."

Chapter 11

Won't someone open a liter of love and pass it around?
Maybe being lost is the only way to be found.
Won't someone open a six-pack of hope and pass it along?
Maybe being found is the only way to belong.

-Liter of Love

"I'm sorry," Camille apologized. Her head pivoted as she faced the wall. Selina had always been able to successfully steer her to a climax with tenderness. Tonight stimulation, mingled with love, was not enough.

"That's okay, sweetheart," Selina said. Her fingers softly brushed scattered hair back from Camille's forehead. She whispered, "We're all too tense now. Things are happening so quickly. I know I'm mighty tense," she comforted.

"I'm stressing over everything."

"BlueJean? Did she bother you? I mean, she makes passes at damn near everyone she meets. I wouldn't be surprised if she did."

"No. She isn't interested in me in that way. And I'm certainly not available if she were."

"She captivates most women."

"Elena and Jesse were definitely captivated." Camille issued a wispy smile.

"Yep. I was pretty sure Megan would end up staying with BlueJean. But I think this time Megan is immune to BlueJean. Sparks were there, but not like in the old days." Selina turned onto her side. Her arm folded and her hand gathered beneath her chin.

"I was amazed that it was so easy for them to resume.

BlueJean must enjoy returning to the scene of the crime." It was said for humor, but there was a sour accusation. Camille had seen Megan's soulful eyes when BlueJean walked toward her. Camille admitted that there was a provocative, savvy glisten to her. As if exoneration had been preassigned, BlueJean gathered Megan and off they went. "I admonished BlueJean not to hurt Megan. She doesn't deserve more hurt."

Selina's long limbs stretched as she gently fluffed the sheet around Camille's shoulders. "That's just like you, Cammy. Always carin' about someone else. Guess that's one of the reasons I love you so much."

Camille's eyes began to flood. Through the liquid in her eyes, she saw the room blur. "No one deserves to be hurt." She felt an ominous chill. Pressing her body nearer Selina, she wanted to whisper of her love to Selina. For Selina. As her eyes shut she felt the tears drifting down and dampening her pillow.

* * *

"A late feeding," Megan growled playfully as she sprawled out on her stomach.

"Mmm," BlueJean's voice was a sexy tickle. She reached toward the nightstand and plucked a fresh strawberry from the platter. Directing it toward Megan's mouth, she giggled. "I surely don't want you leaving my bed hungry."

She lifted her voluptuous body atop Megan's. Straddling, with great acuity, she massaged Megan's back.

"I'd forgotten what wonderful backrubs you give," Megan praised.

"After all that glorious sex, you're still tense." Her fingers pressed circlets over Megan's shoulders.

"You just saw what you still do to me. I'm probably worried about the band."

BlueJean leaned down to nuzzle Megan's neck. She whispered, "Don't worry, it will all turn out fine." She eased back beside Megan. "Stay with me while you're in Denver?"

"Sure."

"Good. You can use my car while you're here. Just get me to work on time in the morning and pick me up after I sign off. That way I'll know for sure you're coming back to me every night. But no intoxicants when driving. Promise sobriety?"

"Certainly. And I'll be coming back to this blazing passion. BlueJean, I won't be coming back to you. There's a difference."

"You know I'm in love with you. Don't you know that?" BlueJean delved. "Know that I love you with all my heart?"

"It isn't relevant. Not any longer." Megan watched out of the corner of her vision.

BlueJean kissed Megan's temple. Her eyes curtained shut. "Do you love me at all?"

"Our love has taken too many convolutions. Remember at one time you pulled an inventory reduction. I was your possession that had to go."

"That isn't what happened. But now I'm asking you to forgive me."

"I know you aren't a total charlatan. I wouldn't be here if you were. But forgiving? Trusting? I left all of that baggage back down the lonely road." Megan couldn't say the words she knew BlueJean wanted to hear. And why should she?

"Well, Megan, I love you. From the top strand of your hair to the soles of your feet I love you. I'm not going to get tired of telling you. I'm not going to be impatient. I am, however, going to wait for you. No matter how remote you are. I'll be there. I love you so much, I'll gladly commit to you. Darlin', I'll even marry you. Not just to show you my feelings, but to be with you for the rest of my days."

Megan's thoughts strayed. For this week Megan vowed to anchor to BlueJean's tenderness. It was a place she valued. But that was all. "Good night, BlueJean."

"Do I have any hope of ever having your love again?"

Megan reached across her lover to turn off the night lamp.

* * *

BlueJean had outdone herself. She had called, coerced, and convinced Jimmy Tanner of Country Crown Records. He implicitly trusted BlueJean's recommendations about talent. And when she raved, he agreed to fly in from Nashville to catch the band's afternoon rehearsal.

Jimmy Tanner was the most successful recording executive she knew. Naturally she charmed him. But she had also played music from his stable of artists incessantly. That didn't oblige him, however he realized she was one of the most powerful forces in country-western music.

If she was hyping these women, they must be good enough for him to consider, he reasoned. Calling in favors was not part of BlueJean Taylor's agenda. However, there was no way of getting out of at least giving this Primrose band a listen.

The band was setting up when BlueJean called Fran. She informed her she would be bringing Jimmy Tanner around after lunch. Prepare to impress, BlueJean recommended. He's a busy man, she coached, so begin with their best effort. Wow him immediately.

Together the band decided to kick-off with "Red Hot Blues," and "Goodbye Embrace" would be second. Through their elation also came trepidation. This was what they had dreamed about.

By two that afternoon, the band was ready. When Jimmy Tanner appeared with BlueJean, tension built. Camille politely smiled as BlueJean's multitude of superlatives pounded away at Tanner. While she extolled the virtues of discovering the band, his skeptical eyes carefully observed each woman.

Tanner, a large, powerfully built, barrel-chested man in his mid-forties, loomed over them. His huge, gruff face with handle-bar mustache added to his menacing appearance.

Primrose began their first song. Camille caught a glimpse of Tanner's foot tapping. She felt encouraged. Before he could even nod for them to continue the band went immediately into their next song. Just as BlueJean had directed.

At the conclusion, BlueJean applauded. "And they can do standards," she clamored, "Why don't you do one of the classics," she suggested.

Tanner uncrossed his arms. "I heard enough," he spoke

slowly. "Why don't we all sit down and talk." The group sat around the table, waiting for his comment. Tanner cleared his throat.

Camille felt her stomach churning. She had been on this threshold before. With a different band, different executive, and different woman at her side. The band's destiny - fate, was in his hands. He unbuttoned the jacket of his fawn-colored, western-cut suit.

"Liked 'em both." He scratched his graying hair a moment. "Now, the question is how much I liked them?"

Fran leaned across the table. "And how much did you like 'em?"

"Enough for a contract," he answered. Looking clockwise around the table, he added, "That much. Now, I can have a contract emailed immediately. We just need to get things ironed out. We'll offer a standard contract deal. What do you say?"

Camille gazed around at the astonished, joyful expression on each of their faces. She saw BlueJean wink at Megan. Megan issued a return smile. Camille was aware that Selina had been watching her.

"We're cookin' now," Fran howled.

"You certainly are," Tanner agreed. "Fran, why don't you find the manager of this place? See if we can't drum up a couple bottles of his best champagne to celebrate." After Fran exited, Tanner frowned. "There is one little thing. As I said, something we need to iron out. We're going to need to ask you women to get yourself a sort of general manager to work with you."

"Fran is our general manager," Selina explained.

"I was thinking of someone we might interface with on an executive level," he prodded.

BlueJean added, "Fran is a great road manager, but Primrose will need someone experienced in public relations, media."

"Fran is our manager," Megan dryly spoke. She sat erect. "She always has been. Always will be."

"Mr. Tanner seems to think..." BlueJean hesitated, searching words. "It might be in the band's best interest to have someone else. Fran is a diamond in the rough, but a little on the severe side. If you know what I mean?"

"We know exactly what you mean," Megan's words were spikes. "Fran doesn't own a tube of lipstick. But she is our general manager and road manager in one package. Like that package or not."

"Surely Fran could see the benefit of this decision," Tanner encouraged.

"We haven't made a decision," Megan blasted.

"Come on, Megan," Selina cautioned. "Fran will understand. She wants us to make it to the top. It will be okay with her. If that's what we want."

Megan's glare fired around the table. "I don't want it."

"Well, little lady," Tanner muttered, "you got more than just your future to think about."

"Fran put the band together. She's the heart of Primrose," Megan reminded everyone. "And she's our friend."

"I got lots of friends. And if they aren't doctors, they aren't operating on me," Tanner debated.

"I'm not talking about your friends," Megan gnashed. "Fran is our manager. That's it."

"Come on, Holloway," BlueJean argued. "Think priorities."

"Look, Taylor," Megan sarcastically lashed, "if we let him dictate our decision, what is going to be censored next? Our songs, lyrics, who we date, what we wear. Don't talk to me about priorities," Megan spat.

Selina quickly interceded, "Megan, let's not be hasty. All they want is to approve an additional manager."

"One Fran will report to?" Megan queried. "No. We have a manager. Fran Tobias is our manager. If she deems it necessary to have another manager, fine. She'll do the hiring."

Selina's concerned glance swept the faces at the table. "I have an idea. Let's take a vote," she suggested.

"Not interested," Megan huffed. "This decision is tantamount to demoting Fran. And it's not happening."

"A vote is the democratic way," Selina disputed.

"I'm doing what I think is right. Dumping Fran isn't right."

"Megan," BlueJean corrected, "Nobody is dumping Fran.

She'll still be handling tours. Be on the circuit with you. As a road manager."

Tanner coaxed, "And you women are going to be major stars. She'll have her hands full just seeing to the road."

"You're right," Megan agreed. "We probably are going to be stars. However, we're going to be selling songs. We're selling music. But make no mistake, we're not selling out."

Tanner's fist went down on the table with a thud. "Look here, girl, you realize what I'm saying to you?"

"And here's what I'm saying to you." Megan's eyes narrowed. She leaned across the table. "No. No Fran. No me."

After several moments silence, Jesse's timid words came with a slow stutter. "I'm g-gonna be w-with Megan."

"Yeah," Elena murmured. "We gotta be together on this."

Selina's survey continued. She looked to Camille for support. "Cammy, talk to them," Selina begged. "She's gonna blow this for all of us."

Camille inspected Megan's staunch, ridged expression. "Selina," Camille affirmed, "she's right. We can't sell out Fran."

Selina threw down the pencil she had been clutching. "You've always had everything handed to you on a golden platter. Everything you ever wanted. Never had to worry. I got a chance now, and you're ruining it."

Megan coolly stood. "Don't sweat it, Selina," she calmly remarked. She then leaned across the table, planting both hands on the tabletop as if they were anchors. She glared into Tanner's flushed face. "He knew he was signing us after the first song. He's just an astute businessman. He wants a reading on how far we'll bend. Now he knows. He knows we are loyal. He knows we stand for what we believe. He is now aware that we are confident enough that we can't be intimidated. He respects that in us because he's probably exactly like we are. And that's what got him to the top." Her eyes penetrated his shocked expression. "Am I correct, Mr. Tanner?" Her smile then flashed wide.

With a bemused, bewitched frown, Tanner stood. He held out his hand across the table. His words were solid. "It's Country Crown and Primrose.

Megan returned his lock-jawed grin. "Yes. It's Primrose and Country Crown."

* * *

After Tanner's cab arrived, whisking him off to the airport, Megan gave a deep sigh of relief. She also acknowledged pain.

The strain between Selina and Camille was evident to each of the band members. Selina had also turned away from Megan. Megan hated that. The confrontation had badly damaged the group. Camille was being even more distant to Megan. She was aware that Selina believed she sided with Megan, rather than stood by her belief on an issue. Camille's remedy was to frost over when Megan was around. Each time Camille's eyes snapped in her direction, Megan felt the sting. The celebration was muted.

Megan's mind recapped the day. Waking in BlueJean's arms had seemed too natural. The afternoon took on moments of a bad dream that intertwined with her most wondrous fantasy. The band experienced the euphoria of getting a contract. But the undercurrent split them down the center. Each sect had gone in separate directions. Megan had gone backstage to chat with BlueJean. Selina and Camille had adjourned to the small dressing room. Jesse and Elena excitedly drove BlueJean's car around the parking area. Their dreams were about having a vehicle like it one day. Fran was having a drink with the club's manager.

Megan reached for the glass of champagne that BlueJean had poured for her. She took a sip. She then sat on a folding chair opposite BlueJean. "Celebratory booze keeps flowing, but the party is over."

"Just be glad there's something to celebrate. It might have been a disaster, darlin'."

Megan slumped back. "I wonder how long Selina's chill will last?"

"Darlin', you are an arrogant bitch. Selina is like me, we don't come from places of magic. You know, where pools of creativity escape the wrecking ball of the norm. She's a terrific musician, but she's a technician at heart. For instance, I figured after you've got your first platinum album and won artist of the year would be a good time to make demands. You creative types fascinate me. You need to surrender to the creative process. You wouldn't compromise. That's not the brightest stance to take when dealing with businessmen."

"It is my flipping stance, BlueJean," Megan said with aggravation.

"It's over my head like a rifle shot. I don't know how you came out of it in one piece. I really don't. You took a chance."

"It could have turned out differently. It didn't. It's over. Why can't Selina let it go?"

"She's been kicked around all her life. She didn't need you to do it to her."

"I didn't do anything to her. I refused to kick Fran around. Fran put us together. She created Primrose. She believed in me. Gave me a chance when no one else would touch me. She's been kicked around too. But she'll never be kicked around by me. I owe that lady."

"Okay, so you were protecting Fran. But think how Selina felt when Camille also did her dirty."

"Camille made her own stand on a matter of loyalty."

"And Selina views it as, not only a conspiracy, but disloyalty to their relationship."

"That isn't how it went down."

"Megan, you could have demolished the deal."

"Maybe I was too abrasive. That's just me. Abrasive. Surly." Megan then declared with a slight lift to her lip, "And yes, maybe sometimes I am an arrogant bitch."

"Sometimes?" BlueJean chaffed. "Darlin', you aren't counting correctly."

Megan's smile conceded. "Okay, so let's stop extolling my virtue. Think Selina is ready to settle for an apology?"

"Just make sure she doesn't have anything sharp in her hands when you approach her."

"And I know you went to a great deal of trouble setting this up. Will you accept my apology?"

"Darlin', I think you can come up with a way to make amends." BlueJean's eyebrow lifted.

Megan considered the oozing warmth that streamed to every portion of her being when they made love. "Yes," she ratified. "I'm sure we can belong to some nice moments." She leaned over to kiss BlueJean's cheek. "Now, I'm going to try to talk with Selina. See if she'll forgive my high treason."

"Darlin', don't offer the same olive branch that you just offered me. Might get your oxygen supply cut off permanently."

By the time Megan reached the dressing room, her smile had wilted. Camille was leaving. She passed Megan in silence.

Megan trudged in to the room. She was greeted by Selina's scalding glower.

"I'm sorry if I hurt you, Selina. It had nothing to do with my friendship with you. I didn't mean to confront you."

"We're damned lucky he didn't walk."

"I'm apologizing to you."

"You took a chance with our future."

"I tried to do what I thought was right. I didn't do that to hurt you. I did it to keep from hurting someone who has been very good to us all."

Their eyes tagged. Selina sighed. "Guess I'm more hurt by Cammy."

"Don't be. She's in love with you. You're punishing her for being her own person. She simply made a stand on an issue that ran opposite to your stand. That doesn't mean she doesn't love you. It just means she does her own thinking. You wouldn't want her to side with you just to appease you. Would you?"

"Naw. It's just that all my life I've had to do battle. No easy way. And that gets lonely. I've been waiting for this break. It's as near as I've ever been. The thought of losing it was too much."

"Selina, we didn't lose it. Come on, it's more important than ever for complete camaraderie. I want our friendship. I want to end this squabble. Get back to normal. Accept my apology?"

"Guess you're right. If we let this bickerin' get us, we

could lose because of that."

"You know how good we are now. You know we're headed for the top. Can we resume our friendship?"

Selina's frown unraveled. She held out her hand. "I figured you'd pissed him off big time."

"For a moment, so did I," Megan confessed. "I remembered an old saying. If you can't impress 'em with your brilliance, you'd better baffle 'em with your bullshit."

They shared a moment of laughter. Then their handshake converted to a tight hug.

Selina's voice muffled against Megan's shoulder. "One thing's for sure. He won't be expecting your behavior to improve."

"Then I'll never disappoint him," Megan joked. "Seriously, his feet were planted firmly under that table. He wasn't going anywhere."

"How you figure that?"

"There was a galaxy of emotion behind his façade of indifference. When powerful people smell gobs of money they can't control the flush of excitement. I caught his eyes calculating our worth."

"You work that high-wire act pretty good, Red Hot." They stood back from one another. Their eyes bonded. Both women valued one another. Selina teased, "BlueJean got anything to do with your spirits bein' so high?"

"Nope," Megan replied. "My positive endorphins are kicking in by themselves."

* * *

The following morning the group decided to get in a quick morning rehearsal. Fran had been up, working phone calls since very early. "Gather 'round," she bellowed before they began rehearsing. "I been heatin' up the ole cellphone makin' arrangements."

"Where's Megan?" Jesse quizzed.

"Had to drop BlueJean off at her studio. Just got here a few minutes ago. Heard the roach-coach honking outside and decided to get us some donuts and coffee."

"I'm starving," Elena confirmed. "Hope she gets glazed."

"I'll tell her about this later," Fran said as she flipped through the tiny date book she carried with her.

Camille checked Selina's expression. Whatever Fran was going to announce, Selina must have already been told while they were setting up the instruments. Selina smiled widely.

"We got the information on our recording sessions." Fran explained. "Country Crown wants to move on this. We got us time booked with a studio here in Denver to lay down the tracks. We'll get the synthesizer, rhythm - all the music tracks down. Background voices, vocal, will be separately dubbed. Once everything is in sync, it goes to a production team in Nashville for a master track. They also got a video team comin' here to work with us this week. Tanner's movin' and shakin' to get us on a CD and DVD. We go into production tomorrow." Fran glanced up from her scribbled notes. She whooped, "Hot damn, this is getting plenty exciting."

Elena hooted. "If each one of my relatives buys a CD, we'll make the charts."

Selina drew Camille to her, kissing her cheek. "A dream comin' true," she whispered.

"Yes," Camille replied.

"Timed a dozen songs – well, fourteen," Fran disclosed, "and our time is exactly on target. We'll go with that new one Megan is working on. 'Liter of Love' will be our fourteenth. You got the lyrics?" she asked Camille.

Camille nodded. "By heart. I committed them to memory when I first read them."

Camille wondered what had inspired Megan's latest song. She had wanted to inquire, but after yesterday's events, she opted to distance herself from her singing partner. It was an insular reaction. It might serve to exacerbate Megan's isolationism. But then, Camille bargained, Megan was spending most of her time with BlueJean.

Although there had been the sharing of happiness about the contract, Camille was aware that Selina's eyes dimmed when they were alone together. Megan had apologized to Selina, but Camille would not. If anything, she was angered by being forced to stand with Megan. And was also angry that Megan apologized for following her heart.

Even lovemaking with Selina had been a reciprocal exercise. They both knew that their love was impaired. Camille acknowledged that her own guilt about her feelings for Megan made it easier to withdraw. Her emotions were precarious, and guarded. The fact that Megan was sharing ecstasy with BlueJean also exacerbated her response.

After the group disbanded, and headed for their places on stage, Fran questioned, "Camille, you and Selina okay?"

"We're fine." Camille glanced over at Selina. Selina bricked out the world when she was involved with music. "I need to work on the phrasing of the new song."

"After rehearsal maybe you and Megan can take some time to work it out."

"No. No," Camille too quickly declined. "I want to take Selina for a lunch date today. And besides, Megan needs to go back and pick up BlueJean after her radio show is over."

"Well, you and Selina can use some time alone. Even if it's just for a couple hours, the time can do you good. You drag her off with you." Fran's eyebrows furled. The pouches beneath her eyes drew upward. "I'm reading a little tension between you. Has Selina been playin' your chords as great as she plays the keyboard?"

Camille's smile was fabricated. "I would never try to vie for first place where her keyboard is concerned," Camille attempted a joke. She turned, walking toward Selina. Selina's eyes were still stern. "Selina, can we take a late lunch? Get away from all this for just a quick lunch?"

Distracted, Selina didn't even look up from the score she'd been working on. "Today? When everything is coming down, you want to go out for lunch? Look, I need to get this song in place."

"Selina, we need to get our love in place."

"Is it really what you want?"

"Yes. Yes, it is."

* * *

Megan had picked BlueJean up from the studio. On their way back to BlueJean's apartment, Megan drove. She hadn't anticipated being stopped by a policeman. Now, she watched on as BlueJean handed the officer her driver's license, since Megan didn't have her own. He took it, examined it, and then peered at her. "Jean Taylor," he read the name. Then he recognized the face and her radio name. "BlueJean!"

Megan's lips budded to a grin. BlueJean had smiled up at the officer. She was a cross between the Artful Dodger and Svengali – and between Molly Seagrim and Cressida. "Officer, darlin'," BlueJean began as she leaned over from where she was seated in the passenger seat. "This poor little ole thing is just a victim of circumstances."

"Miss Holloway's license has expired. She shouldn't be driving." He paused. When he smiled he uttered, "BlueJean. I listen to you on the radio."

"Then I hope you'll believe me when I tell you this is all a terrible mistake. Ms. Holloway hasn't got a current license because she's been tourin' the country. She with the new hit country group called Primrose. They're playing The Palace now. In fact, we'll be doin' a remote from there. Hope you can drop by and hear for yourself how terrific this cowgirl sings."

"I might just do that," he yielded. "But why didn't you drive?"

"Officer, darlin'," BlueJean's voice was laced with Southern charm. "I was tuckered out after my morning shift. You know how tired a cowgirl can get. She kindly offered to drive. Her foot got a little heavy because she hasn't driven in a while. We surely didn't mean to violate the law."

"Suppose you crawl behind the wheel. And the singer gets her renewal license." He smiled down. He handed her ID back. "I hate to write you up a ticket. Then they might toss you in jail and I wouldn't get to hear my favorite George Jones songs."

"Why darlin', it's so sweet of you to be so understanding.

I'm gonna be sending out a special George Jones song for just you."

He watched on as Megan and BlueJean changed seats. With a wave, BlueJean pulled away from his motorcycle.

"Whew, darlin', we are talking a close call." Her laugh chimed. "You're something behind the wheel."

"I was just anxious to get you back to your place. A little afternoon delight. I want you to show me all that goddesses gave you." Megan's hand slowly moved between BlueJean's thighs. The crease was warm and inviting. "I'm ravenous."

BlueJean's hair blew in the wind. Her breasts puffed. "This is so good. Being with you is perfection."

"Yes."

"Are you happy?"

"What's the sudden interest in my happiness?"

"I want you to be happy. That's not a sudden interest."

"You weren't concerned seven months ago."

BlueJean's teeth began to gnash slightly. Her eyes flashed. "Are we going over that again? What do I need to do to convince you that I'm sorry?"

"Don't try to convince me. Let's just make love. Then get me back for tonight's performance. Repeat it all tomorrow. And so on, maybe. Then we say goodbye."

BlueJean swerved her convertible down the off-ramp. When she reached the parking lot her eyes pivoted to Megan. "Do you have a new interest?"

"I have no one," Megan replied. She eased her fingers around BlueJean's lemon colored silk neck scarf. Megan gave a little tug, directing BlueJean's lips to hers. With lips pressing, her eyes closed. "I have no one," Megan repeated.

"You have me. You'll always have me." BlueJean was unflinching. "We can begin again."

"Putting a new suit on an old corpse isn't going to revive it." Megan got out of the car, slamming the door. BlueJean watched the singer in her rearview mirror. Megan turned, inviting, "Are you going to join me?"

"To meet your sexual requirements," BlueJean yelled. She then followed behind Megan.

"That's right," Megan confirmed. "That's all I'm expecting. All I want."

"Fine, darlin'. By the time for you are ready for the performance, you'll think you've been attacked by a gang of nymphomaniacs. That ought to make you hit your high notes."

Megan grinned. "Always keep that homespun philosophy, you hot-blooded woman, you."

* * *

Selina continued perusing the scribbled list she had made before they left rehearsal. The agenda included booking a video company called NashVid. They would be taking live performance shots. BlueJean had suggested that the team also accompany them on a picnic in the mountains that she wanted to host for the band. Great location shots, she had promised. Tanner concurred and set a schedule.

"It's all happening," Selina raved excitedly.

Camille looked across the luncheon table. The restaurant had a soothing ambiance. She hoped it might help. She, however, was beginning to believe she'd taken her lover captive - away from the band. Selina had let it be known that she was accompanying Camille under duress. Even now, Selina hadn't stopped talking about the band.

Camille threw her napkin down. She took a sip of iced tea.

"Selina, I'm glad we could get away. And I'm happy about the band. But hon, it seems to be tearing us apart."

"Things will settle down. We've all got the jitters. Oh, before I forget, BlueJean invited us all over Sunday night for a poker game. We can play cards, get relaxed. Monday we'll be going up the hills for a picnic."

"We were planning to spend Sunday night together."

"We'll be together."

"Just the two of us."

"Cammy," Selina's enthusiasm percolated. "It's for Primrose. Togetherness. Monday night, after our mountain outing, we can snuggle. I promise."

With desperation in her plea, Camille again asked, "Please, Selina? We need to be alone." Her eyes blinked with wetness. Her speech trailed, "Please."

"We can't do that to Primrose. BlueJean will take offense. And after all, we owe her. Sweetheart, we all need to be going in the same direction."

"I'm trying to get us going in the right direction. You still haven't forgiven me for my egregious error. Don't you understand how much I love you?"

Within the moment's silence, Camille thought about her home. She recalled the calm when walking on the beach. There were acres of spongy shoreline sand beneath her feet. Waves lapped against her ankles. She could remember taking Selina home with her to meet her family. All Selina had talked about was one day owning a home on the beach. Camille continued to tell Selina that her real home would be wherever Selina was. But Selina considered a home to be a place. She hadn't listened to what Camille tried to tell her. She wasn't listening now.

Finally Selina spoke. "Cammy, one day we'll have all the time we want. Right now, we need to be with the band. It'll be fun playin' cards."

"I hate playing cards."

"So does Megan. Maybe the two of you can watch a movie."

"Maybe," Camille's voice steamed, "we can watch a skin flick and play with ourselves."

Selina laughed. "I can't imagine you watchin' a skin flick, sweetheart."

"It's far and away ahead of playing cards."

"Well," Selina chided, "as long as you two play with yourselves. Not with each other when you're watchin' this dirty movie."

Camille felt like a spaniel waiting to be kicked. "You probably wouldn't give a damn if Megan and I did play with each other. Not if it promoted the Primrose spirit of togetherness."

Selina was merely amused. "Sweetheart, you've never cheated in your life. You wouldn't even know how." She then laughed, challenging, "But you know the old saying. If you wanna play the field, you need to get into training."

"Maybe I am."

"Naw. You aren't that type of woman."

"What type?"

"A cheater."

"Suppose my halo slipped." The words struck in her throat like a chicken bone. "Well?"

"Babe," Selina laughed, "you don't even like Red Hot. Not really."

"But suppose, hypothetically, I did. Say it was a case of forbidden fruit."

Selina's head shot back. She howled. Through her laughter, she sputtered, "Fruit! Isn't that what they used to call gays?"

Camille stood, picked up the check. Then she began walking away. She felt Selina's hand at her elbow. She turned. "None of this is funny. It just isn't."

Selina's eyes were red from laughing. One of them began to tear. Camille reached, brushing the tear from her lover's cheek. "Sweetheart, I'm sorry if I'm being insensitive. It's just that the thought of you and Red Hot…" she broke with muffled chuckles. "Impossible!"

"I suppose so," Camille conceded. She then considered that even her life was not a risk-free proposition.

Chapter 12

Music with hope is all I've got.
Compared to most, that ain't a lot.
Its wine, cheese, and bread that's warm,
Lanterns to turn back the storm,
Quilts to wrap you soft and near,
And being there to wipe each tear,
And tossing sweet laughter out your way.
But poets aren't heroes on payday.
I can't match what others may have spent.
'Cause poems don't buy luxuries,
And songs don't pay the rent.

- Poet Gifts

The studio was larger than Megan had anticipated. It was also much plusher than the ones she had been in when she was a backup singer. The entire band loved the studio. Selina put down the first track. After which, the band was jubilant. Each note Selina played glistened. Selina was the perfectionist. Her performance showed that. Megan had listened to the precision, hoping that her own work might come near. Jesse followed the engineer around, inquiring about the technical aspect of the studio equipment. Elena watched with an ebullient nervousness.

Fran was off to herself, listening intently. She was aware that there had been a midweek schism within the group, but had not mentioned it to Megan. She glanced over at Camille, who would be adding her sweet fiddle to the next track. Fran gave a nod in her direction. Camille put the headphones on. She fine-tuned her violin.

Megan was experiencing queasiness. Fran approached.

"Selina is magic."

Agreeing, Megan added, "The best. Funny how these sound catacombs are set up. With audiences, well, even in rehearsal, there's a rapport. Coming together. Recording is so autonomous. We go in there and individually empty out our souls." Megan sluggishly fumbled for words. "The first time you hear your song played in unison, it is the song becoming what you'd intended. Now, it's as if the song is being dissected."

Fran snickered. "It'll all come back together, kid."

"Yes. When are we doing vocals?"

"Audio wants instruments first. After those are mixed we'll do background vocals. Tanner mentioned that they may want to work with you and Camille in Tennessee for the final vocals."

"Tennessee?" Megan questioned.

"Only take a couple days. They told me that the publicists could work with you. Get some additional video. Anyways, we're headed down to Albuquerque, Oklahoma City, and Dallas. Might have a line on another booking or two. We got a couple days of travel time in between Dallas. Time enough for you two to fly to Nashville. The rest of us can drive to Dallas, set up and be ready for you two. We'll perform in big D. Then we're all goin' to Nashville, and this time they'll know we're comin'." Fran's eyes glowed. "They hear our sound - they'll know we're arriving big time."

"Wouldn't it be better if Selina comes with us to Nashville? She's terrific at picking out our little vocal glitches."

"They got experts there to do that. Besides, she's my right arm when it comes to setting up."

"Fran, Jesse knows the system. She can set up."

"Those kids are great, but I need Selina to help me with drivin'. I sure as hell can't have Elena at the wheel. She'd have us stopped at every truck dive along the way. She love's flirtin', that one. And Jesse won't drive in city traffic."

Megan smiled. "The kids. Well, I guess you can manage without Camille and me. This is all happening so quickly. Like a dream sequence."

"Ain't a dream. Makes you happy though?" Fran grilled.

"Sure." Their eyes chained. "I just want you to know how much I appreciate your giving me this chance."

"We give each other the chance." Fran issued a shrew wink. "Ya know trouble's been hangin' out with me most of my days. Life can be a real sidewinder. Learned that when I lost my lover. You'da liked that woman. She'da loved you." Fran coughed. She propped a cigarette between her lips, then struck a match. "We got to get you all some new duds tomorrow."

Megan pitched a red hot candy into her mouth. "You want us to look the part."

"Yep. 'Cause when it hits, hold on to your Stetson. You know, we got us a great bunch. I never thought I'd enjoy the road again. After my lover passed on. You five have made it better than I thought it ever would be again."

Megan gave Fran's shoulder a squeeze. "You gave us the encouragement. We owe it all to you. You believe in us."

"Reason to believe. You know, I always wondered about the others groups I had. Some had no talent. Grandma used to say if the tatter is too hot, just drop it. Well, a few just didn't have it. But I tried to make them better, one way or another. Others got a little successful and they off and left me. I always tried to trust my gut instinct. This time I knew it was perfect." She smiled. "It's been a long road to make it to Primrose, but you're makin' it all worth the trip."

* * *

Selina was overseeing the session with Jesse and Elena. Fran instructed Megan and Camille to get their shopping done together since she wanted them in coordinating outfits. Because Megan didn't want to risk a ticket, Camille drove BlueJean's roadster to a country western specialty store.

Camille could tell Megan didn't enjoy searching for outfits. They wanted to be decked out for the evening's remote broadcast. There would be photo opportunities. Megan had shrugged her way through two racks when Camille finally made several selections, then handed them to Megan. "Try these. I'll coordinate to you."

Megan took the hangers dripping with outfits. She grudgingly stepped into the adjoining dressing room. As she began to undress she emitted a huge sigh.

"Shopping isn't that bad, Red Hot." Camille laughed. "If it were horrible, my sisters wouldn't be doing so much of it."

From over the dressing stall, Camille could hear Megan's clothing rustle as she undressed. She was not looking forward to the evening with BlueJean's live remote broadcast. She'd seen more than enough of BlueJean. Even when they drove past one of the huge billboards featuring BlueJean, Camille was perturbed. Megan's eyes had gleamed as she dramatically threw a kiss up at BlueJean's likeness. It wasn't ten minutes later as they were pulling into the parking lot when from the radio BlueJean's voice announced a special song going out to Megan Holloway from hers truly. It was Dolly Parton's "Wildest Dreams" and it brought tears to Megan's eyes.

"Sorry," Megan said as she entered Camille's small cubicle. "Sorry to intrude on your space. Your thoughts." She scrutinized Camille's hot pink bra and matching skimp panties. Camille lifted her shirt, covering her breasts. Megan quickly diverted her glance. "I just wanted to see if this shirt meets with your approval. Also. I'm hooked."

"What?" Camille inquired with a frown.

"My necklace is hooked on the tag."

"Oh. Here, let me see." Megan turned around, lowering slightly so that Camille could see where the chain was hooked. Brushing Megan's hair aside, Camille felt Megan's body heat. With a start, she pulled her hands away. Then slowly began again. With exactness, she unhitched the chain from the tag. "Free."

"Not free, but reasonable," Megan teased. She coiled around to view Camille's perplexed face. "It's a joke."

"I don't like those kinds of jokes." Her glimpse swayed to another direction. But it was a direct hit with Megan's mirror image. When she saw the reflection she realized that she suddenly yearned to touch Megan again. Camille wrestled with her feelings. Their skin was so near. Megan's pant zipper was open, her blouse unsnapped. The warmth surrounded Camille with a menacing tingle that she had never before experience. She stepped back. "I don't want to hear jokes like that."

"You mean trite jokes?"

Fumbling, Camille pulled her shirt on. She looked down at the way it was draped. It was out of kilter with corresponding snaps. She began haphazardly snapping them. Megan reached down to the hem, lining the snaps up, and began to fasten the bottom snap. Camille jerked it away from her fingers. "I'll do it myself."

"You were fastening them all wrong. You would have had to do them all over again."

Camille's throat was parched. "I would have done them over. See, I'm doing them," she said curtly. Her hands began to tremble. She could barely hold the cloth. Camille felt on display. This was an intrusion. She didn't want Megan so near.

Megan turned, drawing back the curtain. "I'm glad you did them over. Sometimes we don't do things right the first time so we need to do them correctly."

"You're better at writing songs than at conversation," Camille indicted. Her eyes flared with a sudden anger. Her face was flushed. Her fingers continued to shake.

"And I'm better at loving than at not loving." Megan walked away, closing the drapery panel behind her. She began whistling "Red Hot Blues" as she went to her own stall.

Camille sat down on the small shelf seat. She shivered with the realization that she had a serious case of the Red Hot blues. She had denied it, excused it, and now she was facing her fears.

* * *

Before going out on stage for the remote broadcast, Megan straightened Jesse's collar. She gave her a kiss on the cheek, and then joined the others. BlueJean was transmitting a two-hour, primetime remote. She gave the thumbs up signal. She was seated behind her microphone. She put on her earphones, gave an introduction, and motioned to Selina.

After the first fifteen minutes BlueJean whispered to Fran that the studio switchboard was going bonkers with calls. Denver had fallen in love with Primrose. Could the world be far behind, BlueJean asked her listening audience. She then blew a clandestine kiss in Megan's direction.

At the conclusion, the women traded congratulatory hugs. When Megan reached Camille's side, she leaned, barely brushing her blonde partner's cheek.

"We're doing it," Selina said with a gasp. She tucked her arm around Megan's shoulder. "Did you see that crowd?"

"BlueJean's a great draw," Megan remarked. When BlueJean approached, Megan made a point of planting a warm, sensual kiss on her lips. When the kiss ended, Megan saw the look in Camille's eyes. She had not only witnessed the kiss, but her glance remained. BlueJean returned Megan's kiss with a saucy laugh. Their bodies stitched together tightly.

"Darlin', let's get home before I climb these dirty ole backstage walls," BlueJean directed.

When Megan passed Camille, Camille glared. "Megan, try not to forget we have a heavy day tomorrow," she snapped.

"Camille," Megan chaffed, "I'll write it on my hand so I don't forget." She then bundled her body nearer BlueJean's.

BlueJean chuckled. "Darlin', don't you be writing anything on those hands. I could get lead poisoning."

Selina had joined in the laughter until she recognized Camille's steely glance in her direction. She then wheeled around. She suggested they leave.

Megan was well aware that there was a problem between Camille and Selina. She had thought the dispute over Tanner's recommendation had been resolved. She also wondered why Camille was being distant with her. Megan thought back to their shopping excursion. When Megan stepped into the fitting room, she hadn't looked at Camille with lust. But admittedly, she had felt stirrings when Camille touched her neck while getting her chain loose from the sale's tag. She hadn't attempted a seduction. But she may have ventured out too far. She wouldn't do it again.

Lamely Megan glanced back at Camille and Selina as they packed their instruments.

"Darlin, would you like to join me in the cradle of contentment?" BlueJean asked.

"I'd love to join you," Megan replied.

On the way to the convertible, BlueJean took Megan's hand. She asked, "You know about the Scarlet Letter? There were public whippings for the unfaithful? The letter A would be scratched on the head of an adulteress?"

"What?" Megan whirled around. She tried to read the lift to BlueJean's eyebrow. "What are you saying?"

"Have you told her you have feelings for her?" she blithely inquired.

"Who?"

"Not that I need to answer. But should I call her Selina's woman, or your singing partner?"

"I'm not some lust baroness chasing down my friend's woman."

"Are you so vain that you don't think I'm bright enough to pick up on your feeling for her?"

Megan was floundering. "I've been told that vanity is what you want others to think of you. Pride is what you think of yourself. And I don't give a damn what anyone thinks of me."

"Don't beg the question on my account."

"Now look who is vain," Megan charged. "Besides, after we leave Denver you'll resume your floozy hunt."

"Let's not divert the conversation. And you don't know what I'll do."

"BlueJean, we'll both be with other women."

Jauntily BlueJean walked around to the driver's seat. "After your rambling days are done, you come back to me." She turned the ignition key. "I'll be waiting for you."

"Working on early bookings for a Sapphic retirement home? Getting your lists and checking them twice." Megan chuckled. "You're the one with rambling ways."

"Let's get back to my original question. Am I correct?" BlueJean's inquiry met with silence. "Of course, I am. Have you told her?"

"It wouldn't do any good. In fact, it would do the opposite."

"At least you know that much."

"You won't say anything?"

"I'm not that adventuresome, darlin'."

* * *

Selina and Camille were reclining together in post-lovemaking bliss. Selina nibbled Camille's neck. Her head rested on Camille's shoulder. "I love you, Cammy."

"Yes. I love you." Camille tenderly pushed the wisps of hair from Selina's face. "I love you so." Her speech wobbled. Accurate memories persisted. She thought of how she felt when she unhooked Megan's chain. Then the image switched to Megan as she flirted with BlueJean. "Selina, I would like to have more time with you. Just you. Relationships need that."

"When we get the album cut, we'll have time," Selina disputed with impatience. "Come on, Cammy." Her tone then converted to an almost placating lull. "Sweetheart, the minute it is finished, we'll take some time for the two of us. I promise."

"But we need time now," Camille debated with irritation. "Can't you see, I need you? You aren't listening to me." She was still in hopes of having Sunday night alone with Selina. "It would be lovely to have an evening together without one of the band members dropping in. We could have that privacy Sunday."

"You always got to have your way." Selina broke from their embrace.

Camille pulled her lover back to her. She closed her eyes to rest them from the incessant blinking of the flashing light sign across the street. She had put everything into love making - into pleasing Selina. She had asked only that they have time together. Selina's condemning glare was telling her that she believed Camille was a spoiled little rich girl.

"Selina, I want to have it *our* way. Us. You and me. You're my priority. Not Primrose."

Selina rolled over. She swept Camille's objection aside. "I do love you more than anything. But this is our big chance. This is what I've invested all these years to get. It has nothing to do with how much I love you. Cammy, it isn't like I'm out chasin'. I want to make life better for both of us. So we can be together in style. I want to be able to give you things. A home near the ocean. A flash car. All the things I can't give you now." She paused. "Don't you want to be famous?"

"I want to be yours. I don't need all the amenities. I could have them if I walked out that door and returned home. I want you." Camille felt bulldozed. She couldn't share her true turmoil. She couldn't tell Selina how tangled her spirit felt. She could only implore Selina to read the distress signals. She could only beg Selina to get her through this.

"You have my love," Selina dueled. "I don't understand you. You know how important this is to me. Us. Sweetheart, let's get some sleep and talk about it in the morning. We have a big day coming up. We got a big career comin' up, too."

Throughout the desolate night, Camille reached to touch Selina's sleeping face. She needed to caress her lover. She understood, and admired, Selina's need to win a battle over poverty. Camille grappled about that. She considered that if she and Selina left the band, they would be safe. They could relocate to California and Camille's trust fund monies would buy them an ocean-front home, and set them up in whatever business they wanted. Even a recording studio, Camille thought. Although that would also be Selina's dream, she would never agree to it. Camille kissed Selina's auburn hair. No, Selina would never come away with her. She measured her own valor in terms of what it might have been like to climb out of the slums on her own – as Selina had done.

But now their relationship was endangered. The band's success was tearing them apart. Camille felt at risk. Her face nestled against her lover. She realized that things were the same when she was a small child. Her sisters controlled her as well as controlled her events. They saved her when she needed saving, but they did it their way.

Selina held that power. She could save them both. Selina

could help Camille brace against her own emotion. Camille's virtue was not as impenetrable as Selina believed.

Camille mostly feared Megan's warmth.

* * *

After an early rehearsal, Megan and BlueJean stopped by a local supermarket to pick up snacks, and ingredients for BlueJean's famous chili recipe for Sunday night's poker game. They decided to return to BlueJean's townhouse for a quick dinner of omelets and another of BlueJean's specialties, buttermilk biscuits.

"You'd make some man a terrific wife," Megan teased when BlueJean served the steaming hot biscuits.

"I'd make you anything you want," BlueJean lulled. "However, my eyes are not glazed over with heterosexual zealotry."

"I can't tell you how wonderful it is to be sitting here relaxing. Enjoying one of your luscious meals."

"Movin' a million miles an hour, aren't you?"

"At least I've got a little life experience. I can't imagine what Jesse and Elena are going through."

"Those kids seem to take it all in stride."

"Jesse's eyes were like saucers when she saw the studio's control panels. She kept telling me that they went on for miles. She spoke with such reverence. She's enthralled with the technical. She likes being alone."

"You must also like being remote."

"Me?"

"Well, you ran off to live up there in the mountains for half a year. In total isolation."

"It was the most productive months of my life. Self-imposed isolation was also self-confrontational. I collaborated with my deepest fears."

"The blustering, snowy night would be my worst fear. Weren't you frightened?"

"No," Megan answered. Then she emptied her heart's

envelope. "To be honest, my deepest fear was that I couldn't live without you."

Silence confirmed their pain. The sentence had expressed the words that Megan thought she would probably never tell BlueJean. For Megan, it had been far more truthful than the empty dialogues they had shared throughout the week. Both women ached. Their eyes still steamed over when they were in the same room.

"You have lived without me."

Megan looked away. "Proving there is life after BlueJean."

* * *

Camille wasn't thrilled about BlueJean's being backstage in their cramped dressing room. But because the production team would be videotaping, more attention to makeup was required. BlueJean had offered to assist with the younger women's makeup.

Each of the band members wore a coordinated outfit that picked up a basic color of primrose. Lavender neck scarves were issued to each of the women. They busily assisted one another as BlueJean applied makeup. Jesse had always shunned makeup, but was coaxed into BlueJean's promise to make her look natural. A towel was wrapped around Jesse's neck, and BlueJean began. After she had finished, the timid young woman beamed.

"Darlin', with a little color, you're even more gorgeous," BlueJean flirted.

"It does look wonderful, Jesse," Camille agreed. She gave Jesse's chin a tap. Then she turned to BlueJean and complemented. "Excellent work. Guess if you ever lose your radio voice, you have a career as a makeup artist."

BlueJean's frame stiffened. With a slight edge, she spoke, "And if your voice goes out on you, you can buy a cosmetic factory."

"I was only praising your work," Camille snapped back.

"Praise away with someone who cares."

Selina grilled, "Jean, why are you snarlin' like a bear with a headache?"

"Sorry," BlueJean backed away. "Look, Megan is out there at the bar. Maybe one of you can bring her back here sober."

Selina made a quick path to the door. "I'll see if she'll listen to me. Where's Fran?"

"Talkin' with the film crew," BlueJean answered.

Jesse and Elena followed Selina. Camille watched BlueJean's image in the mirror's reflection. She sat. She began applying her makeup. After many blank moments, Camille turned and asked, "Was Megan's drinking the real issue in your splitting?"

"I told you, she behaved better with me at her side. It wasn't lack of communication. It wasn't that I don't like cinnamon. It wasn't our sex life. Or music. Or careers." BlueJean walked slowly to the door. "You want in-depth honesty. Maybe it was that I needed to learn about love. I didn't learn in time to keep Megan. I saw her intoxication level begin, and I didn't want that for her. I should have helped her – been there for her. I accept full and complete responsibility. Does that answer your question?"

"I have another question. Do you know about love now?"

"I've sharpened my retentive powers. And yes, I learned."

"Are you saying you wouldn't hurt her again?"

"I would do anything for her. I would give anything to have her back. I would spend the rest of my days showin' her, proving to her, that I would never let her go again. But if she isn't willing to believe that, I'm sure my words mean nothing to you."

Camille watched BlueJean exit. She stared into the mirror. Her eyes appeared weary. She wished they had picked another night for filming. She was glad to see Fran.

"Fran, did you see how great the kids look?"

Fran did the shimmy. Her torso twisted. "We got us razzle-dazzle baby dolls, for sure. And you look like a strawberry sundae."

"Is everything out there ready?"

"Yep. They just need enough footage to splice in with the

music. They manage the sync and added sounds. All you gotta do is just sing the songs like always. Did Selina mention that we'll go on to Dallas? But you and Megan will head for Nashville for the final tracks."

"No. She failed to mention it."

"Well, it's been confirmed. That's the plan. That'll give us a couple of days on the road while you two are in Nashville."

"Two? Won't Selina go?"

"I need her to help me. Driving." Fran lingered, leaning back against the wall. "I already been over it with Megan. She gave me the standard argument that Selina should go with you. Megan said Selina could help with the technical aspects. The truth is - those folks wouldn't listen. Hell, they hate it when band members butt in and try to tell 'em their job."

"Megan wanted Selina to join us?"

"Yep. She was real upset when I refused. It's only for two days." Fran took out a cigarette. She rolled it around her lips without lighting it. She knew Camille didn't like her to smoke in cramped quarters. "Megan got her makeup on yet?"

"Yes. We're all ready to go."

"Hot damn, we're cooking now."

Fran turned, nearly bumping into Megan on her way out. "You're looking' tasty," Fran cackled.

"Were you looking for me, Camille?" she asked.

"I just asked where you were."

"Were you concerned that I might be falling down drunk? Did you think you might have to carry the show?"

"Tonight would not be the best night for your falling down drunk routine." Camille reached for a tissue. She knocked over a bottle of makeup base. After righting it, she laughed. "And I'm concerned about you. I'm the one with the shakes."

Megan knelt down, taking Camille's hand in her own. "You'll be fine out there. A little case of nerves even helps. Just relax and have fun. You'll be terrific."

"I don't know how you can be so calm." Camille smiled. "Your nerves must have been severed at birth."

Somber, Megan's gaze shifted. She pulled her hand away. After straightening her scarf, she answered, "Perhaps. Perhaps at birth my heart was taken out and made into a saddlebag."

"I didn't mean it that way. I'm sorry," Camille apologized. "I just meant that you're always composed. Calm and secure out there."

"Maybe the stage is one of the few places where I don't feel abandoned. There was this old mine shaft near my home. I used to hide out in the entrance. Thought maybe I could live there when I grew up. Then I found out there had been a mining accident. A dozen miners had been trapped. They never exhumed the bodies. Just filled in the shaft with backfill. I figured I must have felt at home with the miner's spirits. That was why I didn't feel alone there." Megan swallowed. "It was a fucking tomb. I felt more at home there than I did at my mother's place."

Camille reached, touching Megan's arm. "I am jittery. Will you carry me if I go up out there?"

Hypnotized, Megan vowed, "You won't go up. But we can always save one another."

* * *

Megan had no idea how much of Camille's warm personality was switched on for the cameras. But her performance seemed an act of love. Megan checked her own glances of desire. But when they sang certain songs, both women were captured within the music, trapped within one another's gazes. They both felt the trap of looking into the other's eyes. It was as if they trespassed.

Sparks from the band were igniting with each song. They had never been more in unison. Megan knew each of them savored the night. When Megan's guitar string snapped, she quickly began singing "Strings fall to Pieces" as she unwound the gear.

Camille reached down to assist Megan with her guitar. Megan playfully cautioned, "Stand back, it could explode at any time." The audience laughed - Camille laughed. Megan was seeing to it that everyone had fun. She realized that the band's magic wasn't just for the cameras when the film crew finished filming, but stayed on for the final set.

Megan's jocular interludes had no doubt calmed the band member's nerves. When they packed up for the night, her good time had dwindled. She'd emptied half a pint of bourbon. As if mourning the loss of the evening, she toasted the empty dressing room.

Disenchanted, BlueJean looked on. If only alcohol impaired Megan more. But it didn't corrupt her musical abilities. BlueJean thought that might save her because Megan loved music enough to give up booze. She wondered how anyone could touch an audience with such love and joy, and be so miserable inside. She had no idea how Megan could go on stage half loaded, and play the guitar and sing as she did. BlueJean admitted she couldn't even have a beer before entering her own broadcast studio without slurring.

When they returned to her townhouse she embraced Megan. Megan extricated herself from the thicket of BlueJean's arms. She took a swig from the bottle she'd brought along. BlueJean stormed away, slamming her bedroom door behind her.

Megan knocked, "BlueJean, what the hell's wrong?"

The door flashed open. BlueJean blasted, "You're being self-destructive. You've been loaded most of the night. If you're riding the fast train, you'd better clean up your act," she blustered. "Before it's too late and you're just another broken-down, warbling lush."

"You aren't my manager," Megan stormed. "The audience had a great time. Primrose too."

"Your little partner had fun. She was cracking up at your outrageous humor. And she was the one supposedly worried about your imbibing." She leaned nearer Megan. "What do you plan to do if you're a naughty girl and get caught?"

"I'd be sorry. Can I show you that I'm not too wasted to make love?"

BlueJean's eyes watered. "I don't think you have a clue."

"You said you love me."

"And once again, you haven't said you love me."

"Let me try to show you how I feel."

BlueJean opened her arms. Time was limited; days were being chomped away by those ticking moments. "I love you. That'll have to do."

"For now," Megan hoarsely whispered.

By the time morning's light created its beige shadows, both women were exhausted. BlueJean issued her final goodnight lullaby. "Megan, I do love you," her rich, sultry voice confirmed.

Megan drew her near, gathering BlueJean into her embrace. "You're beautiful, Jean."

"Aren't you ever going to tell me those words?"

Megan smiled. "Let me guess, you're one of these puritanical women whose conscience can't be eased without the words."

"Naw," BlueJean replied. "My great-grandmother was a dancehall girl."

Megan chuckled. "That's why she was great." Megan lifted her lover's chin and deeply kissed BlueJean. "She passed on her greatness."

"But I'm not great enough for your words of love?"

"Those words were about to be said when you walked out of my life. So they frightened me." Megan hesitated. "Now, are you going to send me from your arms because I won't tell you I love you?"

"Darlin'," BlueJean said with a laugh as she tickled Megan's ribs. "Darlin', I wouldn't ever send you to the other side of the bed. Not ever. And when you believe that, the words will be easy."

Their lips tasted of love. They were on the same side of the bed.

Chapter 13

What's the world speaking about,
When every silence seems to shout?
Words open up the light's glare.
Okay, I'll listen, whatever seems fair.
And what I'll say to the light and to the sound,
Okay, I'll play at lost and found.

- Lost and Found

"Incognito?" Megan queried as she glanced at Camille's lime-colored short and blouse set. "Not exactly the garb of a county-western singer."

"For the day, I've traded my boots for running shoes. Bright neon running shoes. And I am a California girl. Remember, California is west of nearly everything except the Pacific Ocean."

Megan chuckled as she followed Camille onto BlueJean's lanai. She closed the sliding glass panel after them to quiet the noise from the poker party. Camille was aware that Jesse and Elena were impressed with BlueJean's abode. With BlueJean's everything.

"Well, you look alluring in your West Coast duds," Megan stressed. "Guess you've had it with the rolling cacophony of poker chatter, too."

"Very much so. I find it tedious."

"Think about the connotative implications. We've got some truly sexually stimulating buzz words: Queen. Ace. A pair. A flush. Everyone raising one another. Wild. Stud. And for homophobes, there's even a straight."

Camille chuckled. "Even the word 'poker' can be slightly

suggestive."

"I missed that one entirely." Megan gazed at the view of the mountains. "We'll be up there tomorrow."

"Yes." Camille's answer was like a sharp pain.

"I love it up there. I miss the solitude."

"I figured with BlueJean in the picture there isn't time to miss the mountain cabin."

"I still miss the mountains. Don't you miss the ocean?"

"Very much. But right now I miss having Selina to myself."

"That's what's going on between the two of you? I hoped it wasn't over the contract business." Megan's dark, sensual eyes targeted Camille. Moonlight gave those eyes a mahogany luster. Camille was intrigued by their sparkle. "We don't need to discuss it, if you'd rather not."

"I just wasn't aware that our problems are so transparent. I wanted her alone tonight. She gets so intense when she's involved. No matter if it is playing poker, music, or anything else really." Camille smiled benevolently. "And I can tell you, poker will never be her game. She is just too honest. She can't bluff to save her soul. My father wanted his children to be savvy enough to select a terrific husband, or survive the corporate climb. One of his tutorials was learning to play a crafty hand of poker. Card games became my first school subject. Selina would never pass my father's scrutiny."

"Probably not. Last count she'd lost eight bucks in pennies.

"But her honesty is one of the things I most love and respect about her. I find her intensity endearing. Most of the time."

"Difficult to believe anyone's intensity over anything would make a woman pass up an evening alone with you."

"She wants to keep the Primrose bond. I also admire her loyalty."

"Fran picked up on a problem between the two of you. Asked, delicately, if I knew why you looked as though you were stepping on your own utters. Again, an old saying," Megan disclosed with a laugh.

Camille grinned. "Nothing gets by Fran."

"No." With a tremor, Megan's jawline went taut. Her eyes twitched as she sipped from her glass. "In this night lighting, your eyes have a silver gleam."

Camille intersected Megan's words. "I'm glad we've become friends so I can talk about Selina and my problems."

With tempered sarcasm Megan replied, "Feel free." A frown hooded her eyes as she squinted up at the glaring oval moon. "I'm one of love's greatest shrinks. Philosophically, I know that life is a very larcenous odyssey. We have some wild illusion that love exists. Once in a while we hold our hearts up to the window and pull back the blinds. We allow global voyeurism to examine our coronary confusion. Cellophane-wrapped for ease of observation." Megan took a quick gulp then swirled the ice in the bottom of her glass. "I'm a cynic. But I hope I can be there when you need to talk."

"Megan, I'll take that into consideration."

"Need a drink?"

"I'm fine."

"I'll be right back. I dry out if I don't have a steady stream of booze flooding my arterial passages. You need a jacket? Colorado evenings are pretty cool."

"No. What I do need is Selina's arm around me." Her thought with those words were to reinforce her barricade. After seeing the look on Megan's face, she wished she could have them back. There was empathy for what Megan was going through with BlueJean.

Glad for a moment to withdraw when Megan exited, Camille massaged her temples.

When Megan returned, she handed Camille a soft drink. She placed a half filled glass and a bottle of booze on the ledge. "Here you go. I thought you might be running low."

"Thanks, Megan. And thanks for understanding. I worry about losing Selina. I worry about our relationship." The rest of her words became impaled before reaching her lips.

"One poker game isn't likely to ruin your relationship."

"No. I've unloaded my woes. You feel like talking about BlueJean?"

"Some of life is unattainable."

"You're still hurting."

"Yes. Bad times have a way of stockpiling. Like so many of life's edges, you can never forget the travel over them or through them."

"I've heard that your photo is the only one BlueJean always carries. She told me that you're the only one she's ever been completely in love with. That kind of love counts for something."

"BlueJean is an intricate woman. Aren't we all?" Megan grinned.

"I suppose so. Maybe BlueJean has changed. Could change."

Megan took a sip. Her eyes watered. "Love is an instrument of torture. With love she trespassed on my soul. She encouraged my belief in her. She walked out on me. And you wonder why I'm tentative about doling out trust."

Camille reached to touch Megan's hand. The coolness from Megan's icy glass reminded Camille that she must not allow that touch to last. "Megan, I'm truly glad we can talk now."

Megan's throat tightened around her words like a clamping fist. "I wish you could know me. But I stay in a secret place."

* * *

Bleary-eyed, Megan stirred. Her mind drifted the previous night. There was BlueJean's sexy invitation for a relaxing dip in the spa. She'd punned that Megan needed to be well-Taylored before the evening progressed. And BlueJean Taylor was there to offer stress relief.

Megan's heart had been assured safe passage. She was blotto drunk, and was being fully eroticized within BlueJean's steamy domain. That had divested Megan of pain. For the time.

"What a night," BlueJean exclaimed as Megan stumbled to the kitchen. "I doubt if you remember. But you had a wonderful time."

"I remember."

"Amazing." She poured Megan a cup of coffee. "You were tempering the booze until your little chat with Miss Sweet and Chaste. Then you began knocking 'em back."

"It was a party. I had a few drinks. I needed to fortify."

"Megan, sometimes you start with honesty and there's a turn off on the road to self-deception. Darlin', you have a problem with alcohol. There. I've said it."

"You're going to sit there and pontificate," Megan huffed. "In Sapphic hierarchy, you're the woman with a problem. You've got a love addition. And you're going to lecture me on my drinking."

Her eyes pelted Megan. "We're not talking about me. I do think it would be nice if you told me what it is you want. Or who."

"I want to belong."

"Belonging is a self-determined freedom," BlueJean stated. Her long lashes bobbed as she stirred her coffee. "You're within reach of your dream. Before you land yourself in the center stage of fame, you'd better have your own truth faced." She hesitated. "What is going to make you happy? Do you want to come back to me?"

"That's not an option. We both know that." Megan stood, her face flushed as she passed BlueJean. "I'm going to shower. One thing I can tell you. I'll hate leaving Denver. Nobody makes a better cup of java."

"Megan, you're hiding out again. Hell, what's new. You've never even told me what you name your guitars."

"And you've never told me what your favorite color is."

"It's yellow."

"Of course." Megan's lips lifted to a smile. "The yellow rose of Texas."

"Yes," BlueJean confirmed. With a rakish wink, she then asked, "Would you like to put a little morning blush on this Texas rose?"

"Definitely." Megan walked back to the breakfast table. Her arms went around BlueJean and she kissed her forehead. "Let's tiptoe through the lavish, dewy rose garden of romance."

"Tiptoe?" BlueJean chuckled. "Let's romp. Barefoot. And

bare all."

"As long as we beware not to stub our hearts."

* * *

Primrose music filled the mountain side. There were echoes downward from the craggy rock formation where they stood.

Camille was amazed it hadn't become a total circus, since BlueJean had been directing the afternoon picnic, slash, video shoot. The camera team agreed when BlueJean and Fran recommended that they use the backdrop of sky and mountain top. The five women were placed up on a rocky ledge. With blazing blue skies behind them, and pines to the side, they stood high on the mountain's apron of granite.

Cameras zoomed in as the band sang. Fran was excited about the outdoor shoot. A side benefit was that the location was near a small stream. She planned to do some downhome fishing. And the day of sunshine, great scenery, her band, and promise, made it one of her finest. The entire band, crew, and BlueJean were aware of that.

The feast had been excellent. Barbecued beef from the spit had been perfectly seasoned and tender to the touch. Elena had also cooked her specialty – pasole. The pork and hominy stew had been a favorite. Catered side-dishes stretched, luscious pies tempted, and drinks flowed. BlueJean enjoyed entertaining her friends.

Camille was glad when Megan began her drinking with only a sprinkle of whiskey in an entire glass of ginger ale. Megan had commented how it took a couple hours to tamp down a hangover. She sipped cautiously. Camille was also glad Megan wasn't ripped when they climbed the rocks to their elevated stance atop the boulder.

A great shawl of Colorado sunshine covered the land. Camille issued a soft smile in Megan's direction. Megan gave her Stetson a tip as she flashed a return smile. Camille was certain that was the smile that would make it onto the finalized video. The cameraman was as intrigued with Megan's dazzling smile as Camille was.

Although elated that they had made the climb, the height bothered Camille. Their voices soared, and admittedly it would be a magnificent addition to the video. A thrill streaked through her body when they concluded. Applause lifted. With a sudden cave of her heart, Camille realized she was gazing into Megan's eyes. Staggered, she was mesmerized for many moments. She then shifted her attention to Selina.

The songs from above had been exhilarating. The band knew it; felt it. They carefully handed their instruments down, and then began their decent. Megan's agility allowed her to quickly dismount from the jagged rock wall with skill. She reached up toward Camille. There was fear in the singer's eyes.

"You'll be fine. I'm right here. Pretend it's an ocean mantel."

"It's so steep." Camille's footing didn't feel at all sure. She halted. Her fingers tightly clutched a crust of rock. She peered down at Megan's outstretched arms. She wanted to continue, but didn't want to touch Megan.

"Just let go," Megan whispered. "I'll catch you."

Panicked, Camille sucked in air. "What did you say?"

"I said I'll catch you - no matter what. Just ease down slowly."

As if struck by an electrical charge, it was a secret suddenly revealed. Some cosmic force had come to her rescue. She had always wanted someone to tell her that no matter what, they would catch her.

Megan sensed Camille's frozen fear. "I'd never drop you."

She lowered her body. Megan's arms surround her. Megan's body was against hers. There was the press of Megan's breasts, her hips, and the side of Megan's face. But that touch was brief as Megan steadied her. She then quickly stepped away.

Camille didn't wait for the other to descend the incline. She needed something cool to drink. Opening the cooler, she dug deeply down to a can of soda. The ice cubes were a welcoming interlude. Kneeling by the cooler for several moments, she then heard BlueJean behind her.

Whirling around, Camille asked, "Want a soft drink? Beer?"

"Sure. Beer." BlueJean's eyes were steady. Even that had unnerved Camille. It had overwhelmed her. "You two sounded great."

"Thanks," Camille politely responded. "Glad Megan recovered from last night."

"Just barely. She'll be working on a new inebriation in no time at all." BlueJean took the beer as she sat on the ground beside Camille. "Megan searches out life's flaws. They become props."

"You believe that's her excuse for drinking?"

BlueJean flipped her hair. Her eyelids ruffled in thought. "Maybe I didn't do my part in keeping Megan and my relationship together. But maybe I'm getting a bad rap. She goes through a creative process when she writes those songs. There's a time of brooding. It isn't an easy sequence to live with."

"She told me she stays in a secret place."

"That's an understatement!" BlueJean howled. "You know, she's got that guitar named. But she's never told me what she calls it. She's locked in her own secrets. She even refuses to divulge the lyrics of certain songs she's written. Got them in her head, but won't give up the words. Even when she's inebriated. So maybe," BlueJean drawled, "maybe she was frightened to completely give her love to me. Suppressing love can't be easy. And having total love withheld isn't easy either."

"I wouldn't know. My relationship with Selina is based on complete love. I view our love as a marriage."

"You mean if you were to slip, become unfaithful, you would consider it adultery?" BlueJean's eyebrows lifted with mock amazement. "My, my."

"Infidelity doesn't just happen when there's a marriage license."

BlueJean stood. "Looks as if Fran is about ready to find that stream and wet a line. Are you coming?"

"I'm going to attempt to coerce Selina into taking a walk

with me."

"Megan has a standard joke about taking a little tramp in the woods. Once I told her I wasn't any little tramp. She said she knew that. She called me an archetypical prima donna of the microphone."

Amused, Camille laughed. "I'm not even considering going to the woods with Megan. But I'm hopeful Selina can be talked into it."

"You'd better do some fast talking."

Selina was lifting one of the fishing rods. Camille's stab of isolation thrust her to quickly catch up with Selina. "Can we take a walk together?"

Selina turned, "Sure, sweetheart. Come with us. We'll find a nice place to drop a line. Those rainbow trout are more fun than a season ticket to the Mustang Ranch."

"Selina, I want to talk."

"Nice part about fishing is that if you talk quietly, you can do both. Fish are biting this time of day. Come on, babe. We'll do all the talking you want."

"I'll just rest here." The group of women trailed away from her. Under her breath she muttered, Terrific. I'm left behind with Megan and a bottle of bourbon."

Megan was seated on a downed tree trunk. She was strumming various chords on her guitar. Within arm's length, her bottle rested. Camille busied herself straightening up the area. She collected a barrage of paper plates, cups, and napkins. When finished, she looked back at Megan. Megan would push back her Stetson, take another drink, and continue on with a new set of chaining chords. Finally she stopped. "Camille, I thought you were going to rest."

"I just finished cleaning up. I'll rest now. I don't like fishing."

"Me neither."

"Are you planning to stay plastered for the remainder of your life?"

"Very probably. So why aren't you at Selina's side?"

"Because I'm tired of Primrose always coming first," Camille answered bitterly.

"We're family. Selina hasn't got a real family. I can understand her belonging to the group as a family."

"She has me."

Megan's boot tapped against the tundra's stubble beneath. She motioned for Camille to sit beside her. Slowly, Camille sat. With somberness, Camille concluded that the stony bordered, loamy earth with its coverlets of pine needs and paths would not be walked upon by Selina and her. They would not trek, hand in hand, heart in heart, through nature. Loneliness was a laceration she hated to face, but feared this was only the beginning. And once again, she was being left behind.

"Megan, what's your guitar's name?"

Bemused, Megan gripped her guitar. "My daddy used to go to a place called the Denver Folklore Center. They had performances. He always told me that once in a while a woman named Elizabeth Cotton performed there and he never missed her performances."

"She was blues and folk musician," Camille pulled from her memory. "We studied her in a music class. African American woman songwriter. She wrote 'Freight Train' and some great old songs."

"I'm impressed you know about her."

"Megan, I didn't study exclusively about opera. And your father knew her?"

"Yes. He said she was a big woman and her face was filled with love. She could play guitar! She always named her guitars. I remembered that, and when I got my first guitar, I named it Cotton. For the beautiful woman that my dad talked about. I've named all my guitars Cotton."

Megan's calloused fingers then firmly gripped her bottle of bourbon. She placed the rim against her lips as her eyes dimmed with memory. Camille was penitent that she had no words, no miracle, to heal Megan's hurt. Camille rose. She walked away - back to her own ravaging battle.

* * *

Megan's eyelids were heavy. Her head bobbed. Her alcoholic stupor had not eased her pain. She wandered away, bottle in hand, weaving as she walked. She found a quiet meadow where she rested on a tree stump. Another burning gulp triggered a sharp cough. She slipped a red hot candy between her lips. Lifting the bottle, she toasted the women she loved. One belonged to another woman. The other belonged to all other women.

Blinking back tears her eyes misted. She had been so near to Camille that her ambrosial scent stirred Megan's emotions. When their bodies brushed, Megan felt baptized in passion. The ceremony surged through her body. When Camille wobbled against her, Megan yearned to embrace her.

Now she was alone. Her eyes prowled the forest. She shivered with desolation as a wounded animal might. She took another swig as her eyes clamped shut. She pressed the bottle against the ground. Her elbows leaned on her knees with her head slumped into the chalice of her hand. She sobbed for songs she hadn't written; and wouldn't write. For the songs she hadn't sung; and would never sing. For all the guitars that weren't named. She sobbed for loves she wouldn't have; for ones she'd lost. She sobbed out for the world. Her tears became a reprisal of each legacy of pain from the beginning of time. She tried to wash clean the world with those tears.

"Megan," Camille called to her.

Megan uncovered her damp eyes. Camille was leaning over her. Camille went down to one knee. Her arms softly circled Megan. Tenderly comforting, Camille's silken body compassionately clasped Megan.

Lifting her head, Megan began to kiss Camille. Their lips met and there was a long moment before Camille squirmed away. Struggling, she pulled her head away. Injured and rejected, Megan attempted to hold her. When they slid to the ground Megan's searing passion continued. In a dream world she held Camille tightly, so tightly that she felt she might never lose her.

Camille panicked. "Megan, let me go. If you don't, I'll scream." She jerked free and crawled several feet from Megan.

Then she stood. "Damn you, Megan. I was trying to be your friend. If it wasn't for the band, I'd tell Selina." Her glacial eyes were dazed. "Now get up. We're going back. I came to find you. The others are packing up."

"I'm sorry," Megan wept. "I just didn't want to let you go. I didn't mean to frighten you. Or to hurt you."

"You're drunk. You're disgusting when you drink." Camille moved back, wiping her own streamers of tears that were flowing down her cheeks. When she'd dried her face, she gave her hair a shake.

Megan stood, stumbling as she reached for a branch to steady herself. "I'm sorry."

"Aren't you going to bring your damned bottle with you?"

"Leave it for the Indian. I may return."

"I have no idea what you're talking about." Camille stormed toward the footpath. Megan raced behind her. Camille was revolted by any form of substance abuse. When Megan was incoherent, she felt a betrayal. With a quiver in her voice, she ordered, "I don't want you to ever touch me again. Do you understand?"

"Yes." Megan's agreed. It felt as though her heart vault slammed shut. "It may be the only thing I do understand."

* * *

"Where's Megan?" Selina asked.

"Right behind me," Camille answered. She glared at BlueJean.

"She okay?" BlueJean inquired.

"While you were busy impressing the band with your angling skills, Megan was getting loaded."

BlueJean inhaled deeply when she spied Megan stumbling toward her. "So I see."

Camille flared, "I don't suppose anyone will blame you if you cut and run now."

BlueJean's hands went to her hips as her shoulders lifted. "She's the only woman in the world I'll never cut and run from.

Never again." She met Megan half way, looping her arms around the staggering singer. Megan leaned into BlueJean's gripe. As they passed Fran, BlueJeans said, "I'll have her back in the morning."

"Early," Fran instructed. "We gotta get on the road. She'll just have to sleep it off on the way down to Albuquerque." Fran's survey of Megan was a troubled one.

"She's done drinking for the night," BlueJean barked with authority.

BlueJean led Megan to her convertible. She eased Megan's discordant body against the leather seats, and then kissed the crown of her head. Camille scowled as she boarded the bus. Selina was driving since Fran had been drinking all day.

Selina noticed Camille's anger. "Sweetheart, did Megan give you a bad time? You look pretty danged shaken up."

"No. I took a slide on the trail. I was upset because Megan was so drunk. Her drinking makes me nervous. The band is finally making it, and now we have to contend with her antics."

"Cammy," Selina rebutted, "she gets smashed. But it isn't like she's doin' hard drugs. She has been good about watching it on stage. She always performs. And then some. Maybe after she gets away from BlueJean she'll be okay. Hell, sweetheart, what we gonna do, kick her out of the group 'cause she ties one on at a picnic? Anyway, the songs are hers. The sound. Brutal, but consider it. You remember what we were without her."

"And what was she without us? She was playing for tips and drinks in a mountain town barroom."

"We aren't Primrose without her."

"So we've got to become accommodating?"

"What's that supposed to mean?" Selina queried.

"Nothing," Camille lamely remarked. "I'm so tired of her bad manners. Her smartass remarks."

"You're really upset. What's she say to you?"

"Nothing. Nothing important." Camille's back crushed against the seat. She felt drained.

"Maybe you're right, Selina. Maybe I'm just overly sensitive because of the drug thing in the last band. I'll let it all go."

Chapter 14

It always seems those Denver dreams meander through my mind.
Thoughts designed to comfort me won't loosen up and find
The way that dreaming takes me back into my yesterday.
Mellow dreams of Denver times, seems they're here to stay.
We shared so many mountain walks, late night campfire talks,
Mica that reflects the stars, country songs on our guitars -
So many ways that we both seemed to care.
Scouting trickling rocky streams, blending with our wildflower dreams,
Wooded paths we wandered through, cabin smiles I've smiled for you -
So many times I reached and you were there.

- Denver Dreams

Pale light filtered through the noonday clouds. Pressing back her sunglasses Megan studied the shaded highway. Across the aisle Camille had curled against Selina's shoulder. She had obviously not disclosed the incident to Selina, for Selina's disposition toward Megan was unchanged. Camille had been distant, and each glance was another reprimand.

Megan slumped back, her boots crossed at the ankles and her arms tightly folded. She was poised to sleep but faded frames of yesterday were projected against her memory. This morning there had been insufficient time to apologize. And Camille had remained cuffed to Selina's side.

Finally, after the bus pulled up to a roadside café, Megan found an opportunity. Selina had debarked from the bus with Fran and the younger women to inspect the bus tires. Before Camille could follow after them, Megan quickly requested, "Can I talk with you a minute?"

Camille sat back down on the seat opposite Megan's. "There really isn't anything to say."

"I need to apologize for my actions."

"You recall what I told you?" Her expression changed from anger to anguish.

"Yes. I promise I'll never touch you again. Never," Megan vowed. "Of all the people I shouldn't hurt, it's you."

"Megan, I love Selina. That can't change. I won't allow it to change." When Megan's head lowered, she added with guarded compassion, "Are you okay?"

"I've given up trying to chug straight whiskey. And I'm definitely off all aphrodisiacs."

As if stabbed, Camille stood and made her way up the aisle. "Please don't do anything like that ever again."

"No."

Camille rushed from the bus and hurried to Selina's side.

After the group had eaten lunch, the women made their jaunt to the rest room. Megan waited until everyone had finished, and then entered the women's washroom. The last thing she wanted now was to be in Camille's vicinity when either of them dropped their denims.

* * *

After their arrival in Albuquerque the band's setup began. Selina stretched, and then continued hooking up an amplifier. Megan was in a vacant corner strumming her guitar. She had been working on her lonely refrain for nearly an hour when Camille approached, making her first attempt at reconciliation. "Nice sound. Have you finished the lyrics for it yet?"

"Some," Megan replied. She clipped the capo over the guitar's neck. She then sang a portion of the haunting lyrics from "Denver Dreams." When she concluded, Megan's fingers lifted from the frets. "I haven't got it finished yet."

"I like it. Thanks for playing it for me. I know you rarely allow anyone to hear your songs in progress. I suppose that's what BlueJean means when she says you don't open up your heart. She told me that you've never told her you love her."

"Nearly every song I've written since I met her has been for her. Maybe she wasn't listening."

"And Megan, maybe you unlock your heart a corpuscle at a time. Maybe she needs more than that." When the response was over Megan turned. Camille continued, "Well, I like your new song. Too bad we've got the album tracks set. It would be nice to include it."

"We can save it for our second album. Or third."

"I admire your optimism," Camille spoke softly. "I admire so much about you. I'm not sure I have the right to say this, but…" her words bobbled. "I watched someone I cared for go down the tubes because of a drug dependency. She was also talented. Her habit ruined her life, and she took a group with her." Camille implored, "Please Megan, don't do that to yourself. And don't do it to the band."

Megan nodded. With torment, she lamented, "I'd hate the world to miss out on my songs."

Through a lens of tears Camille murmured, "I'd hate the world to miss out on you."

Camille said the words and meant them. Although Camille was always pleasant with fans, it was Megan going out of her way to sign autographs and talk with them. As brooding and complicated as Megan was, she never showed that side to fans. For them she was congenial, friendly, and warm. For those heckling, or not showing some modicum of respect, Camille ignored them. Megan won them over with her humor. The dichotomy intrigued Camille.

"The world hasn't seen me at my worst," Megan munched the words contritely. "You have."

"Chapter closed," Camille said emphatically. "Now we need to move on to a new day."

"And I'll attempt to be a new and improved partner."

"Just be you, Megan. Sans the heavy drinking. I'll settle for that."

"Thanks." Megan's attention returned to her song. Camille's to her thoughts.

She hoped Selina would be weary from the long drive, then their evening performance. There hadn't been many hours sleep the previous night. There was the group confab, planning events, and chatting. Major venue tours were being planned. As were TV and radio talk show circuits. Fran had promised that life would get 'hotter 'n fire.'

For tonight, Camille wanted quiet. She didn't want lovemaking. She also didn't want to look too deeply into Megan's eyes when the duo performed.

There was self-castigation. She would always welcome Selina's lovemaking. And she would lose herself in Megan's soulful eyes.

* * *

"Least wise you're looking' better than you did yesterday," Fran assessed. Megan rolled over in bed to reach down for her guitar. As she lifted it out of her case she nodded. Fran continued, "Red Hot, you know you can die from drinkin'? Maybe you need to soften the drink."

"If I haven't died from heartache, I don't think a little intoxication is going to kill me." After picking a few bars of a bluegrass song, she added, "I'll try to behave more responsibly."

"Now that we're outta BlueJean's range, things might be easier."

"Fran, I wish I could blame it on her, but I can't. I probably wouldn't have made it if I wouldn't have been in BlueJean's arms yesterday morning."

Fran chuckled. "What a sweet cure for a hangover. Turn on the charm alarm. Hot damn!" She crushed an empty cigarette pack. She pitched it toward the waste container. "I remember one time I was playin' El Paso. Went over to Juarez. Shit, I was fallin' down legless. Booze was cheap over in Mexico. Well, we go to this show. I fell in love with a burlesque queen that took my heart by storm. Boobs like ripe melons. Well, I'm all fuzzy and shit-faced, but I know what I like. Razzle dazzle. I go on backstage. Find out the queen is a queen. In every sense of the word," she sputtered. "I back off in a hell of a hurry. He had his thing-ma-jig all taped down and his breast implants plumped up." Fran slapped her knee and cackled, "I just told him how

I'm a crazy dyke and let it be at that. He was enjoying it. Hellova nice guy. And all kind of beautiful."

Megan was giggling. "You are a devil!"

"Hey, that sweet queen couldn't thread a needle in the dark and I'da bounced clean offa them tits. That wouldda knocked me sideways. But it sobered me up quick."

"If that wouldn't do it, nothing would," Megan ratified. "What did he say?"

"Said I wouldn't be interested in his dangly parts. He knew I'd been pourin' shots down, so I 'spose he'd figured it all out when I winked at him."

When the phone rang, Megan answered. She'd expected it to be one of the band members offering to pick up breakfast. It was BlueJean. A longing came over Megan. She glanced over at the brightly colored saffron blouse BlueJean had packed in her duffle bag.

"BlueJean, I was just thinking about you."

When Fran heard BlueJean's name, she gestured she would return later. She left the room.

"Thanks for the roses. Yellow roses," BlueJean's voice sounded soothing.

"And thanks for the surprise shirt. It fits beautifully. I love it."

"Darlin' you used the 'L' word."

"Thanks for everything. For letting me use your car. For everything you've done for the group. Sorry I got so wasted. Thanks for getting me home last night. I was in a lousy condition."

"I'll always get you home. I'll even be your home."

"Jean, it wasn't anything you did. I was in a rotten mood. Seeing my family does that to me. My mother has always made me feel as though my butt is painted on the wall - showing. She still does. It wasn't anything to do with our past."

"I did you wrong. I'd be very amazed if that didn't dredge up some bad memories."

"None of it was your fault. Not really. I loved being with you."

"You're getting mighty good at using that 'L' word."

Megan laughed. "L for lump of ice in my heart?"

"Thank goodness I've got ways of putting you on defrost." BlueJean's words rushed, "Darlin', I've got to run now. I'm back on-air in thirty seconds. I'll catch up with you later. I love you, Megan."

"Later," Megan mumbled as they hung up.

"Just us," Fran announced as she and Selina entered. "Got us some breakfast."

Megan inhaled the scent of breakfast sandwiches and steaming coffee. "I'm famished," Megan said. She dug into the sack, and then dispensed the bagel sandwiches filled with egg, bacon and cheese to the others."

Fran plunked her body on the bed. As she took the lids from the coffees, she said, "Can't wait 'til we get back south for some good ole biscuits and gravy."

Selina took a quick sip of coffee from the cup she'd been carrying. "I just stopped off to see if your new song is ready for me to score."

"Almost," Megan said between mouthfuls of the bagel. "I titled it 'Denver Dreams'" and I just need a couple of minor changes. I appreciate the way you always make them sound so much better."

Selina's eyes beamed. "We're like a tapestry comin' together, you and me. I just hope we don't get off track."

"Off track?" Megan inquired, taking a quick sip of coffee.

"Cammy is concerned about your drinkin'."

"Camille," Megan debated, "is concerned about everything. She's concerned about my imbibing. Concerned about how much time you're devoting to the band. She's concerned about the bus making it to its next destination. She's flipping concerned. So what?"

"I'm concerned too," Selina disclosed. "Fran and I were just now talking about it. Everyone's concerned. And I know Cammy and me have problems. I don't try to go out of my way to neglect her. I love that girl. She's everything to me. I don't have an easy way with women. I'm not like you are. You can have all the women you want along the way. Cammy is my world. She knows that."

"Are you so certain she knows that? Camille is a special lady. She deserves your attention. Maybe you should spend more time with her."

"We're goin' shopping now. Going to see some pottery factory and curio studio. That ought to satisfy her for a while," Selina said.

"If that's your attitude about being with her, no wonder she gets pissed at you," Megan charged.

"We'll have time after the band gets stabilized. But let's not be jumpin' the issue. What I'm worried about is the way you're hittin' the bottle."

Fran interceded. "We all had our say now. And after that hangover, Megan will probably be tame as a lamb. Right, Red Hot?"

"I'll try to cut down," Megan pledged as she placed her hand over her heart. "What could be fairer than that?"

"She'll be fine," Fran ratified. "I know you're concerned because of your folks. And Cammy 'cause of her junkie ex. But if Megan says she's tryin', her word is good enough for me." Fran took a huge final gulp of her coffee, then stood. "I'm goin' over to tip the mechanic at the filling station for greasing and oilin' up the bus. If you don't feed the cat, you'll end up feedin' the mice." Fran's laugh boomed.

As Fran exited, Megan faced off with Selina. "Would you stop about the booze? Life has been a little chaotic. I know I've been doing too much partying."

"We all search description to match our truth. Megan, the truth is that booze can harm you."

"My drinking hasn't hurt anyone really," Megan shielded.

"Maybe you weren't there at the time."

* * *

Camille measured her interest in the conversation. "So how did Megan react when you mentioned it?"

"Megan can get surly. She started out with the typical line

of promises." Selina took long strides as they strode the outer edge of the motel parking lot. "As I was leaving, she opened a brew just to show me. Sucked it down."

"I'm apprehensive about Nashville. Honey, Fran said she needed you to drive and set up. Elena and Jesse can do that. And money isn't a concern. I'll purchase the ticket."

"I'm not taking your money. Anyway, I've got Megan's last songs to work on."

"Please come with me."

Selina's stroll ceased. She took Camille's hand. "Sweetheart, it is best I stay with Fran. It isn't just the setup, I'll have to do the lion's share of driving. She needs me."

"I need you. What am I going to do if Megan's beverage count elevates?"

"Babe, she's not going to mess things up. She had a lot to contend with in Colorado."

"And you won't come with me?"

"Megan doesn't need a babysitter. And you don't need a chaperone. You go cold as a statue when she walks near you. It's only two days."

As if reaching for a banister of safety, Camille made a final request. "Please?"

"You'll be fine without me, Cammy." She leaned to tenderly kiss her lover. When the kiss dissolved, Selina whispered, "I love you."

"Just not as much as you love the band?"

"Cammy," she said with a trace of irritation, "I'm trying to prove my love for you by succeeding. Make you proud of me. It's the only way I'm ever going to make it into your social stratum. You can come down here and slum it, but without money, I can't belong in your family."

"Just say the word and I'll assign rights from my trust over to you. Go ahead," Camille seethed. "Challenge my word. I'm prepared right now to give you every penny I have."

Selina balked, "The one thing I don't want is your money. I've got to make it on my own. I want your family to accept me, but I want you to respect me."

"I am proud of who you are. You're the most valiant person

I've ever known. I have more respect for you than anyone. Selina, once and for all, I don't care about money or power. I care about you. I want us to be together."

"We are together."

From the motel room, Megan's sprint was directed toward them. "Selina," Megan gasped, "Fran needs you. Wants to know why the bus's radiator sounds like gargling."

"I'll be right back," Selina yelled over her shoulder.

There was a sigh of defeat from Camille. "Megan, I tried to convince Selina to accompany us to Nashville."

"You can see that Fran doesn't seem to think she can get along without Selina. But I tried, too."

"I can't get along without Selina."

"Camille, I'm sorry she can't be with us. But I'm not going to touch you."

"Megan, you know why I told you that. You accosted me when you were filthy loaded. It doesn't mean I don't trust you when you're sober.

"My filthy, perverted behavior won't be a problem for you." Megan exhaled deeply. "Look, I messed up and I've apologized for it. I tried to hold you."

Enraged, Camille spat, "You tried to hold me! Megan, you don't pin someone down on the ground if you care about them. You'd been uncontrollably weeping. I was only comforting you. Certainly not coming on."

Distress covered Megan's face. Camille had never seen such a spectrum of emotion on any other face. She'd seen Megan's tenderness through song; her playfulness through exchanges with audiences; and Megan's savage rage. Now it was Megan's overwhelming pain.

"I regret what happened. I needed to hold someone. It was selfish because I had no regard for your needs."

Their gaze scalded both hearts. Camille was uncertain what her needs might be. She heard music from the radio coming from the motel room's open door. Solace was not within the tempered gift of music. Song had been her retreat for so many years. Not now.

* * *

With a precise mental schedule, Megan waited for each night's final encore. She then retreated to the motel to drink herself to sleep. She had barely closed her eyes when she was being shaken awake. "Megan, come on, wake up," Fran instructed as she pulled the covers from the slumbering singer. "We got us an emergency, Megan."

Megan's eyes squinted from the light. "What the hell is an emergency at five AM in the morning?" She looked around at the other members of Primrose.

"Gather 'round," Fran ordered. She gestured for the women to sit. "We got our work cut out for us. It might be five in the morning here, but it's seven on the east coast. And we just got us a call from a Country Crown exec. Seems BlueJean dubbed the remote tape and sent it to every blasted major country station in the nation. They started playin' it last evening. Crown's been getting tons of orders for our album. Pissed off at BlueJean for doin' it prematurely, but they claim due to preorders, we outta be on the charts before the CD is on the retail racks." Fran clamored, "They're droppin' everything else on their schedule. Printin' materials offa what they had on the mountain shoot. They need the last tracks done pronto."

"We were supposed to have another night here," Selina rebutted.

"We'll cancel," Fran said with a quick puff of her cigarette. Crown needs Megan and Camille right away. So," she explained as she motioned to Megan and Camille, "We're getting the two of you on the plane bound for Nashville in an hour and a half from now."

Megan searched out the time on the clock. "Shit, I'm exhausted," she complained, "I was finally getting to sleep."

"Not a second to waste." Fran gave another shake to Megan's bed. "Crown made the travel reservations. Then they'll pick you up when the plane arrives. Take you to the recording studio. Said they'd provide accommodations for tomorrow night. You should be able to finish it up the following day.

Meanwhile, we'll hit the road. Whoa-ee," Fran squealed.

There was a delayed emotional explosion as the band members hugged, and yelped. Megan was doing her best to conceal her condition. Between whiskey and drowsiness, she wasn't pulling off sobriety.

"Fran," she objected, "we haven't worked on a practice tape. We'll be going in with no rehearsal time. We don't even know if they've mixed the sound."

"She's right," Camille acknowledged.

"That's why they said they booked two full days," Fran answered. "They got you a suite so's you'd be more comfortable."

"We'd be more comfortable in separate rooms," Megan grumbled.

"Yes," Camille seconded. Her eyes stabbed at Megan. "And I hope you get a good cold shower before the flight."

"The suite has separate bedrooms," Fran announced. "Outta respect for Selina, I was sure you'd want separate digs. Now, both of you get yourselves packed. We gotta rev up the bus so's we can get you out to the airport." Fran twisted around, doing her little dance. She yelped, "Hot Damn! That BlueJean knows her stuff. She wasn't gonna let 'em put us on hold. She is a fast race horse when it comes to promoting. Hypes like nobody's business."

As Camille passed by Megan her jaw tightened. "I'll be ready in thirty minutes. Think you can be sober enough to be allowed on the flight?"

Megan answered with her glare. Their eyes traced one another's anger. She turned and stumbled toward the bathroom. Megan examined her drawn image in the mirror. Her face had a skeletal, ashen pallor. Her throat was parched. As she peeled her crumpled clothing, she breathed deeply. While the water warmed to a good temperature, she attempted to put her body through a quick series of calisthenics. Once under the warm droplets she felt her coordination beginning to return.

She exited the shower stall, dried, and slipped on panties and bra. Jesse handed her a paper cup filled with warm coffee.

Elena was packing her bag, and Fran was pacing.

"Don't forget to pack my new boots," Megan said as Jesse slid another coffee at her.

"Elena's got 'em. Just wear them, so you don't forget 'em," Jesse declared. "Hold still. I'll get the hairdryer blowing. Elena is gonna dress you."

Megan felt the heat. She batted her eyes and yawned. Elena gave her chin a shake, "Megan, get it together. Come on."

The two younger women assisted her steps into her trousers. When they had finished dressing Megan, Jesse swung the garment bag over her shoulder. Elena gave Megan's jacket a final whisk.

"You're ravishing," Elena chirped. With a playful bob of her eyebrows, she gave Megan a shove. "Yep. You'll do."

Fran inspected Megan. She fluffed her singer's sable hair. Then Fran placed the palms of her hands around Megan's cheeks. "You listen to me. You sing your heart out. Sing like an angel. You do that for Primrose. You do it for those two kids. For me. You sing for all we've been through. We believe in you."

"I'll do my best."

Fran motioned for the younger women to carry Megan's bag and guitar to the bus. Her grasp drifted down to Megan's shoulders. "Whenever I get to needin' a drink so bad I can't stand it, I deputize myself. I'm on watch until it is okay to drink again. You're my hope. Don't you know that?"

"I know." Megan leaned down and gave Fran's forehead a kiss. "I'll be incorruptible."

With exhalation, Fran clapped her hands. "Let's make 'em think we care."

With a final hug they both understood as a pledge, they walked out into an arid evening. Megan's taut chin lifted as she filled her lungs with fresh air. "We do care," she emphatically divulged. She felt newly deputized.

Chapter 15

Of course I'll miss your quiet strength.
The way you'd go to any length
To keep my days full of smiles and sun.
Of course those days will never be undone.
It's a junction in the road where our path takes its split.
I've got to keep a moving on before I commit
The crime of too much loving that's sure to suffocate.
So let me go now, darling, 'cause I'm already late.

- A Junction in the Road

Stale, poorly ventilated air circulated through the airplane. Camille hated commercial airline flights. She was more comfortable in her father's corporate jet. But, she considered, this travel was preferable to gritty bus fumes. The road's dust seeped into every pore.

Within moments of leaving the runway, Camille felt the division from Selina. She wished she'd never heard of Primrose. Viewing the runway lights as they faded seemed to disassemble her heart.

She was thankful that the plane wasn't even half filled. That allowed Megan to take a row across the aisle from Camille's row of seats. Determined to stretch out once comfortably airborne, Camille hoped for a little sleep. There would be little time to rest throughout the rest of the day. Time, she mused, was rushing. And it was stealing her lover away from her. To Selina there would always be time for their relationship once they made it to the top. But as their dream closed in on them, Camille ruminated, time shortened.

When the flight attendant passed by, asking about drinks, Megan playfully ordered a sassafras cocktail. Chuckling, the amused attendant was being charmed by Megan's grin. Megan quickly canceled, ordering an orange juice. She tagged a smile and the word beautiful onto her order. Camille felt a tinge of contempt. She wasn't certain if it was for the attractive young attendant, or for the semi-smashed Megan. Or perhaps it was for Selina. Selina allowed her to be away from her and alone.

Camille crossed her arms, waiting for her drink.

"Camille, this is great," Megan blurted. "The Primrose star is in the ascendant. Up, up and away."

Sternly Camille blasted, "Look, Megan, I'm tired. As soon as I get a sip of something to wet my mouth…"

With a wide grin, Megan whispered, "That adorable attendant coming up the aisle could wet my mouth anytime."

"Sweet Jesus! Quit acting like a child," Camille protested. Her shoulder's squeezed back against the seat. She took the cup from the flight attendant. Camille's eyes fired her displeasure with Megan. She leaned across the aisle to rebuke Megan. "She heard that. She's probably straight and offended. I'm amazed she didn't slap your face."

"I'm glad good sense prevailed. Hey, the woman winked back at me. She certainly did."

"You winked at her?"

"I did."

"Please pretend you're not with me."

"I'm not. I'm with me."

Camille gave the small pillow a smack, then propped it up against the seat. She attempted to make her figure into a comfortable oval. When an overwhelmingly dormant feeling persisted, she sat up again. Surprised that Megan hadn't passed out, she commented, "I thought you'd be asleep by now."

"Nope. Just meditating how messed up my life is. How angry I must have made you for you to treat me this way."

"Damn you, Megan." Camille glanced around in hopes that no one heard her outburst. She moved over to the seat next to Megan's. Leaning near, she whispered, "I don't know what it is with you, but I'm making every attempt to treat you civilly. I've tried being your friend. Of course I'm angry with your behavior. You're this enigma. Your arcane life is some mystery with no resolution. No matter how I treat you, it's incorrect. You turn it on me. If I'm friendly, you assault and kiss me. If I'm not, I'm perceived as being a bitch." She glanced down the aisle, hoping no one was eavesdropping and might catch snippets of their conversation. "The saddest part is that I don't think we mean to constantly declare war on one another. I'm just at a loss."

"I'll be on exemplary behavior if you'll just dispense one more chance."

"It's a deal." Camille's smile was forced. She was even angered when Megan put out her hand to seal their agreement. Camille felt Megan's warmth as her hands cloaked Camille's. "We need to be together vocally for the next couple days. A truce will make it much more comfortable."

"Mutual admiration. Harmony. Speaking of harmony, Fran said the cover photo will be where we were all up on the rock."

"You looked at home up there in the mountains."

"I am."

"I find mountains threatening. They seem confining. Not like looking out on the sea. The ocean goes on forever."

"Maybe that's what I love about the mountains. The security of their wrap." Megan looked out the airplane window at the vast, sprawling clouds. They buckled, rippled, and appeared infinite. "But the mountains are also like being up here. When you're on a mountain's top, you can see across the world."

"Guess our opposite attractions in life are a good thing. We're all different. Locations are different. But it truly is all relative. For instance, you think I'm inhibited. My family thinks I'm a wild woman. It's the irony of vantage points."

"Well, you are mighty tame next to me."

"Tame. What is tame?"

"I once believed that tame people were folks who never learned how to live. Or were too frightened to live."

Camille took advantage of a gap in the conversation to move back to her seat. She still couldn't sleep. She wondered how Megan could script songs with universality, yet be so isolated. And there was a question confronting her about her own life. She wondered if she hadn't learned to live, or if she was too frightened.

* * *

Megan watched through the sound booth glass as Camille sang. Megan had offered Camille her choice as to which woman would put down the first lead vocal track. Camille preferred to go first since Megan had a more natural range. She knew Megan's voice would synchronize, twine, and highlight lyrics. Between cuts, Camille had taken her headphones off and joined Megan in the studio. While the engineer set up, Camille commented that "Goodbye Embrace" was mixed beautifully.

"I agree," Megan remarked. "But I wish they would bring up the banjo in the 'Red Hot Blues' refrain. The timing is so precise - it needs to be brought up."

Camille yawned. "I'll sleep tonight."

"Recording is tense at best."

"Tough to make your voice do what you want when your heart is palpitating in it."

"Are you frightened or just weary from no sleep," Megan delved.

"Both."

"Well," Megan suggested, "do what I do. I give a shameless hussy impersonation."

Camille chuckled. "Would it break our truce if I zapped you by asking why you think it is an impersonation?"

"Nope," Megan said as she laughed. "It would make me confront the truth. Do you think I could ever be like you? Deeply in love?"

"BlueJean inferred that your true devotion belongs to music."

With a serene glance away, Megan moistened her lips. "Maybe music does fill my heart and there's no room left over. I hope that's not the case."

"Megan, you'll be fine one day."

When the producer taped on the window Megan lifted her willowy frame from the chair. Before entering the recording booth, she turned. "If I don't come back in a day or two, send the rescue squad."

"Good luck, Red Hot."

"Thanks."

Without thinking, Camille stood, scooped up a small sack of red hot candy and moved toward Megan. She slipped one in Megan's mouth. "Now, go in there and make me sound like a million."

Megan tasted the spice. "You already sound like a million."

"Make us sound like magic then," Camille requested.

Megan made her way to the microphone. She slipped on the earphones and watched her monitor. She felt the bounce of the steel guitar's rhythm. A shiver ran the length of her spine as she began chaining her voice with Camille's. She finessed the lyrics. She felt the astonishment of vocal lovemaking. When she had concluded, there was a total stillness, then applause from the engineer's booth. Megan glanced through the window and into Camille's eyes.

Their voices sounded exactly like magic.

* * *

Late afternoon was rushed. In their haste to produce the finished product, tempers were flaring. Infuriated, Megan vaulted from the sound booth. The chief engineer was cuing Camille's voice track. Megan confronted him, insisting that the banjo track be brought up. Camille tugged at Megan's shirt sleeve. "Come on, Megan, they'll take care of it."

"You heard it. This mix is a mile off. The master tape has to be redone," Megan disputed.

"It will be okay," Camille attempted to console.

"No it won't," Megan steamed as she resumed her stance of anger. "They need to reprogram it before vocals."

"Take it easy."

Megan whirled around. "I'll take it easy when they've done

it properly." Her eyes blazed and her face held the glare of a gargoyle.

"Let's not have a shooting match over it. You know Fran's old expression about when the cook is angry the sauce comes out too hot."

"To hell with the cook and the sauce," Megan huffed. "And the coffee around here tastes like canal water. I need something cold."

"Here's where you say you need bourbon," Camille spewed before she could catch herself.

"I don't need a drink." Then as if retaliating, Megan hammered, "I need a good woman."

"Don't look at me."

"I wasn't. I said good woman. Not perfect woman."

Camille pivoted. Tears bundled in her eyes. She walked to the opposite side of the room. "Is that what you think of me?"

"I'm sorry." Megan wanted to diffuse the anger. She followed after Camille. "I had no right to say that. In the best sense of the word I think of you as perfection. Please forgive me. I'm still a novice at this spirit of cooperation business."

"Maybe we both are."

When the producer announced that the problem would be taken care of, both Megan and Camille released a simultaneous sigh. Megan listened intently when the engineers played the track. She nodded. "Much better, thanks."

Camille laughed. "Do you always get your way?"

"Apparently not always. But throwing a good snit sometimes helps."

"So I've noticed." Camille returned Megan's grin.

"Maybe I've spent too much time drinking and the tavern lanterns have blinded me to reality."

"Maybe my vision has been dimmed by the glare of chandeliers. The important thing is that we're making the effort to understand one another."

"Camille, I didn't mean that about you. The good woman thing. If I thought I deserved anyone like you, maybe it would be easier to behave myself."

"I see so many fine qualities in you," Camille reinforced.

"And you deserve happiness."

Megan walked slowly back to her seat in the sound booth.

Camille felt chills when she heard Megan's buttery soft, soulful voice. She covered her eyes with her hand. Her spirit felt lame. She tried to envision Selina. She longed for the touch of Selina. But try as she might, her mind was unable to visualize Selina's image.

With a rapid surveillance of Megan's face, Camille quickly looked back and followed her sheet music. It struck her. She was feeling desire. But, she considered, one needn't act on attractions. She was beleaguered by lack of sleep. She had been unable to eat much throughout the day. Begging off from any social exchange would be easily excused. She would turn in early. Above all, Camille meant to put down her emotions.

* * *

Toasting with lavish eloquence, Megan had been completely amazed when they returned back to the suite. Camille had insisted on ordering a sumptuous dinner. In perfect French she had ordered Bouillabaisse de Poulet, Potage Celestine, and Le Glorieux. Before she could turn down the complementary bottle of Pinot Blanc, there was a disconnect.

Megan complained that her two years of college French hadn't prepared her for much more than greetings and goodbyes. She translated it to be chicken and cake.

Camille explained that one of the engineers had told her that the hotel has a famous French chef. That was her reason for wanting to splurge. And, she translated that she'd ordered poached chicken with veggies and herbs in white wine. Celery, rice, and leek soup. A very rich, light chocolate cake for desert. And a bottle of wine.

As they sat across from one another at the table in their suite, candlelight spilled across their faces. Camille lifted her glass. She suddenly stopped to apologize. "Megan, I'm sorry. I was so caught up in the menu, when they mentioned the wine, I failed to decline it. You haven't had anything to drink. We can send it back if it's a problem."

"I promise, it isn't a problem. I don't need to drink the entire bottle. I'll just have this, and then shift to water. I only drink when I'm lonely." Their glasses tapped. The sound of the glass pinged. Megan slowly sipped. "For the first time in a very long time, I'm really not at all lonely."

"I wish you could always be this happy. Like the way you are now."

"I wish life could always make me this happy. When you're at home do you have fancy meals?"

"Yes. We have had extraordinarily fine chefs."

"Have your parents always been flush?"

Camille smiled. "I wish I could say prosperity was recent. Then I might be able to say I've gone through the character building that poverty often provides. But my family has had wealth for a number of generations. Wealth, being flush," she corrected, "can often exile you."

"Both your folks have bucks?"

"Business has been lucrative on both sides. Yes."

"I'll bet it makes your family nuts to think of you're being soiled by the commoners."

"I've mentioned that they wish I were in what they believe to be my element. But they love me and for that reason they're civil to Selina. Not completely receptive, but civil."

"Her introduction to snobs must have been a shocker."

"Thank goodness it didn't rub off on her. I would hate to think her wonderful disposition might be altered."

"Have your parents ever seen you perform?"

"Only school recitals. I was weaned on the classics. You can imagine their protests when I joined a rock group. Anything away from an opera house calls for a public whipping."

"Will they come to concerts and award shows when we make it big?"

"I imagine so. How about your parents?"

"My dad would get a kick out of it. He's seen me in taverns and always told me he popped his buttons with pride. My mother would probably only be angry that she was wrong in her forecast of my failure."

"Maybe the fact that we're all disenfranchised tends to bond us as a band."

"Is it the closeness you like in belonging to a musical group?"

Camille paused. "It's being near Selina. That keeps me with the group."

Loneliness spread across Camille's face as the candlelight flickered. She lingered without additional words. Even when Megan glanced away, she saw the cameo image of Camille's ivory throat, her cheeks, forehead, her light hair angelically fluffed around her temples, lush lips, and the pale eyes with sparkles from the candle's reflection.

The hush was appropriate after Camille had rededicated herself to Selina. Megan suspected that the hush was the only lyric she could have written.

* * *

Before her skin curdled, Camille thought, she should exit the steamy shower. She wrapped her body in a fluffy towel. She loved the downy towels. The towels in cheap motels were scratchy. Inhaling the faint scent of soap, Camille looked into the misty mirror. She was glad that she'd suggest an elegant dinner to Megan. It had gone nicely. Megan had been subdued, but congenial. After a glass of wine, she had quit drinking and taken coffee. Her conduct was measured, but friendly, and most importantly without her usual flirtatious statements. It was amicable. No comments that could be even remotely construed as having any sexual connotation. No glow. As if it were all shut down, Megan had discreetly curtailed her affection.

Camille wiped the haze from the mirror. She wondered if her message had been so strong that it had extinguished Megan's obvious desire. Had Megan finally been convinced of the boundaries between them? Was Megan now reading Camille's words, rather than her heart?

With that realization, Camille felt isolated. There was a collision with reality.

Megan had finally taken her at her word.

When the telephone rang, Camille slipped into a pastel blue gown. She heard the sound of the shower coming from Megan's bedroom, so she went into the living area to answer the phone. She was glad that it was Fran and Selina. She gave a complete rundown on the day's events to Fran. Then she was warmed by Selina's voice.

"I'm gonna miss cuddlin' with you, sweetheart."

"I miss you, too," Camille responded.

"Is Megan givin' you trouble? You sound a little distant."

"No. She's stayed sober. Really." Camille glanced up and saw Megan wrapped in a towel.

"Sorry," Megan murmured. "I didn't know if you heard the phone." Megan looked away shyly.

"Yes," Camille uttered. She then resumed her conversation with Selina, "I can't wait to get back with you."

"Cammy, I gotta run. Fran's getting a call from Dallas…"

"Please, Selina, just talk with me a few minutes. I miss you."

"You too, Cammy. We'll talk tomorrow. I have to dash."

"Selina, please." Camille heard the line go dead. She turned to Megan. She repressed the trembling that was beginning in her hand as she placed the phone down. "Guess everything is going smoothly for the band."

"Great." Megan's fingers formed a fist around the draping towel. "Did you tell them that we're doing our best?"

"Yes. And I told them that your behavior is exemplary." Camille's smile was tender, yet tense. "You've been handling this wonderfully."

"I've been trying not to do anything you don't want me to do." For the first time, Megan was exact in reading Camille's eyes. "And trying to do almost everything you want me to do."

"Almost?"

"You want me to make love to you."

Camille felt her heart cage open to release desire. As Megan's towel lowered to the floor, Camille stepped into her embrace. Their softly parted lips sealed them together. Because temptation had never baited her, Camille failed to believe in it.

Until that very moment.

Chapter 16

Shadows of a morning sunrise,
Watching as a hummingbird flies,
Clouds that ruffle up against the blue,
Are mornings I've saved just for you.
So join in and greet my day.
Listen close to what I say.
I want your world to be so kind.
Never thought that I would find
Your belonging to my morning scheme,
Of realizing my best morning dream.

- Shadows of a Morning Sunrise

Their empyrean excursion had lasted most of the night.

Faintly suffused light spun down onto Camille's exquisitely sculpted form. Megan gathered her near. There was the sheen of Camille's blonde tresses as they sprayed against the pillow. The great oversized bed had become a cloud upon which Megan and Camille were swept along with an erotic glide. She leaned to kiss Camille's glistening lips. A shawl of kisses made reverential paths across the singer's body. For the brevity of this night, they had been cloistered within one another's embrace.

Love was shared as if gathering a treasury of tenderness. It had been long forecast in both women's eyes. As if predestined, passion had been tender and precise.

"I'm frightened of my feelings," Camille confessed.

"Morning-after remorse. Do you regret last night?"

Camille turned her head away from Megan. "Megan, we had last night. We can tell the band we're too weary after taping to fly back tonight. Also the producer mentioned that if we stay over we can hear the finished product. Check for any corrections. So tonight will be ours."

"And will that end it?" Megan persisted.

"I thought BlueJean is the love of your life."

"BlueJean is the love of everyone's life. Camille, I don't want this to end."

"There's tonight."

"And then?"

"Then I'm going home to Selina. I hope we can both handle this with discretion."

Megan had resisted the truth from the beginning. She enclosed Camille in her arms. "I do want to hear the finished songs. And I do want another night with you. And do you want another night?"

"Yes, I do. I often wondered what sharing love with you would be like. I wondered if you make love the way you sing. Seduction. Tenderness. Unveiled passion. There's a combustible fury in your voice. It's fervor is unlike any other I've heard. Your songs and voice are mysterious and yet a known commodity."

"And do I make love like I sing?"

"You make love exactly the way you sing. Had you ever thought about making love with me?"

"You know I have. I still can't believe I'm actually holding you. You're like an angel."

Camille's eyes clamped closed. "Some angel. I hope you know I've never done this before. It isn't a meaningless fling. Being unfaithful to Selina is the most difficult thing I've ever done."

"I care about Selina's feelings too. And I'm ashamed that I wish this could last forever with you."

"It's all so complicated. Life is going so quickly now. It has been lovely."

"Past tense?"

"Yes."

Their frames latched and as Megan's arms chained around her, Camille felt her own tears and Megan's tears. Both knew it must end, but relinquishing one another seemed impossible. Waking in one another's arms was a dream. Romance had hitched a ride on a very delicate spun glass falling star. It was plummeting uncontrollably. Both women knew it would be a costly decision. The price was enduring the loss of someone special.

* * *

Night had finally hushed the sounds of love. The day had been one of rush. They had scurried to the studio, worked diligently, and talked briefly with Fran by phone. Fran was negotiating a headliner tour. When Camille questioned where Selina was, she was told her lover was finishing a new arrangement, but sent her love. Megan heard Camille's voice sag. She asked Fran to have Selina call. She waited, but Selina had not called.

After their songs were completed, and all the techs and execs were satisfied, the women returned to their hotel. They shared a quick meal, a warm shower, and then love.

As Megan woke, Camille asked, "What time is it?"

"We have another couple hours to sleep."

"Megan, if it is our last hours together, I want to make love. And then we've got to end it forever."

"It doesn't need to end. Whatever it takes..."

"Please, Megan, we both know it can't continue. I can't leave Selina. I won't leave her. Not only because she's fragile, but because I'm in love with her."

"Can't you give me some hope?"

"Please, don't make it difficult. Megan, I'm struggling with the guilt of this. Selina doesn't deserve to be hurt."

"No one deserves it."

"I'll have to tell her about it eventually. Ours has never been a deceptive relationship." There was a tension in Camille's voice. Her eyes brimmed with tears. "That's going to be the most difficult thing of my life. How do you explain this to someone who loves you?"

"Love isn't an absolute."

"I've betrayed her trust."

"We didn't do this to hurt Selina. She should have been more attentive. She didn't even return your call earlier."

"I don't want anyone hurt."

"You think ending what we've shared won't hurt? Or maybe you believe if you catch it in its early stages, this affair can be cured?"

"I've always thought Selina and I will be together for the rest of our lives. She's my comfort. Now I'm not even sure she'll want me."

"And if she doesn't?"

"Even if Selina doesn't want me, I don't think you and I would be possible. Fran once remarked that even if Selina wasn't in the picture, you and I would do one another more harm than good."

"And you agree?"

"Fran is a very intuitive woman. Under those simple hillbilly mannerisms is a very bright woman."

"She might not always get it right." Megan took a deep breath. "And basing a potential relationship on what someone else thinks is bogus," she argued.

"Megan, I'm attempting to deal with this through honesty. I consider my relationship with Selina a marriage. Does that give you any idea how I feel about what I've done?"

"How can you just turn off all that we've shared?"

Camille allowed the torment in her throat to escape. She sobbed. "Megan, I didn't think this would hurt so badly. I thought of you as a womanizer."

"Are you telling me that I was nothing more than your tramp for the trip? Did you happen to look into my eyes?" Megan sat, ruffling her hair. "I don't believe it."

"I hadn't expected either of us to feel this way. But now we need to let go. We must."

"Damn, but you aristocrats love that word must. For all you bluebloods it must have been part of your first commandment. Charm school. Haughtiness 101. We must let go."

"Megan, I'm sorry. I honestly didn't realize you would

want more. I believed that this was something we needed desperately. It would contribute to our individual strength. Last night you told me you would do anything for me. If you meant that, then please don't make it harder for us. Please let go. I've got to work on reestablishing my relationship with Selina. If she'll allow it. And I'm not certain I can do it alone. Please."

"Please what? Please take a hike. Please drop dead. Please what?"

"Please don't tempt me. Promise me you'll accept it is over."

With a sarcastic lash, Megan's words jolted. "Is it a protocol of the rich and famous - you have divine rights over the souls of anyone who cares for you? Well, princess, anything I can do to make your life easier, just snap your fingers."

"Megan, why are you wasting precious time attacking my background? I can't help how I was raised. It's this kind of attitude that frightens me."

"I didn't mean to attack you. What is it you want?"

Camille's arms encircled Megan. "I want to be held by you now. Then when we fly home, I need to be released."

* * *

With a strut she was unaccustomed to, and head held high, Fran Tobias had stomped her way through the lobby. Today would be just as if life was planting a huge kiss square on her rear end she had told the group when she boarded the red-eye special for Nashville.

"Rise 'n shine," she bellowed as she burst into the hotel room. Dressed in her new heather-gray western suit jacket and Stetson, she loosened her string tie. Her stocky frame was weary from the rushed flight to Nashville. The hotel site would allow her a couple hours sleep before meeting with the recording executives.

When she heard the rustle of sheets from one of the bedrooms, she entered. "Holy shit!" she exclaimed when she viewed the scurrying nude women. Megan and Camille rushed to cover themselves. "What the hell is going on?"

Camille quickly wrapped herself in her robe. "Fran?"

"What are you doing in Nashville? Megan grilled."

"Sure as hell ain't doin' what you two are."

Megan's head wobbled as she attempted to find something to throw over her body. "I guess knocking went out of fashion," she grumbled. "Look, Fran…"

Fran interrupted, "I ain't breakin' and enterin', girl. And *you* look. They called and asked if I wanted to fly in this morning and listen to the master playback. I figured I'd surprise you two. That's a fuckin' understatement." She leaned against the doorway. "The tragic part is that I very nearly brought Selina. Selina," she repeated. "But she wanted to test the equipment out before tonight's performance. Good thing she didn't come. She'd be seeing her buddy and her woman. Damn good thing, huh?"

Megan pulled the sheet around her. "Fran, I need a shower and dress. I'll go over to the other bedroom and get ready. Then you can scream at me." As she walked by the sturdy woman, a flash of shame channeled through her eyes. "As usual, it was my fault. Don't blame Camille. It was me."

As soon as Megan had exited, Fran inspected Camille's face. She was uneasy, her voice was censuring. "Cammy, I understand her brazen goin's on. Hell, that woman is trouble. Walked off a stage. Can't keep her hands outta lady's dungarees. Boozes. Slicker than STP, I reckon. Thinks she has God almighty by the balls. But you're a classy woman. Didn't you read the warning labels? Cammy, I know she's a looker, but why did you need to give in?"

"Fran, I wasn't a virgin sacrifice. I was a willing participant." Camille clutched the robe around her. She tried to explain, "We didn't mean for it to happen. It was as if we needed to save one another. But if anyone's to blame, it's me. I made the first move. I walked into her arms. I'm also the one in a committed relationship."

"You know that old sayin' of my grandma's. If the tatter gets hot, drop it. Why didn't you walk away if you knew there was feelings? I guess I should a come with you, or sent Selina. I seen some of the looks you two traded up there on stage. I just never figured you'd let Selina down."

"Maybe the truth is I've been unfaithful since I met Megan. I've tried to overcome my feelings. I couldn't."

"Feelings?" Fran grumbled. She scrutinized Camille's face. "And how about your feelings for Selina?"

"I love Selina. It was never my intention to hurt her. I'm sorry it happened. I want to keep my relation with Selina."

"Then go on back to your woman. Make it up to her. I won't mention a thing. You got it out of your system. Now you can go on from here."

"Fran, I intend to tell Selina."

"The more you stir shit, the more stink you're gonna get."

"I won't lie to her. We've always been honest with one another."

"How's this for honesty. You got yourself a choice right now. I'll tell you honesty from the ground up. You go back and unload this on Selina, and you got a chance she'll drop you like a bucket of fried nails. And it will take Primrose down to boot. And you know what this band means to Selina. All of us. But no one more than your Selina. Luck has finally happened for her, and if you tell her, it will all come crashing down. Now then, that's your honesty."

"I've got to think about it." There was an ache of emptiness inside.

Megan finished showering and dressing. When she went back into the room where Fran and Camille were talking, she felt the coolness. "We have time for breakfast before our meeting with the big shots," Megan suggested.

"Unless you two want me to leave," Fran barked.

"Come on, Fran," Megan spoke casually. "We can order a nice breakfast from room service. Go over and you'll hear the Primrose sound." She gave Fran's shoulder a squeeze. "Then we'll catch the next flight back."

"Back to a band full of trouble. You two asked for trouble. I 'spose we all got us trouble now."

"Fran, we didn't mean to hurt anyone," Camille insisted.

"No," Megan confirmed. "Least of all Selina. And Fran,

Camille wants it over. She's told me. I'll abide by her wish. I'm sorry if our actions hurt you. Let you down. I really am sorry," Megan apologized.

Camille nodded. "Fran, you said the band is important to Selina. I have to agree that now isn't the time to tell her. I won't mention it. But she will need to be told eventually. And you have my word we'll behave properly when we get back. This is over."

"Hell, Cammy girl, we gotta make a go of this band. Together." Fran's scowl delved, "Think it'll be okay now?"

"We'll make it okay," Megan promised.

"Like I say, we gotta be together. Or fold," Fran stressed.

"Divided we fall," Megan agreed. "Like in Gorboduc."

Not hearing what Megan said, Fran bellowed, "Duck?" She frowned and then her laughter burst like a storm. She blustered, "Duck, hell. You two are like a couple of rabbits."

Camille chuckled, but there was an underlying blush. "I'll get ready now."

Fran blurted, "Hell, that was your problem, you was both too damned ready." After Camille left, Fran added, "And it is a fuckin' problem."

Megan's eyes seemed wounded. "It wasn't a problem. For me, it was a solution."

* * *

The three women took their first class seats. Fran chuckled. "You know I helped launch lotsa women into the country market. For one reason or another, I always found a way to screw up the deals. But at least some of 'em made it. Primrose is different. It's my band." She closed her eyes for a moment. Her memories were deep scars. "When I left Nashville the last time, one of those movers and shakers called me an old soak. Said I couldn't manage a tea party without caterers. Well, now I'm here with the best band I've ever had. And we're winning."

Megan smiled. "We made 'em think we care."

Fran emptied her glass of bourbon. She made a hasty hand

flag to the flight attendant. "Megan, you're stickin' to sugar-water?"

"Yes. I'm fine." Megan knew that booze was one of Camille's objections. But, Megan rationalized that it didn't make any difference if she drank or stayed dry. Camille was going to be avoiding her. She would become an invisible Red Hot to Camille.

As the trip continued, Megan brooded. Camille severed the affair. Now she was going home to her lover as if nothing had happened. Her lover had neglected her. Megan had been enlisted to punish Selina for her crimes of negligence. Camille extracted both women's hearts, put them in a hopper, churned them, and beat them into submission.

Megan frisked the expression on Camille's face. She was looking out of the window, ignoring Megan completely. Maybe, Megan projected, she was proud of her actions. She had retaliated against both of her lovers. A dose of infidelity to Selina. A dose of broken heart to Megan. Big time retribution. Revenge. Good old vengeance. Then Megan witnessed a teardrop tumble from Camille's eye. Maybe, Megan considered, Camille felt stranded, too. Megan's anger was dispelled.

Fran leaned across the aisle to Camille. "You okay?"

"Just thinking about how pleased Crown was with the album."

"Tanner was kissin' ass. Movin' like stink to make us happy. With our sound, what else they gonna do? By the time we hit Dallas, the album will be released. Prime the pump in Texas. Crown is gonna be goosing the distributors. Most of the time they move like a herd of turtles. Hell, we got 'em going now. I've never been so danged proud in my life as I am of my band."

Megan felt the stab of remorse. She didn't want this woman's dream destroyed. Fran didn't deserve it. "I'm sorry that I let you down."

Fran took her drink from the flight attendant and toasted, "To us." After another gulp, she stood. "I gotta hit the kitty litter. Why don't you slide over here and offer Cammy a little comfort. She's got her wringer a spinnin' the blues. Looks like her spirit has been battered like a kite sailed headlong into a rock cliff."

Megan wanted to object, but couldn't. She moved over to the aisle seat. "You're being quiet."

"I've got so much to face."

Megan's chivalry was sincere. "Can I help?"

"No, but thank you." Camille's answer was stolidly given.

"Have I done anything to anger you?"

"No." Camille's blue eyes finally linked with Megan's. "It's just that I'm frightened to be near you."

"I'm frightened not to be near you."

"It's when you say things like that. Look at me the way you do. I'd rather you didn't. That's how you can help me."

"I don't put down these kinds of feeling on cue."

"Please, just don't say those things."

"Because my feelings run deeper than yours? Well, just anytime you need a couple of nights of pleasure, look me up."

Camille glanced down the aisle as Fran approached. "I'm going to the restroom," she said.

"Gonna have yourself a little rest," Fran snickered as they passed. As she was seated, she spoke to Megan. "Your little chat didn't go down."

"No."

"You aren't needin' a drink, are you?"

"No. I need a perfect woman."

"The perfect woman you think you need is wearin' someone else's brand. Respect that enough to stay outta her britches. Didn't your ma and pa tell you about respecting bonds?"

"No. My mother taught me that if the tip is too small, try to short-change the customer at the cash register. The difference can go in the collection box on Sunday. My dad taught me it's much easier to fail without trying than to bust your ass and still lose. There's a combination philosophy of sorts in all that. But literature taught me about bonds. It taught me that people don't belong to other people out of a sense of commitment, but rather out a sense of love. I studied the great romantic renaissance and therein was my truth. People don't belong to other people."

"Cammy does, Megan. And she knows it and you know it."

When Camille returned from the restroom, Megan noticed she'd been crying. Her eyes were rimmed with red.

Megan grappled with her own tears. She felt abysmally lonesome. Perhaps, she thought, it was only pain's genesis. It would never end. The moment was poignant. It revealed a magnified truth. She was still a vagabond hiding from some phantasmal emotion called love.

Chapter 17

You told me in the morning
We'd talk about our past.
But when I view your morning smile
Our talking doesn't last.
You gather me in near to you
And all that's gone before
Somehow doesn't seem
To matter anymore.

- In the Morning

Camille was savaged by guilt. She ached with disappointment when Selina wasn't there to pick them up at the airport. After the cab delivered the three women at the club, she felt another surge of ambiguity. She quickly searched Selina out. Selina climbed down the ladder, held her briefly, and then directed her to stand on stage, on her mark. Selina positioned the lighting correctly.

By that time it was late. Camille needed to apply makeup, get dressed, and tune her instruments. She hated the pungent stuffiness of small dressing rooms. When Megan entered with the scent of vanilla that had thrilled her in Nashville, Camille found it was producing an adverse reaction now.

Megan was aware that there had been a format change in Camille's emotions.

"Camille, have you spoken with Selina?"

"Not yet. There hasn't been time. But I've got to tell her eventually. I've spent the last year unlocking my heart to her. I can't change that."

"After the show we're having a little celebration party."

Camille's fist went down on the dresser top. "Damn. More Primrose. I feel as if I'm a captive. I'll ask Selina if we can skip the party. I'll explain I'm weary from a full day."

"And a full night last night."

"Stop," Camille fumed. "Please don't dredge it up."

"Did Nashville mean anything to you?"

"Megan, don't do this to me. Or to yourself." Her eyes began to fill. She quickly daubed them with a tissue. "We'll be going on stage shortly. I've got to concentrate on the performance."

"I try not to concentrate. I just excavate dreams while the Muse gives me a nudge."

"It isn't necessary to be so damned flippant. No more, please."

"No more flippant," Megan said as she pretended to write the instructions on the palm of her hand. She slipped a candy into her mouth. "Terrific flavor."

"Stop!" Camille screamed. She slammed her eyeliner case down.

"I didn't say it, but yes, you have terrific flavor, too." Megan walked to the door. "See you on stage. We can pretend we don't care."

As the door shut Camille's head went down into the crook of her arm. She felt cornered by Megan's insolence; she felt bereft by Selina's indifference. When Selina scurried in and began applying makeup, she chattered about small technicalities.

"Selina, I missed you. We need to talk."

With exuberance, Selina said, "Glorious goodness, woman. I did miss you, too. Fran wants to have a shindig..."

"It's been a very demanding couple of days. Can we beg off this gathering? Just go back to the motel?"

"Only a few minutes. Just enough to celebrate. Then we'll leave. I'm anxious to get you alone, sweetheart."

"Please, we need to talk."

"We'll make a quick appearance then have Jesse or Elena drive us back early. I'm mighty glad you're here, Cammy."

Camille felt a rage. She realized she was the ultimate

culprit, but she blamed Selina as well. There were too many intrusions on their privacy. And Selina allowed it; encouraged it. That was no excuse for infidelity. Her conclusive relegation of guilt remained with her.

* * *

"Let's take it home," was Megan's sexy growl as the group finished a verse. She tapped her boots and swayed her hips, and her voice shaped the lyrics of "Red Hot Blues."

After the ripples of applause finally faded, Fran approached the duo. "The radio station wants an interview with you two in the morning. Now, let's break out the bubbly."

Camille motioned to Megan. "I couldn't talk Selina out of this."

"A little beverage isn't going to hurt."

"Just be available for the interview."

Megan pressed her guitar pick in the small watch pocket of her denims. "I'll make it to the interview."

Camille moved back toward the table where Selina was uncorking the champagne. She opened ginger ale for herself. Megan hung behind until Fran grabbed her arm. "There's a party goin' on, girl. Forget your problems for the night."

"I might as well have a contagious disease."

"Cammy got her own troubles now. And you ain't one of 'em."

"Maybe I'm the cause of her problems. I'm not tamed out."

"Not that you're seedy as a strawberry. Nope. But you two are different."

"Fran, I'm tired of being wrong."

"A sip of vintage grapes will put you right."

By the time they reached the table, Megan had been handed a glass. Her fingers tightened around the stem. They lifted their glasses, clinking them in celebration. When Selina began talking about the morning interview, Megan suggested that Selina and Camille do the interview.

Selina balked, "You two are the lead singers. They want to

use you."

"You did the arranging, and backup music. Besides, you sound more country than I do," Megan insisted. "I feel self-conscious because I don't even have much of a Colorado twang."

"Folks wanna hear the one who wrote the songs. I may have a heavy Texas accent, but I don't talk anywhere near as pretty and you and Cammy."

She gave Megan's shoulder a squeeze. Megan's head lowered, she couldn't look back at Selina's friendly, trusting face. She was now powerless to correct her sin. Bells can't be un-rung, and some sins can't be forgiven.

Camille reached for Selina. "Can't we please leave now?"

"Just another few minutes," Selina bargained. "Five minutes, I promise."

Camille turned abruptly. She made her way to the door. Over her shoulder she yelled, "I'll be on the bus."

Megan encouraged, "Selina, go on. Go after her. I'll ask one of the kids to drive you back."

"She'll wait. She's tired from the trip. Maybe she can get a little shuteye on the bus."

Selina spoke with her good-natured lack of concern.

Megan's mouth went dry. "No, she won't." She wanted to lunge at Selina and shake her. "Selina, you can't continue to ignore her."

"She knows I'm not ignoring her." Selina looked perplexed. "Just a few more minutes. Hell we're celebrating."

Megan returned to the solitude of the dressing room. She hoped that Selina had taken her suggestion to leave immediately. She feared that was not the case. Slumping down in the makeup chair, Megan touched the glittery spangles on her shirt. Under the lights they replicated diamonds. Fran was correct. Camille was in another realm, with another agenda.

Megan peered at her image. She had been Selina's stand-in. She was nothing but a romance imposter. Megan quickly stood and trudged to a window. The sky was filled with reflective stars. Stars, Megan pondered, were probably leftover asterisks from the footnotes of lost love. They'd all been pitched out there into the desolation of an indigo sky.

Sucking deeply for air, Megan's chest cavity seemed to have constricted under the crush of an expanding universe. Tears forged in her eyes, she blinked them back, but not fast enough. Many spilled. There was never an intention to injure Selina. Life had inflicted its own pain. She had meant to confront her soul. But Megan had only located a blank space.

Another magic moment in show biz, she mumbled to a mournful blackness overhead.

* * *

Camille had locked herself in the bathroom for a steamy shower. When she exited she sat on the edge of the bed, clutching her robe around her body.

"Cold, sweetheart?" Selina questioned.

"No. Selina, I've been attempting to talk with you all evening. We need to talk."

Selina was staggered by Camille's voice. "What's wrong?" She sat next to Camille, lifted her hand and kissed it. "Cammy?" Tears began spilling down her face. "Why are you crying? Is it because I spent a few minutes with the band? Come on, I'm here now. We're together."

"That isn't why I'm crying. Selina, I'm so ashamed."

"Ashamed?"

"I haven't got any other way to tell you. And I need for you to know. I've been unfaithful."

As if she hadn't comprehended, Selina repeated, "Unfaithful?"

"It was just something that happened. A mistake. Megan."

"Megan?" Selina interrupted, "Megan and you?"

"Yes." Camille's lips trembled. "It wasn't planned. It wasn't to hurt you. Please believe that."

"Did Megan force you? Take advantage?" Her question was fierce.

"No. It wasn't like that. It took us both by surprise. But I'm to blame. I'm the one in a relationship." Camille felt Selina's hand slip away. Selina stood and walked to the other side of the room. Her gaze penetrated the wall. "Selina, I'm sorry. I love you."

With her own remorse, Selina murmured, "You asked me, begged me, to go with you. It's my fault for being so involved with the band."

"It isn't your fault. It isn't even that the opportunity was there in Nashville. Maybe it was inevitable. I'm not sure that anyone or anything could have prevented it from happening."

"I should have seen it coming. The looks you two gave each other when you sang together. Hell, I shoulda known."

"We both should have. I tried to be strong. I realized from the beginning that there was an attraction. But I wanted to fight it myself. When I was small, being the youngest child, I always tried to do things on my own. Maybe if I would have shared my feelings with you, it wouldn't have happened. I honestly thought I could suppress the desire."

"Do you love her?"

"I'm in love with you, Selina." Her words stalled. Through her sobs, she repeated, "I'm in love with only you."

"That didn't answer my question if you love her. Guess I know the answer to that. You wouldn't have made it with her if you didn't have feelings." Selina pivoted around. Large droplets flooded her eyes. "I don't want to lose you, Cammy."

"Please hold me," Camille pleaded.

Selina went to her side and tenderly embraced her. "No one could ever love you as much as I do."

Camille clutched Selina. Her body was grounded to Selina's "I'm so sorry."

"Are you going to leave me?"

"Not unless you don't want me anymore."

"I don't wanna lose you. Not ever. What about Megan?"

"It will never happen again. It shouldn't have happened. I told her it has to be over."

"Are you certain?"

"Selina, I'm asking your forgiveness. I've never lied to you. I'm not lying now. I promise it won't continue. It is all over. For the rest of my life I'll try to make it up to you."

"But do you still love her?"

"Not like that, Selina. Please, I want another chance with you. I want to be with you and only you. If you still want me."

"I'll always want you. I'll try never to ask more than you can give. I'll try to be there for you."

"I'll understand if you can't forgive me. And I'll understand if you want me to sleep in the spare bed tonight."

Selina gathered her into her soft arm nest "I forgive you, Cammy. And if you sleep in the other bed, how can I make love to you."

"You still truly want me?" Camille questioned with grateful amazement. "You love me in spite of this?"

"I love you because, not in spite."

* * *

After the interview was completed, Fran mentioned her parched throat. Megan agreed to stop off with her for a couple of brews to celebrate a successful promotional interview. Selina and Camille had objected, but Fran insisted the bus be pulled over into the graveled lot adjacent a country-western dive. Fran instructed Selina to send one of the younger women back for them in two hours.

Megan rationalized that tossing back a couple to celebrate was in order. The interview had gone without a hitch. Megan lit up the room with her wit and charm. Fran had given the thumbs up sign repeatedly. Camille was congenial and personable. There had been no time before the interview to question her about how her talk with Selina went. Megan was certain, however, that Selina had been informed. There was a reserved, yet angry chilliness exuding from Selina.

Glowering zaps had been transmitted from Selina's eyes toward Megan. They aimed and fired each time Megan was within range. Camille's emotions had all but shut down with Megan. They were walled away immediately after the playful banter of the interview.

Megan conceded she needed a drink after that. She glanced

around the tiny bar's interior. They all looked alike. Cluttered with props, in their dimness and dankness. "Fran," Megan acknowledged, "If ever there was a day meant for us to put down a little whiskey, this is it."

"Yep. Have another," Fran encouraged. She ordered a third round of boilermakers. Her eyes were roving a bosomy middle-aged barmaid.

"I do believe," Megan whispered with heavy speech, "that you're taken with her."

"Reminds me of a brazen hussy I dated once. She was a tart, but she could surely cook in bed."

"This one looks straight."

"You can't grope if you listen to nope."

"I'm not a bringing-out kinda woman. It adds one additional step in the lesbian instruction book."

Fran chuckled. She leaned across the bar as her eyes trailed the barmaid's ample backside when she leaned to dip ice. Fran sputtered, "You gotta learn to strike while the eye'n is hot."

"That was my trouble. I struck. Now I'm being struck off. Honest, I never meant for this to happen."

"You know that old saying, excuses are like assholes. Everybody's got 'em one."

"Do you think someone can love two women at the same time?"

"Lust, maybe. Love, hell no." Memories became dislodged. Fran's eyes strained under the tavern lighting. Her face was pasty white as tears began wringing from her eyes. "Megan, that woman of mine was a one and only. Lost her. Damn it all to hell," she cursed.

"You think there's really a hell? I mean, after the hell we go through in life?"

"Yep. There's this big ole cowgirl heaven. They're waitin' for me. Sure. They got this bar-gate dealy. You gotta put the right coins in it. Admission."

Amused, Megan probed, "Change? You mean like a turnstile? So where do you get this admission?"

"Maybe you get it from kind women. Hell, maybe you shit it. How the hell do I know where you get the fuckin' money?"

Fran's laugh boomed. It stormed with a cackle. She inspected Megan's somber face. "You're really sufferin' over all this, aren't you?"

"I've come full circle with the sweet crazies."

"You know there's one too many of you. You knew that goin' in. Selina and Cammy got 'em a traditional kind of love. I expected 'em to get married soon."

"I knew it would never be divisible by three. But maybe like in the theater. Maybe this deus ex macinea..."

"What the hell you on about?"

"It's a contrived machine they use in stage shows. It plucks you off the stage and takes you to heaven. Maybe all three of us, Camille, Selina, and me, maybe we could go through that tollgate you were talking about. Maybe what's up there isn't just cowgirls. Maybe they have this spinning machine. Maybe it could spin our souls together. Come up with the correct number. A number that's divisible by love." Megan wheeled her stool around, inspecting Fran's bewildered face. "What do you think?"

Fran tipped back her shot glass. "I think Dallas is gonna be mighty good to us. And I still got no goddamn idea what you're on about." With a teeter and a blink, she ordered another round.

"It was just an idea," Megan conceded. "Fran, machines don't have anything to do with it. You're right. The question is where to find the coinage."

* * *

After the final set, the band wearily packed up the bus for their return trip to the motel. It had been a quiet ride. When they arrived, Camille wearily plodded across the parking lot until Fran caught up with her. Camille's coolness had not gone unnoticed. Fran knew it would be futile to apologize for Megan being tipsy. But she also knew an attempt was required.

"Cammy, girl, I'm damned sorry about Megan bein' a little stewed."

"She was smashed. I don't know how she can manage on

stage. Some mystical acuity."

"Yep. She snares the audience, no matter," Fran agreed. "I'm sorry it's tough on you. And I'm not blameless. I shoulda called for a ride back earlier."

"It's okay."

"Cammy..."

"Did you want to talk with me?"

Fran glanced around to make certain they were alone. "I want you to talk with me." Fran dug the heels of her boots into the gravel. "You gonna tell me what's goin' on with you and Selina? And do us both the favor of cutting out the bullshit."

"I had to tell Selina. I couldn't stand the thought of sharing her bed if she didn't know."

Fran squatted down and sat on the sidewalk curb. "Guess I can appreciate that. So where do you go from here?" Fran tipped her Stetson back. She patted the sidewalk. "Sit right down and talk it out. I'm your Ma Confessor. So spill your guts."

Obediently Camille eased to the cement. "I'm in love with Selina. I have feelings for Megan. I don't know what those feelings are all about. Selina's forgiven me. I don't ever want to hurt her again." Her words evaporated.

"Megan is a real enticing woman. She got some good qualities. And some not so good."

Camille spun a brief smile. "Yes."

"Some folks give off magic. They can give the stuff off by the bushel load. But they're the kinda people who get to the bottom of that final bushel, and they got nothing saved out for themselves. Now, Megan, she makes what she does on that stage look mighty easy. We know it ain't easy. I got no firsthand experience, but I just betcha that when she's with a lady, she gives off that kinda magic. She makes it real special. Then she finds out she's got nothing saved out, she gets all terrified. She says it's the sweet crazies. She pains for life. For women. For the empty bushels of life. When she drinks it helps her to blot it out a little."

"Temporarily."

"Maybe it don't take longer'n that. And maybe someday

she won't need the sauce to make it through."

"I have no idea where I'm going from here. Fran, I've wronged Selina. I'm not sure I can live with that."

"I want you to always remember this. Sometimes we got no control over things because we're not supposed to have control. Life rolls on. And maybe - just maybe life self-corrects. Could have been you and Selina needed a shakeup in order to make your relationship strong enough to survive." Fran stood, offered her hand to Camille, and then issued a sigh. "Hell, I'm just an old rummy with no proper schoolin' so I don't know."

Camille stood and gave Fran a hug. "I appreciate you. And I think you are one of the wisest people I know. I don't want anything to disrupt the band either."

Fran shrugged as they made their way back to their rooms. She chuckled. "My grandma used to tell us to put a good face on a bad day. Hell, I just want a good, old-fashioned cowgirl band. I get a pinafore operetta."

Chapter 18

Love's touch is a sharing
For two people's caring.
There's no way to separate.
What is or isn't fate.
Time beams brightly from afar.
I'll forever be where you are,
As well as where you're not.
You're the love I've always sought
But I guess devotion won't be showing
Unless my love is where you're going.
I'll never be too lost or too far
From wanting you, wherever you are.

- Love's Touch

Megan slid the strap of her duffle bag over her shoulder as she sprinted toward the bus. Fran had booked a one-nighter in Wichita Falls, on their way to Dallas. Because they had planned a layover there anyway, Fran insisted it was a good idea. Not only would it be additional exposure for their album, but it would add a little spare cash. As the bus pulled away, there was the grind of the engine and a plume of dust.

Between Camille's elusiveness and Selina's total avoidance, Megan felt the sting of ostracism. The bus ride offered sanctuary. Beleaguered by the ordeal, Megan hoped the band wouldn't be impacted. Jesse and Elena had either been told of the affair, or they had guessed.

There was a distance. With cloistered heart, Megan spent her time scripting lyrics and digging stored-up songs from her memory.

When they'd arrived and were checking into a small motel, Megan inquired about the nearest Laundromat. After hauling her luggage to the room, she made a trip to launder her clothing. She entered the tatty storefront with laundry bag in tow. She loaded two machines She then quietly sat on the molded chair.

"Megan," Elena said as she touched her shoulder.

"You two burdened with laundry chores, too?"

"Yep," Jesse reported. While Elena stuffed clothing into the washing machine, Jesse sat by Megan.

"Jesse, at the studio in Nashville we made them pull up your banjo opener on the 'Red Hot' track. I listened closely and could even hear that little stomp of your boots when you finished. Remember, you kind of jumped with both feet landing. It's on there. I heard it."

"I just wish you w-wouldn't have gone without Selina." Jesse slumped. "It's all changed."

Elena swung around and blasted, "For shit sakes, we all know what musta happened. Well, we do know what happened."

"You know?" Megan queried.

"We were pretty sure. Then we caught Selina crying so we asked. She finally told us."

"I'm not proud of what happened," Megan admitted. "I didn't want Selina hurt, and neither did Camille. It was totally my fault. I've told them both how sorry I am. And now I'm telling you."

Jesse's timid frown wrinkled her forehead. "I just w-wish we'd be a happy band again."

"That's right," Elena added. "Selina trusted you both. I think it stinks."

Megan flinched. She stood to empty one of the washers and put the clothes into the dryer. When she sat again, she watched the whirling, twirling laundry. It lifted, fell, and gave off sounds of its damp bulk as it hit the spinning tub's side.

Megan finally said, "I think it stinks, too. And I'm sure Camille thinks so, too. It was a breach of trust on both of our parts. And we're sorry." Megan emptied the other washer. She pressed her clothing into the dryer. When she turned back, she saw the disapproving faces of Jesse and Elena. She walked between then, knelt on one knee and pressed her hands on their knees. "I swear to you, I didn't mean to hurt the two of you. I'm very sorry."

Both women neared, placing their faces against hers. Their arms tangled around her shoulder. "We love you, Megan. It just hurts," Elena spoke with the fragility of glass. "It's gonna hurt for a long time."

"I hope we can work through it." Megan wanted to promise she would atone. Banished by glances, shunned and chastised by wordless interludes, she was aware of her own expulsion. Her exile was deserved. But now at least there was communication with Elena and Jesse.

"You gonna leave Camille be?" Jesse delved.

With stab, Megan's morose words stumbled, "She can't stand the sight of me. And I can't blame her."

"Time for the rinse cycle," Elena declared.

* * *

The Primrose album was about to be released. It had already been circulated to major market radio stations. And it was set up to light with Amazon. Camille felt chills when the bus approached Dallas. Fran turned up the radio's volume. "Goodbye Embrace" blared. The women howled. As if by automation, Camille's head rotated toward Megan. Smiles had been released before there was time for censorship. Glances painfully dissolved.

Their route to the motel took them by the concert hall they had been booked into. Venues had been upsized, and upgraded. Fran hooted, "Lookey there! Hot damn!" There was a life-sized photo placard. "We are headliners now."

Selina's excitement was visible. She whirled around and clamored, "I do believe we're gonna be in contention for album of the year. Song of the year."

"Maybe," Megan acknowledged. She reached into her

canvas bag to pull out a handful of clumsily scored sheet music. She sauntered to Selina, dumped the sheets in her lap. She staggered back down the aisle of the swaying bus. "One of these might be even better."

Camille watched on as Selina perused the music. "Whew!" She handed one called "Love's Touch" to Camille. Camille had barely finished it when Selina enthusiastically handed her another. "Check this one out, sweetheart." Camille recalled Megan scribbling the first two lines on a napkin when they were having breakfast in Nashville. It was the first morning after they had made love. She tried to concentrate on the notation and placement of lyrics. As she read the lines, 'shadows of a morning sunrise,' she stopped to look away. Then she had slowly sipped her coffee. Camille remembered that faraway look in Megan's eyes.

Selina poured over the dozen songs. Her face flushed with ebullience. She called to Megan, "Want me to arrange these?"

"If you would. If you want." Megan then resumed her taciturnity.

"Terrific songs," Selina whispered to Camille.

Masking her emotion, Camille answered. "Yes. Lovely." She reached to brush away a tear. She could still visualize Megan dashing off those lines. And Megan's smile after she had finished scribbling them.

When the bus rolled into the motel's parking lot, Fran cut the engine and then stood to make an announcement. "Now then, I got a big surprise for you all. Dallas is truly waitin' on us. Crown is gonna put on a big do for us. Party for the official release. Couple of the wigs from Nashville will be here for the event. Bless BlueJean for setting up the bash. She'll fly in and says she's got a dozen other disc jocks comin' in. Promos like this spell success," Fran crowed. "And don't let nobody tell you success ain't sweet. Best damn deodorant in the world."

"BlueJean's comin'?" Jesse questioned as she lurched forward.

"You got it, partner," Fran confirmed. She emphasized, "Ought to make our Red Hot happy."

Megan smiled a smile of decorum. She felt its bogus taste. "I can always stand a little more brothel sex."

"That was tacky," Elena defended.

"Hell, we're mighty beholdin' to that woman," Fran added.

"She left me with the biggest goodbye I've ever known," Megan disclosed.

"Megan," Elena argued, "sometimes people leave people if it is for their own good. She claims she left you so you could get on with your career."

Megan sat forward, her eyes flaring. "Maybe that's her excuse for me being a liability. Maybe she couldn't stand being manacled to a committed relationship." Megan realized too late that her comment had impacted Camille. She half whispered, "Maybe I was a nobody. And still am."

Camille handed the sheet music back to Selina. "I'll take a peek at these later."

"Are you upset?" Selina asked as she squeezed Camille's hand.

"No." How could she explain to Selina that torn dreams come in different shapes and sizes.

* * *

"Darlin'," BlueJean wailed as she swung Megan around in her arms. "My, but you do fondle a song." Then she whispered into Megan's ear, "And I hear that you also fondle a songstress."

"Let's go backstage." Megan took her hand and led her through the crowd. "Glad you made it for the last set," she added, ignoring BlueJean's opening statement.

"Blame it on Denver International. I'd a walked here if the damn plane wouldn't have taken off in another couple of minutes. Guess a mechanical is better taken care of on the ground, but I wanted to be here early so we could talk."

Megan smiled. "Like my introduction?"

Snickering, BlueJean scolded, "Just a little over the top."

"I've always introduced you as the 'lusty, busty BlueJean.' Thanks for everything you're doing to promote the band."

Megan moved inside the small vault of a dressing room. She securely locked the door. She whirled BlueJean around in her arms. When she sat, she pulled the disc jockey onto her lap. "I knew you were on your way to meet us when I heard the Dallas women screaming. 'Yippy, BlueJean's back,' they were hollering. Hoping for a love fest."

"You seem to be working on taking over my reputation as a tawdry slut. Trying to move in the best triangles?"

"News travels," Megan replied. "A two-nighter and then collapse."

"Should any of it concern us tonight?"

"No. You're most cordially invited."

"I hope Goldilocks can handle me spending the night with her rock-a-bye Red Hot."

"I'm not her anything," Megan said with a grimace. "She doesn't even talk to me when we step offstage. We're both feeling bad about Selina."

"It would make it easier if Selina wore a black hat."

"She makes a shitty antagonist. I wish she'd clobber me. Clean my clock." Megan's voice held dejection. "She's just silent except for band business."

"Maybe she's all out of anger. The crap with which she had to contend hasn't even made her bitter. It probably wore her down. The foster homes were often worse than the one she'd left. She met a string of real bad numbers."

"And one more counting me. She loves Camille so much that she's forgiven her."

"Unlike you. You're never going to forgive me. Could it be because you truly don't love me?"

"Jean, you broke my spirit. You didn't even look back."

"I did look back. I followed you to Denver. I'm looking back now. Did you ever consider that it might have unraveled when your brooding started?"

"Maybe my brooding began because I was insecure. You were a major radio personality. Women were wild about you."

"That shouldn't have been our issue. I was coming home to you. I only wanted you to continue writing songs."

"How could I write when you were being pursued by every lesbian within the radius of your air wave. They threw themselves at you in front of me."

"I played the part they expected. But you were always at my side. Even so, the accusations continued. You pounded away with slurs until you believed them. You'd sulk your way into a bottle. I have no reason to lie to you. Nothing I say is ever going to make you forgive me. I never shared intimacy with anyone other than you in the entire three years we were together. I was unfaithful with Colby after you moved to the spare bedroom. That fling was after I realized you were never going to trust me."

"It's back to me. You are the one who betrayed my trust."

"I couldn't have. You never trusted me. How did you think that made me feel?" BlueJean cupped Megan's face in her hands. "I accept my responsibility. But let's line all the villains up in a row."

"So why are you back now?"

"Because I've seen that you aren't any better without me. In fact, your life is far more chaotic. The desperate crush on your little partner - your drinking, it isn't an improvement. You'll be tasting the gutter if you keep this up."

"That's no longer your problem."

"You'll always be my concern. And I'll never let you fall. I am in love with you. And don't bother trying to think up some line to avoid saying those words to me. I've paid my penance, and I hope one day you'll forgive me."

Forgiveness, Megan mused. She had asked for it and wasn't getting it. It all felt hopeless. "Maybe I forgive you, but just don't want to risk my heart shutting off again."

"Your heart didn't shut off, Megan. As long as you're writing songs, your heart is ticking like a metronome." BlueJean laughed, "And I wouldn't mind conducting a little orchestral bliss tonight."

"Oh, yeah," Megan muttered. "Let the show begin."

* * *

Toward the end of the party, Megan had gone to the women's room, Selina and Fran went to the bar for a round of drinks. Jesse and Elena were basking in their newfound celebrity. Camille finally broke the silence. "BlueJean, how have you been?"

"Lonely. Guess you've been keeping busy."

Although her tone had not been censuring, nor taunting, it was designed to let Camille know she was aware of the affair. It annoyed Camille. "Well, it doesn't appear that you'll be lonely tonight. I do question your motive."

"My motive hasn't changed since the day I met Megan."

"She's now on the brink of stardom."

"I don't think you can dispute the fact that I've done everything I could to help get her there."

"You have. And we all appreciate your effort. But Megan's spirit is delicate."

"Your allegation that I'm interested now is just plain ignorant. I do know more about Megan's spirit than you'll ever know. And as long as you've drawn first blood, I'll tell you something else. When Colby came into the picture, I was no longer sharing a bedroom with Megan. Right now I'm more than a little tired of your assumptions."

"You weren't sleeping together?"

"No, darlin'. We weren't and hadn't been intimate for weeks. Not that it's any of your business, but I'll tell you about my famous affairs." BlueJean gave a quick laugh. "Here goes my reputation as a chaser. As long as we're counting - I've only been intimate with one woman since Megan. So in the last four years – we're talking two women. You have tied my record, darlin'. But don't let it get out that I really don't leap from one bed to the next."

Camille was silent a moment. "Unlike me."

"Hey, we both hurt the women we love. That's the bottom line. I honestly don't think either of us meant to hurt anyone. I admit I'm still in love with Megan. And how about you?"

"I love Selina."

"And?" BlueJean glanced away. "I don't need an answer.

Your eyes are giving subtitles. You're still crazy about her. Red Hot. Isn't that what you call her?"

"Things are very complex."

"Love is never complex. Whereas bullshit is always complex." BlueJean scrutinized the singer. Then she turned as Megan approached them.

* * *

The lovemaking of Selina and Camille stalled. Desire appeared to have reached a suspension for Camille. Selina eased beside her. "Sorry, sweetheart. It isn't happenin' for you, is it?"

"It has been a hectic day."

"Was it anything BlueJean said to you? Your mood seemed to change after you talked with her."

"She just gave me a dose of Texas satire. Maybe a little heresy tossed in. But that isn't it. I think I'm feeling an overwhelming guilt."

"Or maybe you're feeling something else." Selina fluffed her pillow. She leaned back against it. "Cammy, you may not owe me fidelity, but I'd like to think we owe one another honesty. Is it because you're not sure about your feelings for Megan?"

"I'll never leave you, Selina." She pressed her head on Selina's shoulder. She began to weep uncontrollably. "I love you, and that is the only truth I know."

"Cammy, listen to me. Things aren't right. Ultimatums don't work on emotions. They aren't fair. I don't want to lose you. But I also don't want you just because the competition was run off. I don't want to see it, but if you need to find out how you feel, I'll be waiting for you."

"I couldn't do that to you."

"If you're frightened I'll do something stupid like after BlueJean left me, don't worry. I wouldn't do that again. I know it's a risk I might lose you, but I don't have you now. Not really."

"Selina..."

"You've got questions that need answers. Those questions

and answers belong to both of us."

Camille tenderly kissed Selina's lips. "You're my very best honesty, Selina."

* * *

"I'm not a good loser," BlueJean commented as she began to disrobe. "And I have eroticism on my side," she chided.

"You are one inspiring woman, BlueJean Taylor," Megan lulled.

"I'm mighty happy we came back to my luxury hotel."

"You know Fran. She finds deals on the cheap." Megan shrugged. With a grin, she added, "She always jokes that money has to be pried from her clenched fist."

"Darlin', the band is going to make more bucks than Fran will know what to do with. She could have splashed out on high-class digs. I'll have a word with her. Image. From here on it is perception."

Megan smiled. "I guess we are on the verge of success."

BlueJean pitched her blouse on the chair. "You're going to be country's leading female group."

"Jesse will vote for you as the nation's leading radio personality. She loves your voice. She wanted to know if you have a good singing voice. I told her the sink backing up sounds better."

"My singing voice is pure noise," BlueJean agreed.

"Well, it is lovely when you talk."

BlueJean planted a kiss on Megan's forehead. "And when I don't."

"That's lovely, too"

"Camille must also have lovely attributes. But I doubt that she believes I have any at all."

"Why would she say that?" Megan questioned.

"Megan, she mentioned that you have an asbestos heart because I've burned that heart so often. Do you know where that rumor started?"

"Come on, BlueJean. We've been over that."

216

"I'm telling you right now, Megan, I'm tired of the ole mea culpa lines. Don't you think you should make it simple? I hurt you. But you were somber because of your own feelings of self-doubt. I blame your mother for some of that. But grow the hell up. I tried to do the same as I'm doing now. I tried to enhance your life. You're on the verge of becoming famous. Maybe when we get back together I'll understand the apprehensions you had when I was in the spotlight. It couldn't have been easy for you. And it probably won't be easy for me. But fans throwing themselves at you is part of the package. You live with it; your lover lives with it."

"Maybe there were times when I should have been more understanding."

"Damn betcha there were. Megan, love is bigger than you were understanding it to be. Or accepting it to be. And I'm sure as hell not going to stand for your prissy partner's evaluation of our relationship."

"What did she say?"

"Why does it bother you what she says?"

Megan glanced away. "BlueJean, come on, I want to know."

"She says you kissed her instep, before you kissed her ass."

Megan issued a quick chuckle. "Did she tell you how she feels?"

"She didn't need to tell me that." BlueJean moved away from Megan. "Come on, Red Hot, I'll scrub your back."

"Why are you calling me that?"

"Because that's what the country will be calling you. But if you've reserved it for Camille, I'll understand." BlueJean turned. "Megan, I'm through chasing after you. But if you're expecting me to ever stop loving you, don't."

"You can call me Red Hot."

"Fine, Red Hot. Will you take a sudsy shower with me? Will you pretend I'm the most important woman in your life?"

"What makes you think I'd be pretending?"

Megan's arms extended. BlueJean fit inside of them. "I'll settle for pretend."

Megan thought about their romance. They knew one

another's terrain. Their passion was mirthful, sensual, steamy, and precious. It was as quiet as her pulse; as loud as thunder. But most of all, it was known by heart. It had never been pretend. It wouldn't be tonight.

Chapter 19

Let's turn our dreams all around.
I'll share with you the songs I've found.
With happiness to pave your time,
The beauty of a simple rhyme.
Turn your tears back into a grin.
Allow my love entrance in
And slide sunshine back into your eyes.
Place rainbows thick against your skies.
Here's my promise, I'll be strong,
If you'll allow me to come along.

- And Have I Ever Told You

Camille turned away from the motel's window blinds. Their Monday night off was an unwelcome interlude. "Memphis isn't really any different from Nashville if you're looking out of a motel room window," her banal tone drooped. "No difference."

Selina looked up from the pile of sheet music in which her thoughts had been immersed. "There is one difference. Our album has been released. We're on the charts. By the time we arrive in Nashville, we could have song number one. We have two shots at it. 'Red Hot' is number four, and 'Embrace' is seven. We're bound to hit the top with one or the other." Her words cascaded with energy. "You and Megan have a shot at duo of the year. And we could even get album of the year. Well, that's what Fran said is the latest buzz. That ought to make us all happy."

"Megan isn't happy. She drinking herself to death since we

left Dallas. She hasn't stopped trying to take sanctuary in liquor." Camille's remark was without trauma, yet each word was a harsh thud of pain.

"If Megan wants to live her life through a bottle, there's nothing we can do. Is she still out there drinking on the bus?"

"She was walking across the parking lot. Headed toward the fence."

"She's loaded. Maybe she's lost. She'll probably fall."

Camille's voice was constricted. "She's already lost and she's already fallen down."

Selina sat back. She rumpled her hair. Looking up at the ceiling, she directed, "So find her. Pick her up. I know that's what you want."

"Well, one thing's for sure. You're not going to help her." Camille slipped into her denims, pulled a blouse over the tank top she wore, and quickly tied the laces of her running shoes. "I'll be back," she said when she reached the door.

Approaching, Camille heard Megan's cough. Megan was leaning against the chain-link fence's steel mesh. Her Stetson was tipped forward over her eyes. Her hair was stringing down, curtaining her emotions. Her long legs were directly in front of her, crossing at the ankle of her boots. Both hands clutched a bottle of bourbon.

"Does Selina know you're out here?" Megan questioned.

"She knows. Are you drinking over BlueJean or me?"

"Can't I just be in the midst of my own jamboree?"

"You held yourself and the drinking together in Dallas, so I'm going to assume that you're drinking over BlueJean. I was probably only a BlueJean stand-in."

"You were never that."

"I've been told that BlueJean is dynamite in bed, so maybe being a close runner-up isn't so bad. Sorry, it sounds as if I'm doing a comparison check."

"Don't worry about it."

Camille attempted to keep the conversation light. "Do you grade on the curve?" Her smile faded. "Megan, look what you're doing to yourself."

"I'm too drunk to do anything to myself or anyone else."

Kneeling to one knee, Camille lifted Megan's sagging chin. "Once I reached to help you and you pulled away from me. You're on a downward spiral. Will you let me help you now?"

Megan's voice was scratchy from the booze. She rasped, "I'm in my secret place. I'm waiting."

Camille neared, her lips closed out Megan's words. She whispered, "I'll get us a room. Get you cleaned up. You're a mess, Red Hot." Camille's eyes blurred with tears. "It's killing me to see you like this."

"Are you on a mission of mercy?"

"Maybe I'm just allowing my love to be visible. Let's go in. I'll stay with you until you get to sleep."

She steadied the sagging Megan as they stood. After checking in, Camille took Megan to the ground floor room. They showered together. In bed, they tenderly cuddled until Megan drifted off to sleep. Camille withdrew from their embrace. She covered Megan, and then kissed her temple. She left the early morning love of one woman and went to the early morning love of another.

Although she had not made love with Megan, there was an exchange of love. Fran's most recent slice of wisdom, when trying to convince Selina to forgive Megan, was to live each day in that day. Living in tomorrow loses you a day. Camille reasoned that she could no longer allow the larceny of believing in the future to destroy today. She vowed to make every attempt to help Megan. Megan's life was valuable, and reverence for life is known by the fraction, not by the unit. Music had taught her that much.

* * *

Selina's snarl was a command. Her eyes were deadbolts. Fran had mentioned that she was giving off a jabbed terrier imitation. She played the final bars of a new song's arrangement. "Did you hear the difference?"

Megan acquiesced. "We'll do it your way. I trust your judgment."

"That's because my judgment is trustworthy. I'm trustworthy," Selina growled.

Megan approached the keyboard. She sat on a nearby folding chair. When Selina didn't look up from the score she was editing, Megan blurted, "I agree. I'm trying to become a trustworthy person like you."

"And if your statement is that you're trying for integrity, it is a bad fit."

"Meaning?"

"Meaning you've got my woman." Selina's shoulders stiffened and her eyes scowled.

"That isn't true and you know it. She tried to help me. We didn't make love last night. We sorted things out. She's told you that. I've told you that. If she was going to lie to you, she never would have told you about Nashville to begin with. Selina, she was trying to comfort me."

"There's no obligation to tell me if you laid her or not. You say you didn't do anything. I suspect that's another lie, just like it has been since day one. I do know she'd showered because her hair was still damp."

"First off, she has never been a lay to me. Second she got into the shower to steady me because I could barely stand. She didn't want me to fall and break my neck. Not that you give a crap about my neck. But it would ultimately hurt your all-important band." Megan realized the argument was escalating, but she continued. "There are times when that's all you think about."

"It's better than thinking about someone else's woman. So while I was thinking about the band, Cammy was helping you out. In the shower and in the bed. You are a drunken lush, and you use people. You aren't strong enough to stand by yourself. You think Nashville meant something to you – love? Love. You don't know what love is. You've never loved anyone in your useless life."

"Do you want me to agree? Fine. I'm a self-obsessed, no-good drunk. Useless. What other confessions do you want? I disappointed us both. I was disloyal to our friendship. I've let the world down. Fine. But don't ever tell me I tried to hurt you."

"Get out of my sight."

"Selina, you put your stamp of approval on her coming out to help me last night."

"And she helped you."

"Not like you think. I was too smashed."

Selina seethed, "But if you wouldn't have been?"

"If I wouldn't have been, Camille wouldn't have come out to help me. You insisted that she help me. It was like you were throwing her at me. Maybe so she wouldn't get in the way while you're busy working on music."

Selina's fist hit the power switch on her keyboard. "I neglect her so she screws you." Her flashing eyes filled with tears.

"Selina, we didn't do anything. Why did you tell her to go out and get me?"

"I thought she'd select me."

"You were playing a little ego game to see who she'd choose. You make this magnanimous gesture to save a drunken down-and-outer, and then you blame her. That doesn't sound like love to me."

"Don't talk to me about love. You've never said the words. You're incapable of feeling them. You've never been good for anyone in your entire useless life."

"That's the second time you've said useless, and the last time I ever want to hear that."

"It's true. What the hell do you do except drink, screw, and write songs?" Selina said through her teeth. "At least I tried to fight for the woman I love. You ran off to the mountains. You've hurt everyone you've ever touched."

"You're right. And I guess those months in my cabin taught me nothing. I even flunked Recluse University."

"That's another thing. You and Cammy both have college degrees."

"I've only got my degree." Megan attempted humor, "She's got her pedigree."

"Stop with the self-depreciating routine. It doesn't work on me."

"Look, while I was learning a batch of crap, you were perfecting your craft. So don't use that one on me. We're all in awe of your musical skills, Selina. Your genius astounds us. You have this great retentive mastery of the thing we most love. And you make it look easy. I would trade you for that any day."

"What good is music?" Selina asked with a sudden release of deep emotion. "Maybe that's what is costing me the woman I love." Selina trembled and then she sobbed, as her rancor dissipated. "She's my world. And you couldn't keep your hands off of her."

"Selina, I understand your resentment. What I've been trying to tell you, and what she's been trying to tell you, is that you're her world. But she thinks music is your world. I'm not saying this to hurt you, Selina. I'm telling you because it needs to be said. Sometimes you treat her like your groupie. She's about to become a big star, and so are you. But if you doubt her love now, it will get nothing but harder. Ask yourself why she's stayed with you this long. This isn't even her world. It is yours. You are her dream."

"Do you believe that?"

"I'd like for you to forgive me, Selina. But if you can't, I understand. But with all my heart, I hope you and Camille forgive one another."

Megan allowed silence to mark her exit from the rehearsal hall. She returned to the bus where Elena and Jesse were waiting.

"Selina will be a few minutes getting everything shut down."

"She okay?" Elena asked.

"I hope it will all be okay."

Jesse leaned her boot on the bumper. "BlueJean called last night. We t-told her you was in a motel room with Camille."

Megan's head whirled around. "You told her what?"

Jesse and Elena giggled. "Got ya."

"BlueJean would have understood," Megan said with a laugh. "She has a passerby heart. Just like a true drifter."

"So what's going on with you and Selina?" Elena pried.

"We'll have to see how it shakes out," Megan answered. "I know what it means to you both. It also means plenty to me."

"If we lose this band, it will really piss us off," Elena said.

"Yeah," Jesse agreed. "I feel safe here."

Megan's hug wrapped around Jesse. "I want you to feel safe." She gave the younger woman a kiss on the forehead. "You, more than any of us, know it isn't a safe world. But we need to keep trying and believing it might get safe." Megan's arms spread to loop around Elena. "I'll try harder. I promise."

"We want you happy," Elena spoke softly. "We really do."

"Where did Fran go?" Megan queried.

"Fran took off walking across the street to the bar. Said she wanted to get a damp start to the day." Elena offered. "And I think she meant a drink, not a woman. She's still celebrating our album."

Megan laughed. She turned to see ponds of light splashing over the brightly colored bus. "You two stay as sweet as you are. Don't let fame impress you. Like Fran always says, the higher a monkey climbs, the more you can see of its behind."

They shared true laughter for the first time in too long. It felt good.

* * *

Camille had been taking the brunt of Selina's anger. She had always seen her lover's disposition as bright and cheery. This, Camille considered, was the worst punishment of it all. Selina was no longer happy. That made Camille's spirit wilt. Conversations always seemed to deteriorate in the same way.

Camille insisted that they needed to get away. She planned a pleasant luncheon alone with only Selina. She'd selected an elegant restaurant with a relaxed atmosphere. To her amazement, she didn't need to ask several times to get agreement. Camille dressed in a periwinkle blue pleated skirt, white over blouse with matching blue scarf. Selina looked lovely wearing a peach-colored jacket and tan slacks and matching boots.

It began with the harmony of toasting their iced teas. "To us," Camille toasted.

"Us," Selina repeated. She didn't take a sip, but rather put the glass down. "Is there an us?" Her eyes became weapons.

"I'm trying," Camille answered. "Will you tell me what you're thinking?"

"I try to get by without thinking about anything at all. Thinking would anger me more."

Camille sat in silence until after they ordered steak and lobster platters. "Your favorite is a specialty," she added. "They say the cheesecake is marvelous here. You don't need to watch your weight."

"You don't either. And you could even give up jogging. Just stick to running from lover to lover. Then you could order anything you want to eat. Pull out your platinum card and order the very best."

"If this is another dig at my wealth, forget it. Selina, I've had it with your sniping about something I can't help. Would you be happier if I were a scullery maid? I've offered you my money. I'll offer to reallocate my inheritance, any future trust funds, every nickel I have, if it would just make you love me."

"I don't give a damn what you do with your money."

"Then tell me what you do want. I just want your love. Selina, I went to Megan as a friend. We were both sharing pain. You told me to go. Why?"

"I didn't think you would go. I figured you'd stay at my side."

"I thought you wanted me to sort it all out," Camille disputed.

"I told you to do what you wanted. You did."

"I did what I thought I should do. Selina, it is as if we're hostages. Primrose has become our prison." Camille's voice wobbled. "I love you."

"I'm losing you."

"No. And you aren't sharing me. You allowed me to be a friend to someone who is in big trouble."

"Megan is trouble."

"I'm not certain I can explain any of it. Or that I understand it. It was as if Megan and I tried to save one another."

"From what?"

"Maybe loneliness. I'm not sure. For instance, if we weren't having problems, would you have cleared your schedule? Would we be sitting here having lunch together? Or would you do what you usually do – beg out. I've asked you repeatedly to do things. Before this, we only had one lunch alone together in months. We at least have two hours to share now."

"Then you can go back and save Megan. She should be well-lubricated by now." Selina's eyes were grim. "It must be nice to have a backup. Or maybe she's a replacement."

"I only want to save our relationship."

"Megan wants you to save her."

"Megan wants BlueJean." Camille was suddenly livid. She spoke with muffled anger. "And I want you. But if you want a breakup, then don't look for any more damned excuses. If I wanted to leave you, I would have before now. I don't need the band or the fame or the money. I don't need to waste my time following your dreams. Riding a decrepit bus, eating at gritty diner counters, sleeping in cheap motels! I don't need any of it. But as I've said before, I would travel anywhere to chase down your dreams. To be with you. Make up your mind. If you want me, then let's try to make it work. I'm not going to be treated shabbily. And I'm not going to be ignored by you. Those are the conditions, Selina. What do you want?"

"Cammy, all I ever wanted was to bring the stars out of the sky for you." Her hand slid over Camille's fist.

"You do exactly that. Not the band; not the music. You do that." Tears welled in her blue eyes. "Can you forgive me? Can we just go on?"

Selina squeezed her hand. "Sweetheart, I do, and we can."

"Thanks, cowgirl."

* * *

Night ended their gig in Memphis. Taking BlueJean's

advice, Fran had booked the women into an upscale motel. Each woman was offered her own room. Camille and Selina had opted for one room; the younger women also. Fran had taken a room of her own, saying that Megan needed a little privacy. And that she was tired from the excitement. Fran's weariness showed. With her wobbly wide grin, she had told the band that she was beginning to feel her years.

Megan missed Fran's camaraderie, but enjoyed sitting at a desk to compose lyrics. The quietude of the room was appreciated. Not that the laminated desk equaled the sunken inkpots and plumbed pens on an escritoire. Escritoire was a word she'd recalled from a long ago literature class. Fancy named furniture was a sign of success. It was a sign of upward mobility. Luxury made life seem flexible and precious. But the two places most precious to Megan were her cabin and being in BlueJean's arms.

Megan considered this to be a new dawn for not only the band, but for her. Ending forever would be old days of the band. Certainly once they hit Nashville, things were going to change. Each member of Primrose would be bathed in her own reflective stardom.

Megan sat back. She shuffled her notations and quickly written lyrics. When her eyes clamped shut for several moments, she was seeing how gorgeous Camille looked when she took Selina to lunch. But mostly she recalled how much in love Camille appeared to be.

During their performance, Megan recalled, Camille only gave a quick nod of approval. She then followed Selina.

Megan lifted the ballpoint pen and began writing lyrics that had been swirling in her mind. She was mid-rhyme when she heard a knock on the door.

"Camille," she greeted her partner. "Is anything wrong?"

"I just wanted to talk with you."

Camille entered with a formality. She sat on the chair Megan had been sitting on. Megan sat across from her on the bed. Their eyes intersected briefly. "Talk away," Megan encouraged.

"Megan, Selina and I talked it through. It's time we did the same."

"I'm listening." Megan braced.

"You know how much I care for you."

"And all bets are off. Your decision is made."

"I'm in love with Selina. And be honest, you're in love with BlueJean."

"BlueJean is back in Denver."

"Megan, if Selina and BlueJean didn't exist, we might set the world on fire with our romance. We're both astute enough to know that we would burn out in a hurry. Extinguish. It wouldn't matter if the people we love existed or not. Our love could never survive. But Selina and BlueJean do exist. Admit to yourself that you're glad they do. It gives us both a second chance with our respective first choices."

Megan thought of Nashville. They'd shared one another. Problems were delayed for another time. Perhaps another realm. This was the time and realm. She slid down to her knees, pulling Camille with her to the floor. Their embrace tightened. The only sounds were from their shared cathartic sobs. For many moments, if there would have been a way to have been nearer, they would have been. Yet they both knew there was a secret inside of darkness. They felt its wrap, and its sadness.

And then Camille returned to Selina's side.

* * *

By morning, Camille knew that the ordeal of infidelity had changed her relationship with Selina. Selina now was making time for her. And Camille wanted to belong exclusively to Selina. She hoped it would be for the remainder of their lives. Although there would forever be memories fastened to her thoughts, she knew her heart now.

She and Selina sat in the diner booth, waiting for the other band members. She sipped steaming coffee and perused the menu. "You can tell we're in the south. Biscuits and gravy."

Selina smiled. "Good taste is makin' a comeback."

When Camille looked up she saw the others making their

way through the swaying doors. "Fran said she couldn't wait for coconut cream pie, Nashville style."

"Sweetheart, I love you."

"That's so nice to hear again. And I love you, Selina."

Fran's face was jubilant as she howled, "Mighty fine morning, women. We did it." She slid into the opposite side of the booth, motioning for everyone to gather around. "Primrose is number one! Break out some red hot candies! 'Red Hot Blues' did it. We just hit number one on the charts!"

There was a massive cheer. Fran pitched her Stetson in the air. The younger women yelped, and Selina kissed Camille's cheek. "We're there, sweetheart."

"Today we're arriving in Nashville at the number one spot," Fran boasted. Her eyes filled and she hurriedly wiped them. "This makes up for all the times I left with my ass draggin' on the pavement. This makes it right. It makes me right for once. Twice. I loved me a good woman."

Camille reached across the horseshoe shaped booth to clasp hands with all the band members. When her hand met Megan's it was a brief breeze of a handclasp.

They ate quickly and with elation, and with excitement boarded the bus. Camille had only glanced up at Megan once. Megan had taken the seat across from Fran. There was a slight smile before her vision drifted back to the long highway ahead.

They were ten miles outside of Nashville - ten miles from the town of dreams.

Camille's head rested on Selina's shoulder. She had just shut her eyes. She felt a sudden flapping of the tires as they rattled over chunks of ground. Fran's gasping, guttural cry for help echoed through the bus. Camille watched as the bus began swerving out of control and headed down a ravine. She clung to Selina. She tried reaching across the aisle for Megan, but Megan had made a leap toward the driver's seat. She was grappling with the steering wheel in an attempt to keep the bus upright. Camille feared they could not save one another, as they had promised.

Then she protectively cleaved to Selina.

Chapter 20

Someone planted willows long ago,
Someone I didn't even know.
Now I'm planting willows of my own.
Now I'm loving the willows that are grown.
And tomorrow someone just might say
Thanks for what I did today.
Like I'm thanking that someone
For the planting that was done
One spring day a long, long time ago.
Someone I didn't even know.

- Willows

There was no time for Megan to do anything but react. She had only considered getting to Fran. Getting the bus righted before it rolled and crashed. She pressed her body against Fran's as she wrestled the jarring of the steering wheel. Her legs kicked toward the brake pedal. By the time she had slowed the bus enough to ease it from an embankment, Fran had slumped down to the floor clutching her chest.

Megan twisted around to make certain Camille and the others hadn't been injured. She saw Camille holding Selina. Blood was oozing from Selina's forehead, but she was conscious. Camille's face was a blend of shock and panic. Megan screamed for Elena to press her jacket against Selina's head.

After Jesse and Megan carried Fran from the bus, Jesse searched for her cellphone. "I can't find it. M-Megan maybe it's in the bus."

"Flag someone down. Someone is bound to have one," Megan instructed.

Jesse frantically waved her arms until a trucker pulled over.

Camille found her cellphone. "I've got mine. What's our location?"

"About ten miles out," Elena reported.

Megan tried to shut out the voices as she leaned over Fran's listless frame. Fran wasn't breathing. She was ashen gray. Her hand was clammy to Megan's touch. Megan realized she would need to attempt cardiopulmonary arrest resuscitation. She tried to recall the CPR instructions. The information seemed stale in her memory. There were no vital signs. She skirmished with her recollections. She tilted Fran's neck and began mouth-to-mouth. She tried chest compression, then returned to give mouth-to-mouth. She felt Fran stir. She gathered Fran near. "Fight, Fran. We need you." Fran struggled for breath. "Stay with me. Stay with us," she ordered.

Fran's gasps had become shallow irregular gulps for breath. Megan reached down and took the pint bottle of whiskey that had been stuffed into Fran's back pocket. With a vengeance, she flung it out against the emptiness of the vacant field.

"We need you," she seethed between clamped teeth. "Don't you leave us now." Over her shoulder she screamed, "Where's the ambulance? What the hell's keeping them?"

"On their way," Camille shouted back. "Jesse says they'll be here anytime." She leaned to pull Selina back to her feet. "Come on, honey, please, don't sit down. You've got to keep walking," she encouraged.

Elena crouched near Megan. "Her heart?"

"That's my best guess. She's said she had heart trouble."

"She's been having problems breathing. When she coughs she always blames it on smoking," Elena offered.

"Can you get a blanket? Maybe we should try to keep Fran warm. And make sure Jesse is okay. She was limping. Looked plenty white."

Elena murmured, "She always looks plenty white."

"What about Camille and Selina?"

"Scratches and cuts. Selina's head is gashed. Things were flying around like crazy."

"You okay?"

"Fine. Your hand is bleeding."

"Just a cut," Megan said. "I must have smacked my ribs, too." As she touched them, she moaned. Her bloody crimson fingers were still clamped around Fran's limp hand.

"Here, let me put my scarf around your hand."

Megan started to pry it away from Fran's. "Naw. I'll have someone look at it later."

"You better..."

"Fran needs my strength. Besides," Megan spoke softly, "it isn't my pickin' hand. Are you sure Camille's okay?"

Elena squeezed Megan's shoulder. "We're all fine. Fran'll be fine too. She's got to be."

"Yes," Megan agreed. "She's got to pull through. It isn't just her heart. She's Primrose's heart."

* * *

Camille walked down the hospital hall and directly inside of Megan's arms. Their encounter lasted many moments. Megan then spoke. "The doctor said it's a massive coronary. Arteriosclerosis. Lots of damage. Years of abuse. They're trying to stabilize her. It isn't good. How's Selina?"

"They want to keep her overnight for observation because it's a head injury. They think she'll be okay. They're having trouble keeping her down. She wants to see Fran. Elena and Jesse tried to reassure her that they'd seen her in intensive care. Selina thinks we're lying to her and Fran died."

"For now, Fran's stable. But they said it isn't looking good."

Camille's arm slipped from around Megan. "When will they let me see her?"

"They said she's resting. If you like you can go back with Selina and I'll send Jesse or Elena when we're allowed back in to see her."

Camille lifted Megan's bandaged hand. "Any permanent

damage with your hand?"

"No. Just scrapes and bruises."

Camille turned to go back to Selina's room. She then stopped, turned and began, "Megan, I'm not sure how to begin with this. I want you to be the first to know of my decision."

Megan leaned back against the beige tile wall. "Decision?"

"Yes. For the last hours I've been thinking about life. About the accident. How narrowly we escaped death. Megan, I'm through. I'm going to try to convince Selina to come with me. I'm going back to California."

"What will you do?"

"Teach. Maybe play violin with the symphony if they'll still have me."

"Do you think Selina will go with you?"

"I'm not sure. Now that Primrose is on top, she may not want to leave the band."

"There's no band without any one of us."

"I can be replaced. There are thousands of singers with voices superior to mine. You were always the star anyway. You have an intuitive feel for working the crowd." Camille smiled. "Or a woman."

Megan looked away. "No. That isn't me. Not really me. That's BlueJean."

"Is that the part of her that frightens you?" Camille touched Megan's arm. Spotted blood droplets had dried, hardening, on Megan's sleeve. "Megan, fear can ransom life. Give her a chance. You don't need to be self-contained to pull lyrics from your soul. You just need to be honest, giving, and trusting. I've seen you be those things. BlueJean loves you."

"What about you? You're leaving. With or without Selina."

"Selina's true dream isn't to score country songs. She wants to arrange symphonies. Motion picture scores. She's capable of doing that. She's got the talent. I'm not going to stand by and watch her throw it all away because she doesn't believe in herself as much as I believe in her."

"Selina says she hasn't had enough training."

"There are going to be profits from the album. And I'll help her get all the training she needs."

"Selina's too proud to take your help."

"But she's brilliant enough to realize I'm not going to watch her silly pride cost us our happiness. The accident has made her think about happiness. It's made us all consider what means most to us. "

"You're a tougher woman than I thought."

"Megan, I'm a tougher woman than either of us thought."

* * *

Fran's voice was weak, but her eyes smiled up at Megan. "Couldn't spike that saline drip for me, could you?" she queried.

"No. We've got to get you back on your legs." She rubbed Fran's tobacco-stained fingers. "Just rest."

"I've never rested a day in my life. And I'm well past the age of consent. So pass the bottle." Her tallow facial flesh was swollen with fluid. "I know you're probably carrying a bottle on you."

Megan nodded, "No, Fran, I'm not."

"Hell, you ain't no fun. You'll have me grouchy ."

"Drinking now could kill you."

"I'm fixin' to leave this earth. Megan, we both know my road is runnin' out. But I've had me some times," she mulled. "Hell, from fetus to fossil, life is a blink. Seems like it was no time at all I was just a little girl back playin' away. I'd be swingin' on tires, walkin' on train rails. I'd be eatin' raisins. I had a pony once. She was the cutest little ole thing."

"What was her name?"

"Primrose."

Megan's eyes watered. Fran had savored life. Along the way, she encouraged young entertainers. With grand abandon she extracted performer's ultimate. She taught them to be more than they believed they could have become.

"You loved your pony?"

"Yep. I love my band. But don't stick that on my

headstone." Fran coughed, her body shuddered slightly. "Naw, just have 'em carve 'Tomb of the Universal Dyke' in big, bold letters. Stick that on my tombstone - make 'em think I cared."

"I've got a better idea. How about you get well?"

"I'm not afraid to go. Hell, life is a space between the death of all the people we know. I'm about out of people from the old days." She called, "Megan!"

"I'm right here, Fran."

Her erratic breathing seemed ragged. "Megan, put it away." Her breath continued to gust in spurts. "Do it for me. For you – for the music you can make."

"What?"

"Put your bottle down. Take your life and live it like it counts. Megan, I had nothing for all those years after I lost the woman I loved. You got time. Always be ready to meet up with your dreams. If you've got a chance at bein' happy - take it. Don't make life an unhappy blur 'cause you're drinkin' and can't believe in nobody. You know what I'm sayin'. That's all I'll ever be askin' of you. Give me your word."

Megan had never seen tears run so quickly or flood a face so completely. "I give you my word."

"And there ain't nothing in the world wrong with your word. Live up to your lyrics."

* * *

Under the great gauze of Nashville's morning mist, Fran Tobias was buried. Surrounding her gravesite were the members of Primrose, and a multitude of other people from the music industry. Camille recognized many of the country legends in attendance. More amazingly, many of them had been helped at one time or another by Fran.

"Sweetheart, are you holdin' up okay?" Selina asked.

"Yes. And you?"

"Okay. I can't believe the people here. One of the most famous country stars just told Jesse that Fran heard her doin' a lounge show twenty-two years ago. Fran gave her bus fare to

Memphis and told her to sing sweeter songs. The rest is history."

"Fran would have been pleased that all these people are paying their respect. A regiment of the famous." Camille hesitated. "If you keep the band together, one day you'll belong to that regiment."

"If I don't, you'll see that I'm not lonely."

"Selina, if we return to California, it won't be costing me anything. You'll be giving up friends and the group."

"You believe that one day I can arrange for an orchestra? And make movie scores?"

"I believe it with all of my heart. Will you come with me?"

"Maybe the problem with our relationship had to do with the fact that we were chasing my dreams. My pride wouldn't allow me to chase our dreams."

"Our dreams. I've longed to hear you say those words. And mean those words."

"Cammy, I want to be with you."

Camille felt the strength in Selina's clasp. She smiled. "Maybe that bump on the head did you some good. You won't change your mind when the bump goes down?" she teased.

Selina's lips curved wide. "No chance. These stitches held my brain in. I'm yours."

"We'll miss the women." Camille surveyed the other band members.

"Yep. Elena wants to go back to her family. She misses 'em. You know her, always finds a joke somewhere. Claims that after bein' raised in such a large family the clubs just aren't noisy enough for her."

"And Jesse?"

"When she went to pick BlueJean up at the airport, she explained that we would probably be disbanding the group. BlueJean promised to get Jesse in with the best recording company in the country. Told her to take her pick. Studios know who plays their songs," Selina joked. "Jesse has always wanted to learn the technical aspects of the business. You know how she loves those control boards. She'll still be making music."

Camille's glance drifted to Megan. Red Hot was standing beside BlueJean. They peered down into the rectangle of carved earth that was Fran's grave.

"Megan hasn't had a drink throughout this entire ordeal," Camille remarked.

"I'm not sure what she's going to be doing. But she claims she isn't going to be doing it intoxicated. She's determined to dry out. She promised Fran she would hang it up. And I'm not sure about where BlueJean fits in the picture."

"Maybe Megan doesn't even know. It would be easier on her if she could cry. She went through the services dry-eyed."

Selina and Camille walked quietly back to the waiting limousine. As they entered, Selina uttered, "She looked as if she might cry when I hugged her."

Camille's arm slid around Selina's neck. She buried her head against her lover's shoulder. She sobbed. She could never recall loving Selina more than at that moment.

* * *

Megan's gaunt face was blank as she gazed down at the primrose coverlet that blanketed Fran's casket.

"Wonderful eulogy," BlueJean said.

"Probably would have been too long for Fran's tastes. I shortened it as much as I could. I didn't want the primrose to fade."

"Primrose doesn't always last long, but maybe that's what makes them so special."

"BlueJean, when she was a kid she named her pony Primrose." Megan glanced back at BlueJean's questioning face. "And my guitars are always named Cotton. Always." Megan noticed that they were the last to leave. "Sorry, I'm taking so long."

"That's okay, darlin', our limo doesn't have a meter."

"It's just like when we walk away from here, we abandon her."

"You didn't abandon her when it counted."

"I never wrote a song for her. There was only one other woman. The rest of my songs were for you." She glanced at the cemetery's perimeter where a magnificent willow trees stood.

"Megan, that must mean you love me. Okay, so I wish I could hear the words. But I could get used to not hearing them. If we were together."

"When you love someone you don't place requirements on them. And I could never again take your womanizing. Flirting. You were correct when you said I'm too insecure."

"Megan, you told me that you're giving up booze. You've just gone through one of the most trying times a person can. The loss of a loved one. And you've been strong. I've watched you the last couple of days. It hasn't been easy, but you've done it. I believe you have changed. You'll continue staying sober. Do you believe you can do it?"

"Yes." Her resolve was firm.

"Then why is it so damned difficult to believe that I can change? Do you have the corner on courage and willpower?" Her lips spread a veil of kisses across Megan's face. "We can believe in one another. Isn't that what love is about? We can return to Denver until my contract is up next year. I've been offered a fulltime syndicated talk show here in Nashville. You can write songs. I can talk. And more importantly, I can change my image. Megan, that's what it is – image. I didn't sleep around. But I knew you wouldn't believe me if I told you there wasn't intimacy."

"You didn't need a scorecard?"

"Two sides of a card with two names, one of them is your name."

"You should have told me?"

"You wouldn't have listened. But now we can attempt to make one another safe and secure within one another's love. Megan, remember the very first song you wrote for me? It was spring. May 12th. At 9:45 in the evening. You jotted it down on the back of a telephone bill. It was titled 'BlueJean's Blues' and you were smiling."

"You made me smile."

"Let me make you smile again. Lend me a lifetime of your

smiles. I'll promise you an exclusive on my heart. Megan, give me the chance."

Megan inspected BlueJean's solemn gaze. "I'm going to miss the band."

"Maybe in a decade I can promote a Primrose reunion."

"Ten years. We'll all have changed."

"Yes. Precisely, Megan. You'll forever be Red Hot. And change is fine."

"Change!" Megan suddenly exclaimed. She put her hands in her pockets. Quickly she pulled out her loose coins. She requested, "BlueJean, take all the coins you have in your shoulder bag. I almost forgot."

"Darlin' we don't need to tip the driver." Bewildered, BlueJean rummaged through her shoulder bag and fished out a handful of coins.

Megan's hand opened. Coins sprayed down into the grave. "Throw in the money," Megan directed. "Just do it. It's for heaven's turnstile."

BlueJean's coins scattered. "You realize nobody else will spend a lifetime with somebody who throws money in graves. Nobody else will spend a lifetime married to someone that wild."

Megan smiled. "And no one else will spend a lifetime loving you like I will. Do."

"Darlin', what did you say?"

"You heard me," Megan's smile lit up.

"Say again?"

"I love you. There's never been a time I haven't been in love with you, BlueJean Taylor."

"Was that also a yes to my proposal?" BlueJean questioned.

"It's more of a probability than an actual commitment."

BlueJean Taylor took Megan's hand in hers. She felt confident with a probability. And she felt electrified by the word love.

Walking away together was part of Megan Holloway's dream. She could feel BlueJean's love now. Hand in hand, simultaneously their clasp squeezed gently. Megan turned once to look back at the lonely gravesite. She was confident that the floral cape of primrose would last a very long time.

Author Kieran York

Kieran York

ABOUT THE AUTHOR

Kieran York has authored both Sapphic fiction and poetry. Her lesbian mystery series, *Timber City Masks,* and *Crystal Mountain Veils,* featuring Royce Madison, were originally written and published in the mid-1990s. A second edition of them was recently released by Scarlet Clover Publisher. *Shinney Forest Cloaks* was published in 2015 and is the third mystery of the series. All three Royce Madison mysteries have been on the Amazon 100 Best-Seller's List – LGBT Mysteries. And *Shinney Forest Cloaks* was Amazon's Hot New Release.

York's fiction also includes *Appointment with a Smile,* published in 2012. It was a 2013 Lambda Literary Society Award Finalist in the Romance category. *Careful Flowers* was released in 2013, followed by 2014 releases – *Earthen Trinket* and *Night Without Time.* In 2015, *Touring Kelly's Poem, Loitering on the Frontier,* and mystery *Trevar's Team: 1* were released.

In 2014, her volume of poetry, *Blushing Aspen,* was published as Sappho's Corner Solo Poets book of poetry. It won The Rainbow Award Honorable Mention for poetry, and was a Finalist in the poetry category of Golden Crown Literary Awards. In 2015 the poetry book titled *Realm of Belonging,* was published by Scarlet Clover Publishers.

York has had two collections of lesbian short fiction. The first was entitled *Sugar With Spice,* and was published in 1989. The second was released in 2015, and was called *Within Our Celebration.*

Previously, during the seventies and eighties, Kieran worked as a reporter and reviewer for both newspapers and magazines, and was a magazine publisher for three years. She also wrote and performed songs with a regional women's band. She has been guest lecturer and panel member at various events, including Rocky Mountain Book Exhibition and Colorado

Musician's Series. She is a member of Lambda Literary Society and Sisters in Crime.

She has written for *Journal of Mystery Readers International.* In addition, she has given numerous campus and coffeehouse poetry readings, as well as teaching poetry and creative writing workshops. She graduated from Fort Hays Kansas State University, and attended Mexico's University of the Americas her junior year.

Kieran lives in the Rocky Mountain Foothills of Colorado with her schnauzer, Clover. She enjoys music, literature, and art. She considers her valuables to include Clover, and her other family and friends, her library, her antique typewriter collection, and her guitar.

Additional information is available on her websites: http://kieranyork.com and www.scarletcloverpublishers.com – in addition, her Amazon Author's page at: www.amazon.com/author/kieranyork.

Kieran York

SCARLET CLOVER PUBLISHERS
COMING ATTRACTIONS

ASTRAY

Randa Florez is an award-winning reporter. She is the only member of the press granted interviews with murderer Jona Bell. The drifter/drug addict avoids the death penalty by using the insanity plea. But when she escapes, her enemy's list not only includes Randa Florez, but the reporter is at the top of Bell's execution list.

That is not a healthy place to be, as Randa learns.

The women in her life concur. Alison Pagette is the stunning executive that glides in and out of Randa's life. She strongly suggests Randa take precautions. Randa meets Officer Nevada O'Bryan – and has feelings for the adorable cop. Nevada would like to be her bodyguard.

Her discordant family agrees that Randa needs to be careful. The paternal Florez side of her family worries about her safety. A rift with her mother, Erika Randolph, and her maternal grandparents, becomes its own worry.

Life is a puzzle and Randa Florez desperately needs to find the solution – terror is near.

SCARLET CLOVER PUBLISHERS
COMING ATTRACTIONS

BALLAD OF RAINDROPS

Troubadour Magnolia 'Nolie' Cassidy's existence had always been unorganized. Although Nolie's life had settled down, it was now once again disrupted. Events had suddenly shrouded Nolie's life. Her precious old Irish setter had died. Her inkwell dried up, and her guitar was in hibernation.

She was in love with Libby. But Libby had let her down. Nolie was once again a vagabond. But now she was without a song, without a lyric, and without love.

Nolie previously wrote poems and songs that came from some magical Muse. She believed that it was her Muse that had gone missing. That was until Nolie herself became lost in the middle of the Rocky Mountains. Then she realized that she was the one that had gone missing. And she was assuredly lost.

To be found, it took a storm, the friendship of a dog she despised, and the love of a woman who never gave up on Nolie.